A D … S

FOR SIXPENCE

Leonora Wilson

To our Dot
With Best Wishes
Leonora Wilson

Cover by Mark Wilson.

ISBN: 978-1-0687622-0-8

Dedication

Sincere thanks to my family and friends for all their support for 'A Dozen Words for Sixpence'.

Thanks to my reader friends and my writing group for their constant encouragement, especially Megan and Mark.

Loving memories of my mother Cora, and my grandparents Polly and Gil for their stories which inspired me to write this novel.

LEONORA WILSON

PROLOGUE

London, 10th August 1923

Sailing to Canada today STOP Will send for you all STOP Come soon STOP Love George STOP

George Haddon chewed the end of the pencil and quickly counted the words on his telegram. The postmistress had said a dozen, and he knew he must watch every penny now. One two three… twelve, yes that would do. Dorcas would understand. She had to, she must. She was his wife!

He guessed she might not agree at first, though he was sure this was their only way. He'd promised he'd do his best for his family. There was no employment in the Welsh village where they lived and there was none here in London either. The past week had taught him that. The London trade fair he had travelled to in the hope of finding work, had been a total wash-out. Not a sniff of work anywhere. Dorcas had been right about that he supposed, although he'd never admit it.

Clutching the form, George joined the queue in the post office, dreaming of his adventure. Tossing back his fair hair he shuffled his feet looking over the heads of the queue. This chance sounded like a new life for him, a future. Something which would bring a fresh beginning for Dorcas and each of their children. Why hadn't he thought of it before? It sounded like the perfect solution, a glimpse of promise. Yes, he'd take the chance. George sighed as he considered Dorcas's reaction to what he was about to do. Would she understand, agree with his decision?

In the past few days he'd seen the problem on the crowded city's streets, men and women scraping by, begging, holding out an enamel mug, eyes withdrawn. George saw war veterans with damaged bodies and fragmented minds, standing, abandoned against a wall. Other ex-soldiers, some very young, looked down-at-heel, worried and scrawny, scurrying from dole queue to work queue, worse than back home in the valleys. He did not want that. He must do something. After all, he was the man of the house, their breadwinner. A proud husband and father to seven youngsters, it was his responsibility, he must find a way.

Grinding his teeth, he jutted out his chin, determined he would make a worthwhile start in a young country that welcomed men like him. That was what the poster offered, a chance for a man who'd roll up his sleeves. Men who weren't afraid of hard graft. Pushing his hair back from his eyes George shuffled forwards and shoved the telegram form through the grill at the postmistress behind the counter.

'Pencil please,' she demanded not looking up at him. He rolled it through to her. She pointed her rubber thimble as she checked and said, 'That's thirteen words.' She peered up at him over her glasses. 'Do you want to pay a shilling?'

'No, no. You said a dozen words was sixpence?' George blushed, cursing his mistake.

'Well either change it or go back and think. We're very busy at the moment.' She pursed her lips, tapped the pencil, then stared at him, her eyebrows raised. Confused he grabbed the pencil and heard the impatient sighs of the queue behind him. Hastily he read it through. Without thinking but sure Dorcas would understand, he dashed his pencil through the word 'Love.'

'Right,' the postmistress muttered, her hand extended, 'that'll be sixpence please.'

George paid for his lodgings in the East End, picked up his bags, caught the tram and found his way to Tilbury docks. 'Dorcas will know by tomorrow, no cause to worry,' he muttered as he slung the tool bag over his shoulder. 'It'll be the new start we need.

Later George's telegram lay on top of the bulging pile behind the postmistress waiting for the postmaster's return when he'd tap them across the wires. As the door was opened, a huge gust of wind blew in from the street whisking them about the counter. The postmistress grabbed those within reach, banging her hand down on the desk where she counted postal orders, tight-lipped and tutting as she called, 'Someone, close the door!' Behind her the telegrams lay everywhere. She grabbed those on the floor and thrust them back in the tray not noticing the one which had slid down behind the cupboard. George's telegram would not be found for a week and Dorcas expected him back.

CHAPTER 1: George, August 1923

As George Haddon hurried back to the sailing ticket office he remembered when only a week earlier his wife, Dorcas, had stood in their small kitchen with hands on hips, her cheeks flared, and lips pursed as she accused him again of daydreaming. The evening light from the window shone on her auburn hair with a few stray signs of silver at her temples.

'You always have these grand ideas George. You think the world's going to bend to your wishes and everyone will want whatever you choose to sell them. To make any real money is not so easy, you must have learnt that by now.' She shook her finger, her dark eyes sharp and determined, her neat frame rigid. Dorcas folded and refolded the tablecloth smoothing it with the flat of her hand on the table, turning away from him.

'You're not fair, love. Tell me when I've ever let you down?' he protested frowning at her.

'It's not that. It's just we don't make enough now with the shop, let alone with your plumbing work. The people here are as broke as we are and it's getting worse. It's never been the same since the war.' She put up her hand as he tried to interrupt. 'Don't you understand? We both know they won't buy fancy baths in this village or pay you for installing them, so what's the point of you going to this stupid London fair? It'll cost money to get there, money we don't have.' Her voice rose as she stomped to the scullery, trying to hide her frustration, her fists clenched.

George took a deep breath. 'Listen Dorcas. I could offer folks different ideas. Perhaps a few of them want to change their homes, buy something a bit special,' he called, his voice following her. 'What alternative do we have?' He ran his finger around his neck inside the shirt band moving his head from side to side.

He was so tired of this endless wrangling, the feeling of gloom that settled over their house. Seated at the large table, he looked about the kitchen seeing all they had worked for, despite the growing family.

Her voice echoed from the doorway. 'No one here has the money to pay for them. Ordinary people like us are still paying for their so-called Great War! It's another of your pipe dreams.' Dorcas grasped the chair, her knuckles white.

'Some men made a packet from all that, why not me?' Angry, George stood up, shoving his chair back and turned away from her bitterness. His cheeks flushed red. Why did she always make him sound like a fool and feel like one too? She was too clever by half. George knew he'd always relied on Dorcas's quick wits and her advice but in this he was sure she was wrong. He had to do something. It was up to him. It was his duty. They could not go on like this, always worrying about money and never having enough for bills. He looked at her as she came across, teapot in hand. He saw defiant tears spilling from her hazel eyes. He put out his arms to make up the row which hung between them, 'Come on love, don't let's fight.'

Turning her back, George saw from her look she'd not let him. Today's news about the rent increase was the last straw, a crippling blow. Finding the rent for the house and shop was always a priority for them both and with seven children money was tight but they'd always managed. Until now. What else could he do?

Dorcas had served in the shop and on his market stall, even when the babes were due. Meanwhile he dealt with all the plumbing problems in the village and recently with boilers and heating. Locals knew they could rely on him to fix things. He'd had a knack with practical problems since he was a lad. He understood his job and persisted with even the most difficult repair until he solved it. If George couldn't mend it, customers trusted his word that it was damaged beyond hope.

Now no matter how hard he tried, staying here would not fix their money worries he knew. He needed to do something before winter bit again. He looked up when Dorcas rapped on the window, as she called, 'Girls, stop bouncing those balls against the wall. It's giving me a headache.' His young daughters giggled then looked contrite and George secretly grinned at them raising an eyebrow.

Most of their neighbours had no bathroom, not even a bath. They had tiny outhouses and sculleries with coppers for laundry and the tin bath hanging from a nail in the yard. Only a few of the wealthier houses needed George, as they had Geysers or the new back boilers where the fire heated the water. This provided work for him at times. He sorted leaking gutters and any problems with their modern flushing, indoor, lavatory cisterns, since the new drains had come to the village street. Such work barely covered the rent.

Dorcas clutched a handkerchief in her apron pocket hurrying into the dark scullery, her head held high. He guessed she did not want him to see her tears, it was pointless to argue. He always lost. But George was determined to go to the plumbing fair in London. Something had to change after this terrible year of financial stress and he was sure he was the one to change it.

The country was getting worse, he'd read in the newspaper. The urgent need for steam coal had gone after the end of the war and miners were on short time with reduced hourly rates. Money was especially tight in South Wales.

'There's never enough to go around, George. I can't make it stretch any further.' Dorcas nagged him about it making him feel he was failing her and others guessed their problems in this village where they knew everyone's business. Sighing he watched as the scullery door opened. A silent May crept in and climbed on his knee. She snuggled against him wide-eyed, aware of the sharp atmosphere in their kitchen. Dorcas flashed a sharp look at her so the five-year old closed her eyes defensively.

As the silence between them lengthened, George climbed the stairs to their bedroom and got out his bag. He would pack it himself. He didn't need her help, just enough for a few days, a decent shirt, an extra collar, his best jacket and carefully pressed trousers. He'd take his tools, in case he got a chance to prove himself, to earn a bit of smart London money. Snapping the clasp shut George nodded. He wanted to prove he could solve their problem, to make her smile again. This last year had tested their love and he wanted to mend that, to get back to their familiar warm feeling.

After he came down he was silent for the rest of the evening as his older children quietly moved about their chores, aware of the fraught atmosphere in their home. Their four younger girls went to bed with none of their usual protests, kissing their father with querying glances. He winked back at them. Dorcas hurriedly tucked them in.

The kitchen clock ticked loudly as the evening light faded and their shadows passed across the wooden floor. He lit the lamps. Dorcas drew the cotton curtains and sat at the table opening her bulging work basket. He pretended to read the paper, watching her determined mending and waiting for more comments.

The older three children fell silent. Tilda, at nearly sixteen and the eldest, always felt responsible and tried to be helpful. She said to Roger and their younger brother, Peter, in a quiet voice, 'Come on you two, I think it's time we went up.' Roger pouted but seeing his sister's warning stare he said 'Goodnight' as they disappeared without their usual moans.

The silence was only broken by the coal shifting in the stove. George sat in his chair before the hearth stretching his long legs and meticulously threading a pipe cleaner through the stem of his pipe as he waited for Dorcas to speak. She didn't say anything, studiously hemming a dress. He watched her squint at the light as she threaded a needle and he waited breathing gently. The silence stretched on. The smell of the lamps and their occasional splutter added to the creak of his chair. No word was spoken. The air between them hung thick and waiting.

Later in their bed he put his arm across her hoping to soften her, but she shrugged him off. He whispered to her, but she plumped up her pillow and shrank away. Let her be like that, stubborn woman. Why couldn't she understand, he only wanted to make things better for them all. Rejected, he turned over. He'd prove her wrong. Just wait and see.

Early next morning, as George sat at the table, he watched Dorcas cook his breakfast. He glanced across at her hoping to catch her hand, but she neither spoke nor raised her eyes. His sheepish grin faded. Clearly, she wanted him to understand she thought this was foolish, a waste of time and money. Doubtless she'd say something soon. The dam would break. The early warm sunlight coloured the floorboards stretching the distance between them. He stayed silent, ate his food, waiting. His hands about his mug, he finished his tea, then held it out for a refill, hoping she'd smile, touch his hand perhaps, but she didn't.

Finally, she burst out, 'Why do you need to go to some London Fair with at least four days away from home looking for work while you expect me to carry on here, making excuses to the rent man and telling your customers they'll have to wait with their problems? Do you think I can do wonders? All this with a shop, a home and children to care for, who do you think I am? A miracle worker?' Dorcas banged his mug down on the cloth and turned away. George caught at her hand, but she snatched it back as she shrugged.

'Trouble is, you have no faith in me,' he said. George wiped his plate with the bread. 'Well, I'll show you. I'll come back with some good contacts, see if I don't. And some real money. Prove I'm right!' Swigging the mug of tea, he scooped up his bags and went to give her a peck on the cheek. Dorcas brushed him aside and stood back, her lips clamped.

George went through to the shop, opened the cupboard which hid his small safe and took eight crisp white notes from a cotton bag, folded them and put them in his wallet. That would buy several baths and wash basins for him to sell and install. He did not mention the money as he went out, dropping the key back in the pot on the mantle shelf. He'd not told her he'd been paid for some work he'd finished before Easter or Dorcas might expect some for the rent. He'd left her a bit, enough for now. The shop would make up the rest. This fair was the only way to make some more. The rent could wait a week or two.

'Get on with you. You'll miss the carter,' Dorcas called. Once more she turned away. As he went he banged the door behind him. She was becoming crotchety these days, just crotchety. His dad had warned him that women did.

He stood with his hand on the gate post, tempted to turn back but thought better of it. He hadn't time. He loved Dorcas and she loved him. Their love had prevented real arguments even when unexpected babies arrived. She had got over each childbirth quickly and made a happy home for them all. She was a hard worker and clever too. He could rely on his Dorcas. Yes, he'd made a good choice of wife all those years ago.

For the past few years, since the end of the war, families had felt the pinch. Work for the men in the village had dried up, everyone tightening their belts but this year, 1923, it was getting worse. George wasn't frightened of rolling up his sleeves, of getting his hands dirty for a few shillings. Though in the past year his previous success at finding any work had changed. Now there were queues, lines of men, often before dawn, for every single day's work. Maybe Dorcas was right. Men with no work did not want expensive new ideas in their homes when the rent, a fire in the hearth and food on the table were their priorities. But George did not turn back. He knew he must try.

As he came to the end of the street, he looked back at his home in the warm morning light. They had lived there for over sixteen years while the family had grown, filling each corner. It was a tidy house despite the scaffolding around the back yard where he kept his ladders, handcart and gear, with a neat shop in front, his name above the door. The sun warmed his face promising it would be another hot day. His eyes searched for his wife perhaps smiling and waving, but no one stood at their door.

The mountains glimmered along the ridge as he looked upwards. Sounds from the town square drifted up punctuated by the constant whirr of the mine wheel, as it pumped water to the river, thumping rhythmically. George ran his fingers inside the stiff collar loosening his damp neck as he turned away, strode down the hill and across the bridge to the square.

When Dorcas heard him stamp out of the house, she shook her head. Stubborn man, she knew she was right. She grabbed the mug and plate he'd used and took them to the draining board, looking up out of the back window at his cart and tools.

She remembered their good times together, seeing again the strapping young plumber who had worked hard for them all. No, she could not send him off with only cruel words. She hurried through the shop and struggled with the bolts on the door. Pulling it open as the bell tinkled, she stepped out and peered down the hill. Had he gone, was he there? She lifted her hand in a wave as she saw his back disappearing over the bridge. She had missed him. He had gone.

Waiting on the cobbles, George looked up at the black mining tips between the mountains, the only work for many. Coal dust tainted this whole valley. He knew the damage it could do. He frowned arguing with himself. No, he'd not work down the mine. Never again.

Only a few people were about so early, hurrying to work or to set up their stalls, in the early August heat. It would be a good day, lots of new places to see. He started to feel encouraged. He hailed Mick the carter as the horse and cart approached and jumped onto the box, finding coins in his pocket. They chatted as the mare plodded along the lane, but he didn't intend to satisfy Mick's curiosity, only said he was going on 'an important business trip.' That'd give the locals something to chatter about, keep their tongues wagging. Mick loved a bit of gossip, spreading secrets he'd heard, so Dorcas always said.

'The newspapers are full of reports of strikes and this unemployment has certainly hit the village. Now it is every man for his own.' Mick moaned watching George's reaction.

'Never was much money about, but I must admit it's got worse this last year.' George nodded. He had no intention of telling Mick any more.

As they neared the station, George saw the wisps of steam and smoke trailing along the skyline over the fields. It was his train. He leapt from the cart with a quick, 'Thanks Mick,' and ran through the barrier as the great engine shuddered to a halt. Screaming steam escaped in billowing clouds around the waiting passengers on the platform surrounded by cases and large trunks.

Doors banged open as people emerged, with luggage and goods unloaded, porters with wheeled handcarts dodging around. Not many families visited the village but several men, obviously wanting work at the mine, passed George.

As soon as the few early passengers were seated, the guard slammed each carriage door and blew his whistle while George slipped into the front of the train clutching his return ticket. He loved trains; all those moving parts, the pressure gauges, the smell of burning coal and the hiss of steam on hot metal. Often, he wished he'd driven a train, gone places, seen the world, but that was before he'd met Dorcas and their children had arrived.

Sitting in an empty compartment, his head thrown back. George's eyes flicked up to the string rack which held his case. The carriage smelt musty, the velour seats hinting at past travellers. He let the window down and fastened its leather belt on the notch which held the glass in position. With his elbows on the ledge, he looked out. The hills trundled by, the morning sun flashing between, encouraging him. Soon the smuts from the engine made him close the window and brush his jacket with his hand. 'Got to look smart,' he said to himself. Leaning back against the seat George planned what he must do. He needed a chance that's all. He'd make Dorcas eat her words.

He guessed the old lady, her ma, had something to do with her negative comments. That tight-lipped old woman had never quite accepted him although she'd been adamant the two must marry once Dorcas had admitted little Tilda was already on the way. It had been tricky then. Once the old girl made up her mind she was determined. Stubborn he called it. That's where Dorcas got it from, he was sure. Whenever he suggested anything different, his ma-in-law gave Dorcas a piece of her mind for free. He was sure Dorcas defended him but later he'd hear the old woman's opinions. Her ma had never been out of the village. Little and stout, dressed in rusty black, she was short tempered and bossy. He'd kept his tongue for Dorcas' sake. What did the old woman know anyway? No, Dorcas must do as he said.

Drawing into a station, several passengers got into the carriage. He bought a newspaper from a news vendor walking along the platform and read the headlines. Prime Minister, Stanley Baldwin, had been unable to do much it seemed. Since the war there had been frequent general elections with no one party having answers. The whole country was struggling. Stories of bread queues and soup kitchens were told everywhere.

The morning was warming up and he loosened his tie. He nodded at a young woman in a pretty hat offering to put her case up on the rack. 'Can I help you Miss with that?' Her smiling response made him feel better and he drew himself up to his full height straightening his back.

'Thank you, sir.'

'Beautiful day, isn't it?' George smiled. He wasn't entirely useless whatever Dorcas said. He checked his pocket watch for when they might arrive. Railways necessitated more accurate time. George was fascinated by time, by having things in order, like King George, he'd read. It's where he differed from Dorcas. She had this dreamy side, a love of music and books. George found that irritating.

He dozed and woke quite thirsty. Stretching George stood up. At the next station, women walked along the platform selling cold drinks. Buying a lemonade, George joked, smiling at the sultry girl who took his coins and flashed her dark eyes at him. He nodded, noticing her slim waist and figure. Not long to London, as he checked his wallet and put it safe inside his hidden pocket. Born a Bristol man and having grown up amongst crowded tenements, George knew you can't be too careful in cities.

George caught his reflection in the train window and straightened up, brushing his forelock back with his hand, a flicker of pride at his image. He knew he still made women look. It felt good to be free for a few days, see what the big city had to offer. Sitting back, he closed his eyes and day-dreamed till the train eventually drew into the hubbub of Paddington Station. Rousing himself, he stood, brushed down his jacket, grabbed his case and stepped from the train. George had arrived.

CHAPTER 2: Dorcas, August 1923

Dorcas felt the tea pot beneath its cosy. It was cooling but it would do. She poured herself a cup and reached for the knife. With a slice of bread and homemade jam, she sat gazing into the yard. Light peeped over the high gate, promising a drying day for their laundered sheets. For now, she'd leave the children to sleep for a while longer. On their school holidays, she preferred not to be disturbed until she had to be, relishing the peace and quiet.

Her fingers followed the checks on the red gingham tablecloth as Dorcas remembered her argument with George. Nothing she'd said had made any difference. Once he got an idea into his head, he'd go for it regardless. It was not that George was unkind, for he'd always shown he loved her. He invariably finished things he started, seeing them through to the end. He was so full of ideas, always a new project, another dream. Meanwhile she trailed behind sorting the family out, coping in the shop, picking up the pieces.

The younger children, enthused by his energy, thought their Dadda was exciting and loved him for it though the older ones noticed the reasons for some tensions between their parents, looking sceptically at his adventures. Tilda helped her mother but always dutifully accepted George's authority. Roger, as the elder boy, still at school and not yet fourteen, was often sulky at his father's enthusiasms. He'd throw Dorcas a silent look, although Peter, only a couple years younger, adored George. The younger four girls usually fell in with anything their Dadda suggested. 'Good little maids!' George would say, patting their heads and distributing toffees.

'If I didn't love him too, I'd make more fuss. The children adore him. Only my Mam doesn't fall for his smile and she never did. She'll tell him to his face what she thinks, so he avoids her.' Dorcas smiled at the thought of her tiny mam, head on one side wagging her finger at her tall husband. George never dared answer back!

She refilled the kettle for the children's washes, put it on the back of the range along with a large pan of porridge, and wandered into the yard, through the gate and up onto the grass. The summer daisies on the mountainside were opening to the early sun, still fresh before the day's heat. The smell of the grass damp from the dew calmed her mood as she breathed deeply. The children would soon wake so this would be her last chance to be alone today. Birds' song was clear and sharp in the crisp air. Dorcas sat on a cushion balanced on the wall and daydreamed. A tune came into her head and she thought of her piano and of her beloved father. He was long gone, his heart worn out too early, but he'd had such grand ideas for her when she was young. She heard his deep voice in her memory. 'You can do anything my girl. You are clever, you could teach, play music, write. Don't marry too early or you'll become some man's slave.'

Dorcas had done just that, though her father had never lived to see it. Love for her family filling every waking hour, she knew she would not have it any other way. George was a kind and loving man, but their children were her responsibility. Taking a deep breath of the morning air Dorcas relaxed, closing her eyes and lifting her face to the sun.

The children were generally good, helping each other with their chores. May, their youngest at five, left everything to her sisters, although the others noticed that when she cried in protest, there were no real tears. Olive, neat and quick-witted, at ten last spring, often dealt with her, helping her dress and wash. Dorcas thought of little Ethel, her brown mouse of a daughter at nearly seven, completely outshone by May. How would she cope with this brave new world? She feared for her. And Marjorie, at nine next Christmas, was broader and taller than Olive although a year and a half younger. Always tears and laughter, kind but Olive's enemy. Dorcas thought about their spats. She loved each one of them, yet on quiet summer moments like now, she longed for a more tranquil life. Maybe one day …

'Come on girl, you've a lot to do this morning,' Dorcas told herself standing up. 'I'm afraid you can't go swanning off to London like some people!' She hurried back to her kitchen to the sound of voices. Her children were awake.

After a noisy breakfast they started on their chores with mumbles and false starts. Olive sat and wrote the shopping list, as Dorcas called out items to her before her daughter collected May with the basket and the two girls disappeared to the market square. Olive loved shopping.

Tilda filled the copper in the scullery with a hose from the tap, grated soap in and lit the coal fire beneath.

Dorcas watched each one and felt a love and pride for them all. Noise and bustle radiated throughout the small house. Giggling together, Marjorie and Ethel stripped the beds, to take to Tilda. Top to bottom for some, then eiderdowns were spread. Ethel patted and smoothed them with her small hands, before they were free to play. Roger and Peter burst in, loaded with vegetables from the allotment. 'Don't bring them in here covered in mud! Wash them off outside under the yard tap,' Tilda insisted shooing her brothers outside.

Dorcas tied her apron and opened the shop, greeting some early shoppers. She drew up the blinds and put cash in the till. Strong sunlight warmed the tiled floor. By mid-morning, Tilda was serving customers while Dorcas pummelled the washing with her dolly stick. The boys returned to their allotment chores, and Olive bustled in with groceries and a grumbling May, before joining her sisters in the yard.

Longing to sit down with a cup of tea, Dorcas gave a sigh of relief when Sarah, her neighbour, called over the fence. 'Got a minute for a break Dorcas?'

'It can only be a minute, but yes. Come in.' The two women sat in the kitchen relaxing tired limbs.

'How did George get off this morning? All well?' Sarah raised an eyebrow.

'We argued again. I was sure he'd not change his mind. Stubborn man!' Dorcas bit her lip, clenching a fist on her lap.

Sarah smiled and patted the cloth. 'He's a good man Dorcas, whatever you feel at this moment. George won't let you down, you know.'

'Yes though I find it hard to keep up with his enthusiasm. For a practical man he can be very short-sighted.'

'Give him a chance. He may actually get some work, lassie.' Sarah stood stiffly, her knees creaking. 'Well, I mustn't hold you up anymore. We both should get on, but if you need a hand getting those sheets through the mangle give me a call.'

Slowly Sarah made her way out of the gate and Dorcas returned to the steaming copper, the soda smell pervading the whole house. Scrubbing collars on the rubbing board, she opened the kitchen window. 'Tilda, I'll take over in the shop and you can take the girls to the local park for a bit, but girls, you must be good. Oh and wash May's hands first. Are you ready?' She waved them off.

Tilda sat on the bench in the small park trying to read as her sisters dodged between a few trees and ran wildly around interrupting her. She felt cross with them as she wanted to enjoy her enthralling romance. By the time the church clock struck twelve they were weary, starting to squabble before wandering home.

Tilda knew their brothers would work on the allotment all morning, but after some food they would meet with other lads on the mountainside kicking a ball and sharing jokes. Doubtless, muddy and dishevelled, only hunger would eventually pull them home. The smell of simmering gravy always brought their smiles.

As Dorcas came in from serving a customer, Tilda left the scullery, tied on the apron and went into the shop while her mother fed the others, crowded around the large kitchen table, silent at last. Meat pie and big dishes of vegetables disappeared before a squabble started.

Dorcas wondered where George was eating and who he was with. Maybe he was sharing laughter with a new friend. A flicker of resentment shot through her. Men always get the best of it. We women have all the hard work. Looking around at her children Dorcas felt lonely. She bit her lips. It would seem strange without him, when the children were in bed. When the time came Dorcas decided she'd get an early night, taking advantage of the extra space in the bed. Hours later she was still awake, missing his warmth, unable to sleep. Surely only a few nights without him, she thought as she turned over.

CHAPTER 3: George, August 1923

Confused by the noise and the traffic, George struggled to find his way across London. Large buildings loomed everywhere jostling for dominance. The air tasted thick on his tongue, smelling of smoke and fumes. Horses, carriages, trams and a few motor buses thronged the streets. George stood on the pavement, amazed. How would he ever find his way in this? He had no idea of his route. Surrounded by crowds of people, who seemed to know their way, George stopped a man delivering goods and asked for directions. In the end he found the right tram and asking again, the conductor pointed out an enormous building with wide steps at the entrance. George stepped down from the tram, looking up. Coloured flags along the façade flapped in the breeze. A bright banner across the doorway told him he'd found the right place. Dozens of men waited noisily, hands in pockets, in a long queue snaking down the steps and he felt encouraged. He gave a silent nod and stood in line. Yes, he'd done the right thing. There was an air of promise about this place George thought, glancing about and brushing his lapels with his hand. Some of the other men were very smart in decent suits. Probably bosses who'd want to hire men, he felt. At least he did not look like those others, the more desperate types who appeared deflated before they even got inside. No, he knew he looked like a real plumber, successful but practical and business-like, willing to take his jacket off and roll up his sleeves. George hoped it was what they were looking for despite the depressing national mood talked of in the newspapers and shouted from the news-stands. The queue moved forward, and paying with a few coins, George passed inside where it was full of bustle, noise and amazing displays, shiny brass fittings and gleaming porcelain.

George had never visited a business fair before, never had to struggle for work like now. Back home in his Monmouthshire village, there had been months, no maybe years, of miners battling with the mine owners with talk of strikes and pay cuts. Men were in and out of work, angry men on the streets and thin wives queueing for bread.

George spent the first hour walking about, staring at so many new things and asking questions. He touched spigots, tried faucets watching the features and mechanisms, becoming excited thinking through new ideas, different ways of working. Many of the displays were in the luxury class, elegant and stylish but outside of the average family pay packet but perhaps some of the managers who lived in big houses might want them.

'Anyone hiring workers here, today?' he asked at various stalls. No one seemed interested, their eyes lowered when he spoke. George wondered why. He heard others ask the same question. By the end of the first day nothing useful had happened. He spoke to men from all over the country; different dialects, different products, a lot of boasting but little sign of any work. The salesmen looked forlorn, a little desperate as no-one was buying. They had the same look, tight eyes, dropped shoulders. Companies seemed more interested in contracts, in profit, with no need of working men, he guessed. By late-afternoon the place became quieter. Many men drifted away and although George determined to come each day, a small doubt began to worry him, when he returned to the cheap lodging house he'd found.

The next two days at the fair meandered by in a warm haze, the filtered sunlight from the skylights moving across the gleaming enamels and brass fittings, smelling of warm Brasso, as the hours ticked on. George saw others like himself, eager and experienced yet, despite being there early each morning, he had no success. Small clusters of men talking in low voices between the tables. Lots of stalls with interesting displays with eager salesmen but he was surprised at how quiet the fair became daily by midday. The prices shocked him with little sign of sales. If this was what they charged for baths and boilers, no wonder few villagers were interested. He decided not to buy anything, his plans upset by the prices.

Several times he spoke with a cheerful couple of young men who wandered through the fair each day. 'Nothing doing here mate. I thought there'd be some decent work, but it's all a dud!' George nodded at their comments. Each night he stayed in a run-down house where the landlady cooked a greasy breakfast and meagre supper. One evening in the gloomy dining room, standing arms akimbo in a grubby overall, she asked where he went each day.

'I'm attending a business fair for working men, plumbers like myself. I run my own business see? Just looking at what I might order, baths and sinks and all sorts,' he boasted. She smirked at him glancing at his workman's hands.

'No work this way not nowadays. Not like before the war!' The landlady turned down her lip. 'Perhaps it's better where you come from 'though it's not what I heard. Wales ain't it?' She raised her eyebrows in a question, casually brushed crumbs from the cloth into her hand, and shuffled away as George was silent. He guessed she'd read the newspapers so she knew. He ate his meal in silence.

During the late evening George lay alone in the narrow bed with mild indigestion thinking of home. Flashes of street light broke through the shadows, highlighting the dingy paintwork and bare floor. He couldn't sleep and turned on his back. Noises from the street below echoed through the thin walls. He missed Dorcas's cheerful smile and his children's chatter. He longed for her warm cuddle and their love. But most of all he realised the pointlessness of his journey. He'd spent good money on this but he did not go home with nothing to show for his efforts. He could not admit defeat. George wanted to be triumphant, for his family to be proud of him.

He tossed beneath the sheets, tangled and unable to sleep. He had imagined arriving home with orders, new work and to a warm welcome. But it didn't look likely. There was no more work here than at home. It had been the waste of time and money Dorcas had predicted. Whatever could he do? George slept fitfully disturbed again by street noises, the clatter of horses' hooves and loud car horns. He wished she slept beside him but dreading how he would explain it to her.

At midday on the final day, feeling disgruntled, George went to the bar and recognised the two young men with bowlers pushed to the back of their heads that he'd seen going around the stalls each day. Over a beer they told him of their plans. Both single men, they'd served together in the army and fought in France and Belgium but since then could only find day-work queueing each morning for a chance and often turned away jobless.

'Yer see mate, there's no security and no future in Britain nowadays. No one's taking blokes on. They ain't paying as much as they did before the war either. The war's done for us I reckon.' Jim wagged his finger at George, 'I didn't fight the bloody Kaiser for all this, yer know!'

The tall one nodded, wiping froth from his moustache. 'Yea George, and there's too much talk of strikes and dole queues and yer put a foot wrong and yer out on yer ear. They changed the ruddy daily rate down too. Daylight robbery I calls it, bloody robbery. They don't need no excuse. Unions can't do much it seems. We're only labourers not men anymore, donkeys more like!' Bert mumbled pulling at his crumpled waistcoat which kept riding up over his belly. 'This week has proved I'm right, ain't it? Nothing 'ere for us I tell yer.'

His mate Jim looked up at them both with a knowing look as he leant on the bar. 'Yea, so we reckon Canada's the place for a new start. Stands to reason, don't it? Mightn't make a fortune but everyone says there's a good life there, new country, plenty of land, and we got a cheap deal with this government thing,' he boasted. 'Almost paying for us to go. It's obvious ain't it?' Jim picked at his hairy arm and flicked something off his skin. 'Why don't you try it mate? No more scratching a living.'

Bert chipped in. 'I lost mates in France behind the lines, good men. Saw terrible things I couldn't begin to tell yer. I reckon I was lucky. I came back with all me limbs, so I wants to make something of me life. I ain't going to flog m'self to death all me days like me old man, Lord rest his soul. I want a decent job and somewhere cushy to lay me head, if yer know what I mean,' he winked.

'We had a mate who went over there a couple of years ago, for a few quid they say, and we've heard he's got 'is own 'ouse and a pretty wife, lucky blighter. We didn't ever 'ave much when I was a nipper, though I never saw people beg in the streets in them days.' Jim drained his glass with a slurp. 'And it's getting worse I reckon.'

'So that's our plan, ain't it? Cheap Government scheme. We sail next Thursday from Tilbury, booked our tickets and hello Toronto!' Bert grinned showing broken teeth, his shoulders doing a little jig where he sat on his bar stool. 'I hope there'll be some easy women there too.' He winked again.

George thought more about their plans as he strolled back towards the lodging house in the late afternoon. Their words echoed in his mind as an idea gradually took root. This could be what he needed. It might be a chance for them in Canada. A new life. Why not?

He remembered the long talks with his own brothers late at night when they were fancy free, sharing their great plans of seeing the world, travelling to exotic places. His older brother Billy had gone to Canada later, though George had heard nothing from him since. Probably making his fortune. George's two sons would find it hard to get any work back home except down the mine and Dorcas was adamant mining was not for her boys. She'd lost one brother down there and another damaged for life. In Canada maybe, they would get a second chance. A bigger house with a garden, a clean start with jobs for their boys. Maybe a new beginning. He'd seen the advertisements in the paper so he knew Canada was cheap too.

George sat in his room thinking. He could not decide. He thought through the arguments in his head. Would Dorcas agree? What would she say? He wished he could ask her. It would be a big step for them all. What else was there for them? It was up to him. He must do something.

He sat on the bed then paced in his socks across the squeaky boards. George opened the catch and looked from the window down at the crowded street. Lads ran about dodging traffic. Then he noticed a man sitting on the pavement against a wall, slumped forwards, a stained and crumpled cap on the ground. He watched him for several minutes. It was true what they'd said, he never remembered beggars when he was a boy.

George went down to eat. The dingy, dining room with its green walls and stale smells of past meals, depressed him. Someone had left a newspaper on the seat and he picked it up. More reports of unemployment, rates-of-pay cuts and talk of union strikes robbed him of any hope. Fear of riots and protests filled the pages. Mounted police attempting to keep order. Then on a back page an advertisement for "A Life in Canada." George read as he chewed, arguing with himself. Maybe he'd not start back home tomorrow. Give himself time to think this through, to sort what he'd do. Back in his stuffy room he washed his face and hands in the cold water, pulled on his jacket and went back out.

The streets were damp from a summer shower as he mused over his idea. The air smelt fresher. He walked around not sure of local streets, as his mind went over the chances of a new life. Maybe he could do this. George felt a tingle of encouragement as he strolled past the public house where light and noise spilled out onto the pavements, shining off the puddles. He jingled the few coins in his pocket, hesitated then drawing his shoulders back he turned and pushed open the patterned glass door. Noisy laughter and the strong smell of beer hit him and some rousing music from a worn piano cut through the general buzz of men's voices. In the yellow gaslight he looked around. The same two men he'd met earlier lounged at the bar.

'Bert. Jim. You still drinking?' As George greeted them he ordered a beer and the three took their drinks to a table in the corner. The warm atmosphere with the music-hall tunes plonked out on the piano and the jovial chatter lifted his spirits. Once more their enthusiasm encouraged him as he listened to their young hopes. If he went, maybe he could find Billy, see how things went for his brother.

Billy might even be able to give him some useful introductions to help him with work.

The men said they were to collect their boarding passes on Wednesday morning at the docks. George remembered the details as later on he wandered back to the cold narrow bed. He lay there with his eyes tracing the stains on the ceiling where the single candle threw vague shadows.

George had already spent more than he'd intended. He imagined Dorcas's scorn, her look of frustration. Slowly he made up his mind. He would do it. He would grab this opportunity for them and turn this hell of endless effort and worry into a more comfortable life for them all. A bigger house with a fancy white porch perhaps. Dorcas would like that. He would show her how much he loved her!

George imagined her reaction, the smile on her face when he showed her a new home with wide steps and a veranda, perhaps some of those colourful trees in the garden he had seen illustrated in books .He imagined sweeping views, without being surrounded by tall mountains, and blackened coal tips. A feeling of freedom for them all. He turned onto his back again, put his hands behind his head and frowned into the darkness. Yes, he decided. Tomorrow he would book his passage and before he sailed he could send her a telegram. She couldn't argue then, could she? Shaking his head, George decided that he might avoid any bitter rows about this. Dorcas would surely agree for once.

Early next day George found the office where emigration officers, looking up at the strong man and hoping to fill their quotas, checked his details and approved a subsidised passage. By midday the following day he'd bought his one-way ticket third class. On Thursday morning George queued in the post office to send that telegram.

CHAPTER 4: Dorcas, August 1923

Dorcas glanced at the clock on the mantelpiece several times as the afternoon slowly moved on. What was preventing George from returning? Was he coming loaded with stock for the shop or working somewhere to make some money? She knelt and swept the ashes in the grate, talking to him silently. Why hadn't he contacted her? Had he got work? Had George taken her harsh words to heart, showing her he would not rush back? Though she worried about their argument, Dorcas was sure she had been right. Thinking about it she pursed her lips.

'It's unlike George not to let me know. Surely he'd send a message or a telegram at least,' shaking her head she murmured, seeds of doubt beginning to sprout in her mind. What could have happened? Was he safe? Had something happened? She frowned all afternoon and the children saw she was distracted. Their Sunday tea was quieter than usual before the two smallest girls started to squabble.

'She's taken the last of the jam and she knows it's my favourite.' Seven-year-old Ethel pushed her elbow across May's plate and grabbed at the slice of bread. May slapped back at her and they both yelled.

'Come on you two, stop it. Someone's got to have the last of the jam Ethel. It can't always be you.' Dorcas closed her eyes weary of their quarrels.

'Yes, she always gets everything she wants because she's the little one Mam!' Ethel looked tearful.

'It's true, she is getting quite spoilt I think,' said Marjorie quietly, normally defending her two younger sisters.

'When I need you to interfere Miss I'll ask. Ethel cut that piece of bread in two and you can share it. You, May, had better learn not to make such a fuss. I can do without your noise at present.' Dorcas rapped the table.

'Mam, when will our Dadda be back?' Olive asked. As the eldest of the younger four she missed her father and his jokes.

'I'm sure he'll be home later tonight or perhaps tomorrow morning after you've gone to the park.' Dorcas smiled around the table. The children asked more questions and she found reasons, more excuses, though not believing her own answers.

When the children were in bed, Dorcas sat for some time by the hearth. She crocheted hairbands for the girls, knowing they could wear them for Sunday best, while trying not to think of train crashes or accidents. Eventually, glancing at the clock at midnight, after plumping up George's cushion and raking through the dying fire, she went to bed leaving his meal ready, staying warm on the stove. She tossed in her bed for an hour before dreaming of disasters.

When Dorcas woke next morning, her hand felt across the bed for George as usual. He was not there. After breakfast she shooed the children off to the park fussing over them to cover her concern. Their school holidays stretched for weeks. Once they had gone she opened the shop and swept the floor, keeping busy to stop her nagging worry. Customers came in grasping shopping lists, and the takings that morning were better than usual. The busy hours passed, and Dorcas closed the shop for lunch then managed to hang out more washing in the warm air, arguing to herself as to why George had not returned. She called over the fence to Sarah next door who was sweeping her yard.

'Where can George be, Sarah? You'd have thought he'd let me know if he'd been held up? Perhaps sent a telegram.'

'Look Dorcas, anything might have held him up. He's probably following up some work or got a few days labouring at least. You know George, he'd want to earn anything if he had half a chance. Perhaps it's difficult to tell you he's fine. Maybe it means he has got some real work. I'm sure you'll hear soon lass.'

Sarah was older and a Tyneside widow with no children of her own, so her special care for them showed in her concerned frown. 'Come in and have a quick cup of tea and stop worrying, hinny. George is a big chap. I'm sure he can look after himself.'

'Yes, but Sarah, I said some awful things to him before he left. I feel bad about it. What if he's taken them to heart?'

'Oh, don't be daft, you two are a splendid pair. George loves you, so he'd ne'er do anything to worry you. He can'na send a message, that's all hinny.' The two women swallowed their tea, and Dorcas hurried back to the shop to find three customers banging on the door.

By Wednesday Dorcas was sure something terrible had happened to George. She went into the village telling herself she'd shop for food but her first stop was the post office where she spoke to the postmistress.

'Good morning Mrs Watson. I am expecting a letter, or it may be a telegram. It's rather urgent so I wondered if there is anything for me, anything which may not have gone out with Mr Watson's round perhaps?'

' Well, no, Mrs Haddon. Everything we've had in went back out on the round this morning, but I will get Mr Watson to check when he comes in. If we find anything has gone astray, I can assure you, we would send it out directly with young Joseph this afternoon. We don't usually have problems,' her mouth pursed, annoyed at the implication.

Dorcas thanked her and went on down the street to the police house. Here she asked the constable if there had been any problems with transport or accidents he had heard of in the past few days. He shook his head.

'You worried about George, Mrs Haddon? I expect he's got held up on business. Give him a few more days and then if you've not heard, come back and I'll put in a report. He's a big chap. He can look after himself so don't worry Mrs Haddon.' P.C. Thomas smiled with a sympathetic nod, stroking his chin as he speculated what George might be doing.

It was more than ten anxious days during which she imagined every kind of disaster before Dorcas saw the telegraph boy cycle along the path. She hurried to the door, her worst fears constricting her chest. She snatched it from the lad's hand and, without a word closed the door, leaning her back against it, her eyes closed. Slowly she read his message. What was this? Whatever was it about? Her mind whirled.

The words stared back at her:

'Sailing to Canada today STOP Will send for you all STOP Come soon STOP George STOP'

Canada? They had never talked about moving, never even thought of leaving the village. What kind of madness had got into George?

Then she heard Sarah's voice at the back door. 'Dorcas, Dorcas lass, what is it? I saw the lad on his bike. Is it bad news? Is it George? Can I help?'

'Come in Sarah. He's gone mad, completely mad. He must have been drunk when he sent this. Whatever has happened? It can't be true. It's crazy!' Sarah gave her a hug and read the telegram, her head on one side and shaking it, she said nothing.

'Sarah, tell me George can't have gone to Canada without even speaking to me, can he? What have I done to deserve this? Does he realise what a mess he has left behind? How am I going to cope with the shop, his customers and the children without him? It's been chaos this week with the school holidays. I haven't stopped. How can we follow him? The stupid fool. Do you think he has gone already?'

'Look at the date stamp on the telegram, it should tell you.' Ever practical, Sarah squinted at the smudged date. 'Not sure. It could be a week old, delayed perhaps, which explains it.'

'When I see him, I'm going to give him something to remember for the rest of his days. He can't do this to us. It's his big ideas again. Always got to be right!' She stamped her foot. 'Look and he doesn't even say "love George," just "George," like giving me an order.' Dorcas's shoulders sagged in disbelief.

Sarah moved to the kettle, 'Sit down Dorcas. You need a cup of tea.'

Her whole body shivered, and she slumped in a chair. 'Well, I don't care what he says, I'm not going anywhere. George can manage without us, and we'll manage without him.'

Sarah gave her the cup, putting her hand on Dorcas's shoulder. 'Calm down a bit before you make any decisions lovey. He'll write to explain more any day soon I'm sure.'

Dorcas spread the telegram on the table smoothing it with her hand repeatedly.

'And how ever am I going to tell the children? What will they think? I can't face them.' Leaning her elbows on the table she put her face in her hands.

'You'll do it and they'll understand. He's their father, they know him. Remember they love their Dadda too.' Sarah sat beside her.

'Well so do I but I can't understand one bit of all of this. Something must have gone wrong. Perhaps he's not well!' Dorcas frowned at her friend, stroking the tablecloth with a nervous hand.

It was late that night when she shared the news with her three older children. They became silent and obviously puzzled. 'I will tell the little ones tomorrow, but I thought you needed time to take this in. Then I hope you will help me break the news to them. I know no more than I've told you and I think for the moment we will let everyone think your father is in London on business. Soon I'll must tell people if he really has gone to Canada though not until I have had a chance to talk to your grandma. I will go to see her, but she mustn't hear from anyone else. You understand?' Tilda hugged her mother, and then Peter clung to his mam.

Roger frowning, his voice husky, said, 'Why Mam, why would Dadda do that?' Dorcas lifted her shoulders in bewilderment and sighed.

Peter, the youngest of these three at nearly twelve, looked closely at his mam and asked, 'Will we have to go back to school or are we going soon to Canada?'

'Oh, nothing will happen in a hurry Peter. Your Dadda's got to get himself settled first. We'll hear more in his letters I'm sure.' Dorcas felt she had to reassure them but she no idea how she'd explain this to her four little girls, but she was amazed when they thought it sounded like an adventure. Smiling at their glowing faces, Dorcas dreaded the enormity of the task ahead.

By the next weekend Dorcas decided she must tell her mother about the telegram. It would not be easy. She planned to visit on Sunday. Still angry and confused herself, with no idea of why George had gone off, Dorcas worried she must counter her mother's arguments and questions. She could not let him down even though she was seething that he'd disappear without discussing it with her. Dorcas knew nothing about Canada except it was north of America.

'What is their weather like … and the animals? Do they have proper schools?' Every time she thought of it she fumed. Her mother wouldn't curb her feelings either. The old lady was always outspoken and today proved no exception. They sat drinking tea in the cramped kitchen before Dorcas told her.

'I felt it in my bones there was something wrong my girl. What did you do? Has he got someone else? George always had an eye for the women, I've noticed.' The old lady looked knowingly, eyebrow raised, lips in a tight line.

'No Mam, he's not like you think. He's always been a good husband and a kind father. You can't say things like that. I won't stand for it.' Dorcas stood up putting her teacup down on the saucer with a rattle, as she leant towards her mother with a furious face.

Her mother crossed her arms and sat upright. 'You'd never know my girl. Wives are always the last to find out. Men can be so cunning when they want to. I always said he was too good to be true.' She plucked at her apron. 'And how much would it cost to go all the way to Canada I'd like to know? Good money which he should have left with you for the housekeeping.' She nodded. 'Has George got any work there? How does he think you are going to feed those youngsters, tell me?'

'I'll manage Mam. I've got the shop and there should be some money coming from the work he's done recently. I won't let them starve you know.' Dorcas worried how she'd really manage if George was away for long, how she could pay the rent. She had no idea why he'd gone or when she'd hear more.

Her mother put her head on one side staring up at Dorcas. 'And how will I explain this to your brother, to Ernest, I want to know? He will be upset George isn't here to take him to the pub.' Since the accident in the pit, when both Dorcas' brothers were trapped, with only Ernest coming out alive, her tall, favourite brother had needed George's care for many things, though her mother never remembered to thank George, her son-in-law.

'Everything is always from your point of view, Mam. What about our children? Anyway, I'll must be getting along. They will be back from Sunday School any time soon.' Dorcas pleaded, picking up her bag and coat. She pecked at her mother's cheek and hurried out, going over her mother's words as she walked home. Dorcas secretly seethed about George's thoughtlessness, but she would not admit it to her mother.

Much later, when the young ones had gone to bed, Dorcas heard crying. She stood at the bottom of the stairs and listened.

'My Dadda, it's my Dadda … I want him!' A little petulant voice came from the far side of the girls' bed. May's sobs silenced her sisters.

'Come on,' said Marjorie as she hugged her little sister and stroked her fair hair. Her sympathy drew a fresh wave of tears and sobs. At barely five May had no idea where her father had gone and had not absorbed anything about Canada. All she remembered was her Dadda had disappeared to London early one morning before they had gone to the park. London was somewhere else, somewhere beyond her world, on a train her sisters had said. And he had not come home by the time she had gone to bed … and he hadn't come home after lots of days.

Where was he? She wanted to see him, to be picked up and carried about the streets on his shoulders. She missed her Dadda's special hug and sitting on his knee. She wanted to put her hand out and close her eyes as she waited for a sweetie or a special treat which he always brought in his big tobacco-smelling pockets.

May's sobs subsided, tears dampening her plump cheeks as well as Marjorie's nightdress and she snuggled up to her sister while Marjorie crooned a lullaby. May moved as she was rocked. The little room the girls shared became still as Marjorie hummed the bits where she had forgotten the words. When they heard their mother's footsteps on the wooden stair, the others scrambled back into bed.

'What's this?' Dorcas stood hand on hips. 'Marjorie, back in bed with you. And May? What's the matter child?'

'She was crying Mam,' Marjorie replied, relinquishing May to her mother's arms then jumping into bed with her sisters.

'What are these tears for? Tell me May.' Dorcas stared at May, wiping the child's tears with the corner of her apron. The other girls pulled up the blankets, wide-eyed and silent as May turned down her lip at her mother.

Her daughter lowered her chin onto her chest as she muttered, 'I want my Dadda. I don't want Marjorie. I don't want you!' Dorcas, no longer patient with her youngest, stood up and put May in beside her sister pulling the blanket up over her small body.

'Now don't be a baby, May. You know Dadda can't be here, he's gone away to work. A long way away and he can't come home each night, it's too far. We'll go and see him soon I promise. We'll go on a train together. You'll like that May, won't you?' Distracted, Dorcas asked herself whether she meant this.

The girls' faces were questioning. ' Mam, what...?' Olive frowned hoping for an answer.

'Now you girls, no more talking tonight. You're not to disturb her and May, I want you to be a bit more grown up for me. I'm too busy to have this fuss.' Dorcas bent to the lamp near their bed and turned it down. As the light disappeared, she whispered, 'No more noise tonight girls, you hear me? Sleep tight,' turning away lest they see the tear in her eye. She wanted him back too.

Marjorie's arm went around May and she winked at her youngest sister. May resolutely closed her eyes and pouted as she decided she did not like her mam today.

When Dorcas came downstairs, she looked at her three older children seated at the kitchen table. Peter was sketching, his pencil skimming over the page, while her practical Roger carefully tried to solder a piece of metal, twisting the strip of solder over a candle flame, some invention in his mind. Tilda, sucking her pencil, was writing a letter to her father to be included with her mother's next reply.

The room was cosy and quiet in the soft lamplight. Dorcas looked at George's empty chair by the hearth. The sight of his scarlet cushion brought a lump to her throat. His absence made a big gap in their lives, bigger than she had realised. The children really loved him, and she missed him more than she had expected. Something massive was missing in their home.

'Mam, I've been looking up Canada in the lending library. It's a big place, much colder than here in the winter, loads of snow. There's lot of new things, railways and roads and the big things being built. It sounds an exciting place to live. Perhaps Dadda's right.' Peter put his hand on his mother's, trying to be helpful.

'I hope so Peter, I hope so.' She went to the scullery for a drink of water and stood clutching the edge of the wooden draining board. Looking out of the window above she pictured George stacking lengths of pipes and planks on the scaffolding covering the back wall. He'd climb there despite her pleading with him to be careful, seeing his mischievous grin at her concern. Where had her handsome young lover gone? What had happened between them? The love they both relished in the first years of their marriage had matured but had the caring dwindled? They no longer had those secret shared moments because their children and work filled every minute.

When George had not returned from London before the telegram arrived, Dorcas had worried for his safety, in part because he was the children's father, and the family breadwinner. Had any of her fear been for the man himself? She questioned her feelings. Had she forgotten how to love him for himself? Reflecting on her haughty attitude before he left she regretted being so dismissive of his efforts for them all. If she'd talked to him – maybe this wouldn't have happened. As she stood biting her lip, she planned when they met to show him she loved him still. No, not the tirade she had imagined in bed each night; that would not help at all.

Her mother's bitter words from earlier went through Dorcas's mind. Had she done something to make him go and stay away? What could she do? She tried to remember their argument, with her words echoing inside her head and her indignation which she had spat at him. Had she been fair? She regretted not allowing him to go with good grace. Why hadn't she turned to George and been more understanding. If she had maybe he'd have come back, talked it through. Had she challenged him? Did he feel he must prove himself? Was that what had caused this, or was it only lack of money? Perhaps George had got a good opportunity for a new life? She had never doubted him before this last year.

Dorcas peered at her reflection, the mirror no longer showing the young girl he had met long ago. Please don't let there be another woman though, she thought, closing her eyes. Anything but that!

CHAPTER 5: George, August 1923

As George entered the huge dock gates he looked up. The greys of concrete and stone mingled with the blackened wood which surrounded the dark water of the dock. The place was vast with only a wedge of sky above. He'd had no idea it would be so big. The ship 'Caronia' rode on the oily water stretching the length of the dock. Layer after layer of decks rose up, towering over him. People crowding everywhere, men shouting, as motors, vans and horse carts wove through the dockside, dodging the crowds and the packing boxes. Giant crane arms swung crates and even vehicles in huge slings on board. Their precision fascinated George as the dockers lowered them carefully to the deck and into the holds.

The smells of the great engines and the crowded quay were pungent. Stinking water mixed with fuel oil, crates of food and bellowing animals added to George's confusion. Even big expensive motor cars were being loaded. Dockers guided large quantities of goods on to the ship and smart officers checked documents as people bustled up the gangplank, some seeming wealthy from their clothes, their self-assurance, while others appeared anxious, working families, and single men in cheap jackets.

'Mind yer back sir if yer please.' The docker pushed a cart loaded high with crates, stacked one upon another through the crowds. George had never been on a large ship before, never even seen one as big as this. He stood back craning his neck as he looked up at several decks. Gulls swooped everywhere in a frenzy, scavenging for scraps between crates piled on the dock and screaming at their finds. Gusts of wind blew around his ankles.

Feeling confused with a cold moment of doubt curdling his stomach, he stood back against the wall clutching his bag. Where was he going? What was ahead? So many people knowing what they were doing, sure of their future. Frowning, he took a deep breath, overwhelmed by his decision. George suddenly felt alone without Dorcas, without his family. Plucking up his courage he shook himself. This was right. It was up to him to make a new life for them all.

'Can you tell me mate, where the booking office is?' he asked a porter.

'The shed over at the entrance. You'll need your papers ready, 'cause they'll be busy. She sails on the next tide.'

George queued for more documents which he'd been told to collect before he could find his way on to the ship, showing his pass and bounding up the gangplank. This was a challenge he told himself as he breathed the cold air with its rancid dockside smells. Excited by the scene before him, George stretched his shoulders, rolling them, thinking of his boys. They'd both love this, he was sure. It would be a new beginning for each one of them. He must remember to write to them about it all. Standing by the rail he looked down at the scum and debris swirling in the water. Had he really done this? Booked to have a new life, to start over again in a new country. Would it be a real adventure? He glanced over the high walls of the dock and saw the grimy bricks of the London streets, remembering the beggar sitting by his cap.

"No, this must be better," he thought. He picked up his tools and his bag and began to climb the lower gangway.

Within half an hour George found Bert and Jim again, who had grabbed an empty cabin in the third class corridor not far from the wash rooms. They dumped their bags on the four bunks looking through the locked porthole realising they were just about the water level, very low down in the ship. When others asked if the bunks were taken Bert said they were.

'We'll be grateful of somewhere to stow our stuff so if they don't check we can keep this cabin to ourselves. S'pose it depends if the ship's fully booked,' Bert grinned. The two men sat on the bunks opposite him smoking, and George felt they both knew a lot more about some things, had travelled more, understood the way things were in the world.

'We'll keep an eye out for you mate,' Jim grinned, winking.

When George put his bag on the bottom bunk and stowed his tools beneath, he realised he'd need to lock the cabin whenever he was out, for he did not trust any passing passenger who might fancy his precious tools. They were his passport to work, each one bought with hours of extra work throughout the years, some he had fashioned for a specific purpose himself. His tools were special, honed to his hands, each one with a history. George had always lived in his own secure home, wherever it was, and these temporary lodgings made him aware of their vulnerability, a problem he hadn't foreseen. He hoped he'd need the tools when he found work, but he'd keep an eye on them. George would be foolish to trust to luck here. There were so many strangers around finding their own spot, their own bunk. A man never knew!

Bert and Jim were both in their late twenties, seeming more aware of the world, having been abroad and in the army. When Bert clambered onto the top bunk George noticed how thin and fit they both seemed. He was fit himself, much more so than many his age but he was no longer so young. Not quite forty, he hoped these lads wouldn’t ask. He would walk the decks each day to keep up the exercise. Back home in his own back-yard, George swung his large wooden Indian clubs to keep fit each morning, always had and always intended to but he'd left them at home. He prided himself on his muscles. The ladies liked strong men.

' Right then, we're off to make a recce,' the others said. 'Yer coming?'

'No. I think I'll get my bearings later, thanks,' George decided. When they left him alone as they went to explore the ship, he drew out his wallet. He'd already paid for several nights' lodging and bought his government-subsidised ticket. It took several of the crisp white five-pound notes. When he needed to declare on the form the amount he was taking out of the country, it was thirty pounds. He guessed it would about stretch until he got work and more pay. He would not have time to waste when he arrived. He would look for a job straight away.

With the sound of hooters and an enormous blast George guessed the ship was about to move at last. He locked the cabin door and went up to the rail. Two sturdy tugs hauled the great ship carefully out of the docks dancing on the water in a formal pattern. He realised the pilot must be steering it out until they were in open water. He turned to look back at the dock.

No one to wave to but he raised his hand as he said goodbye to Britain, maybe for the last time he began to realize. A moment of fear checked him, a questioning of his decision, of the wisdom of such a big step, feeling panic rising in his throat. He started as the ship's siren hooted, people cheered as many on the dock cried too. George had not expected to feel like this, suddenly sad Dorcas wasn't beside him or their children. He couldn't stop it, could not change his mind. It was too late as he watched the water between the dock and the ship widen, flotsam swirling in eddies. He swallowed hard to check his tears reassuring himself they'd soon be together. First he must find them a home. It'd be hard work he didn't doubt but he'd succeed, he was sure. George squared his shoulders, put his head up and, with a serious look in his blue eyes, he lifted his hand and cheered too. The sharp breeze ruffled his blond hair as he took a deep breath. He felt a tinge of guilt but was sure this would be a fresh start for them all. It had to work. George must make it work.

He went below and found the third-class dining room, more like a canteen he felt. After a dinner of sausages,

George walked around the decks and found where the lifeboats were. He rubbed his hand along the rail, contemplating for the first time the terrible possibility of being in these open boats on the vast sea. No, he'd not worry about that!

As he rounded the stern of the ship, the wind hit him. He leant against it as he walked, amazed at its bitter strength. Rubbing his hands together he realised the dock had protected them from this stiff breeze, but they were heading out into some rough, open seas. The rolling deck surprised him as it was his first time on an ocean-going ship. Several times George swayed sideways and then he went through one of the many doors out of the driving wind. He made his way back to his cabin counting the doors. There he lay tossing about as he worried about what he'd started. He tried to doze but his stomach began to rebel. George felt slightly nauseous, so he lay still. Bert and Jim were not back so he felt no need to hide his feelings. Soon he needed to go to the lavatory where he stood waiting for his sickness to subside. It did not, and he retched. Creeping back to his cabin he fumbled with the key and sprawled across his bunk. He had not foreseen this. He felt bad. For several hours he suffered before he slept. He didn't hear when his cabin mates returned much later.

When George woke next morning, he felt a little better, but he couldn't have eaten anything. He remembered Billy his older brother who had gone out years before to 'make his fortune.' Had he suffered like this? George had no idea because there had been some mystery about Billy's departure, some reason no one mentioned. Young George had gone to bed one night and in the morning, Billy had gone. Ma raised an eyebrow when he asked, and he'd guessed it was either the law or a woman who had forced Billy's hand.

'Well it's not me. I will try and find him of course though I've no idea how. Worry about it later,' he thought. 'I'll write to Ma, she'll know for sure.'

Throughout the next few days George struggled with bouts of sickness and loss of balance before getting his sea legs. The three men were grateful they had a spare bunk to stow things on for everything seemed so cramped. Yet one day, George learnt what cramped meant when he found his way by accident down into steerage. Here whole families shared rooms with strangers. Crying babies and elderly couples struggled for air in a foetid jungle of humanity. He noticed the mothers, young and old, trying hard to keep things sweet, to sort the problems of their families and after great provocation yelling in different languages at their neighbours.

It made him think of Dorcas. She did the same, always trying to get the children to sort their differences. She'd ask questions and then at last she'd blow her top when they were determined to argue. She was so different from him. George smiled to himself. He would bang the table with his fist at the first sign of trouble and they'd jump into silence. Their looks told him they understood who was boss!

He glanced around wincing at the relentless noise down here, the constant thumping sound of the engines grinding against the nerves endlessly in the background. He smelt the coal mixed with the human smells of too many people crammed into the crowded area. Old men snored while babies cried and the young men gambled. No, he must send Dorcas enough for at least third-class fare when they eventually followed him. No steerage for his family.

The next day George retraced his steps finding his way down into the boiler room where sweating men shovelled fuel into the hungry iron mouths which glowed red in the vast dim belly of the ship. In the past he had worked for a while in mines or with great engines helping the pumps to function. He was interested in how the ship worked and his curiosity made him ask questions.

'Go through to the engine room and ask if you can watch if you're interested,' a stoker yelled. There the noise overwhelmed him. Giant greased elbows danced a jig in sequence and huge oily wheels and cogs rotated in unison.

An engineer shouted, 'Hey, you can't stay down here mate.'

'I'm only interested in how it works. I'm a plumber back home. I won't get in the way, don't worry. What's the tonnage of the ship?' George shouted, and seeing he was interested the man let him stay. He stared at the smooth rhythm, fascinated and managed a few questions. After a short while he could no longer stand the noise and the choking fumes. He climbed through the ship back to a deck where he went to the rail and breathed fresh air. George thought about all he'd seen, feeling sympathy with the poor men who worked down in the bowels of the ship day and night.

'I wouldn't want to do that, not for a fortune!' he told Bert and Jim later as they lay on their bunks, hands under their chins, reading the ship's newsletter. 'The heat was terrible. Those men were sweating buckets. Must be desperate for work. Just bloody galley slaves!'

With nothing to do every day, George noticed the different members of the crew, polite to others, instructed to keep the different classes of passengers apart where they could. Mainly uniformed youngsters with a few senior officers wearing braid on their cuffs, they seemed there only to serve the first-class passengers. George chatted to Bert as they sat on their bunks. 'The crew want to keep the riff raff like us away from those fancy women on the top deck.'

'Well they're the only ones who are likely to give them a tip, I s'pose,' Bert replied. 'Well, them or their sugar daddies. Got to keep their women folk on a tight rein with us handsome chaps about!'

'Mind you, some of 'em are a bit of alright, don't yer think?' Jim chipped in with a wicked look.

'Yea, I like that red head. I swear she winked at me yesterday.' Bert grinned, his hands outlining her shape. 'Might try me luck on the quiet. What yer reckon?' George said nothing, remembering he'd seen that girl and Bert was right. She was beautiful.

He noticed there was another unseen crew, not only those who stoked the engine but the cleaners who worked late at night, the cooks and kitchen staff who sweated in tiny galleys. A silent crew kept the ship going, carpenters and engineers having to be invisible, working around the troublesome passengers like mother hens with muddled chicks. George watched the ship's crew dance around them as he absorbed this new world.

Each day he kept up the walks and varied his route about the decks, determined to stay fit. At first, he noticed many new things around the ship, clever devices which intrigued him. Hinges and locks which held doors and internal windows closed in bad weather, adapted for the special circumstances of an ever moving ship. Ideas he might be able to adapt he thought.

Soon his days dragged. Used to the bustle of daily work with the shop and family life, George felt trapped with nothing he could do except walk and watch. He smiled at some of the lovely women he saw but, although tempted, he left it at that. Each day he missed his family's chatter and most of all he missed Dorcas, thinking of her as he lay in the darkness on his bunk at night.

One calm night George took a stroll around the decks, stopping, as he smoked his pipe leaning on the rail. He watched the strange lights making zigzag patterns on the water. The moon shone bright and he looked up to the stars.

'I never have much time for things like this, always too busy back home in the village,' he thought. He wished he could share this vast different world with her, remembering a few times when he and Dorcas first met, when they had taken secret strolls beneath the moon, desperate to be alone. Sometimes she talked about the stars and her hopes, about her beloved music and books. George remembered how he'd watched her soft hazel eyes and a fluff of fringe giving a solemn look to her young face and his feelings of love for Dorcas returned. He took slow breaths hoping it wouldn't be too long before they were together again. She was a good wife, a good mother. He had chosen well he knew.

George had not thought about such things for a long time. Probably he had not told her how he felt either. He missed her laughter, her support, her comforting body in bed beside him. He promised he'd write to her about this when he had the time, but he always found it hard to say things, to express himself, to show her how he felt. George wasn't good with words.

The next day he went to the ship's stationers, bought paper and a pencil vowing to keep his promise. Each day he tried to write, he got stuck. George couldn't express what he meant, to find words which didn't sound false or excessive. After half their lifetime with each other they never spoke about their feelings, often too busy with their family and work to choose the words for their close relationship. Everything had become accepted and taken for granted. Both slipping into bed exhausted or irritated, they had often fallen asleep before there was time to talk. They had little energy and even less opportunity to show affection or love. George realised it had become an awkwardness between them, a way of using tiredness as a barrier preventing them from talking of their love.

Crumpled pages of letters littered George's bunk whenever the others were elsewhere, and he quickly pushed the evidence aside when the men returned. He did not want them to wink at him and joke about his wife. So he had no letter to send to Dorcas when they arrived in Canada. He promised himself he would write soon, any day now.

The final days of the voyage dragged. When they eventually approached the shore, he was very relieved to see land. He stood at the rail, bag packed, wearing a clean collar and hair slicked back. He watched the tight manoeuvre to close the gap between the ship and dock, judging the band of dark water as it narrowed. George felt very alone although his new friends stood beside him waving to no one and making loud calls. He sniffed the air full of strange new smells with shouts and sounds of engines and hooters. He shook himself silently vowing, 'I'm doing this for you, Dorcas my love. Somehow I'll make this work!'

The journey had been challenging with little to do except try to plan his future. There were so many questions, things he wasn't sure about, which he didn't know. Dorcas must have heard by now, and George hoped she had started to plan. He wondered what she felt. He guessed she'd be pleased, see it as an opportunity, surely. He must write a letter. George looked at the distant skyline and picked up his bag taking a deep breath before walking to the gangway. 'This is our chance of a new life. Dorcas will see the sense in this,' he told himself as he hurried down onto the dock, unaware of what had happened to his telegram.

CHAPTER 6: Dorcas, September 1923

When Dorcas explained George's absence to customers and others in the village, she mentioned business in London in a voice which spoke of important work, though her neighbours doubted it was the whole story. She guessed they whispered exaggerated tales of rows or money and other women. She saw their sidelong glances, their downward looks. Dorcas thought hard about it. She had to support George, to allow them both to hold their heads up whatever the outcome.

She said nothing, guessing the truth of the telegram had leaked out and the gossip was spreading. Soon the village heard he was on his way to Canada. Dorcas must have faith in him. Gradually the idea was becoming a possibility. Surely, he'd sort a new life for them and she would help George? They'd always managed together. Raising her chin and withdrawing her look, she hurried through the village speaking to no one as their speculative glances hurt.

Sarah got through to Dorcas later one day as she stood in the kitchen. 'Come on lass, sit yourself down. Take no notice of them old gossips. They've got nothing better to chatter about.' She took hold of Dorcas's hand and rubbed it reassuringly. 'Your man's doing what he thinks is best for you all. You mustn't worry. I know your

George, he's decent. I'm sure there isn't anyone else if that's what you're thinking. I've seen him look at you. He loves you and your young ones. We women must leave it to the men to make these decisions. What alternatives have we? It's the way it's always been.'

'Oh, Sarah, it's just I wish he'd come back, and we could have talked about it. Is it too much to ask? Is my opinion worth nothing?' Dorcas raised her eyebrows in a query, as she ironed on the kitchen table and she banged the flat iron on the back of the stove, picking up another hot one, spitting on it to test the heat and scrubbing the surface clean with a rag.

The bell on the shop door rang and Dorcas went to serve a customer.

'Good afternoon, Mrs Haddon. Can you tell me please, when is Mr Haddon returning to the village, only we have this dripping gutter and my husband says we need it repaired soon or it will make the house wall damp? He's asked me to find out.' Mrs Townsend put her head to one side with a smug smile waiting for Dorcas's reply, her eyes darting about the shop looking for any indication of a change.

'Well, I'm sorry Mrs Townsend. My George is on his way to Canada on business at present, so I think it will be a while before I can tell you whether he'll be back working any time soon. I believe young Fred in the new houses is coping with one or two jobs in the village, so it might be best if your husband contacts him for the present, if it's urgent of course.' Dorcas hated giving away opportunities of work but asked outright she had little alternative.

'All right, we'll do that then,' was the reply and Dorcas guessed Vera Townsend would soon be feeding the general gossip on the street corner.

A commercial traveller held the door open for Vera as she left. He came in, tipping his hat at Dorcas as he opened his order book. 'Good afternoon Mrs Haddon. I was in the area and wondered if you had any orders for me today?' He nodded. His smile suggested he'd already heard George was not there.

'I'm sorry Mr. Burton, my husband is away at present and I have no idea what he might need. Perhaps we could leave it for this month?'

'Are you sure? Well, I wonder if you have any cash off the account as it's been over two months since we last had anything from Mr. Haddon?' Mr Burton's pen hovered over the page.

'I'm sorry, I always leave the business to my husband I'm afraid. He deals with the purchases. I only work in the shop.' Dorcas fidgeted with the price tickets, avoiding his glance.

'Oh, I'm sure I've dealt with you in the past Mrs Haddon. You always have a good idea what he needs.' He was persistent. 'I hope he hasn't had to go for any family trouble which may have occurred?' He smiled at her in a gesture of pretend sympathy.

'No, no. Nothing like that. Well thank you Mr Burton. I will bid you good afternoon,' she said with a polite smile as she ushered him across the tiled floor and closed the shop door behind him. Hurrying back to the kitchen, red-faced and furious, Dorcas realised Sarah had finished the ironing and a neat pile of clothing lay folded on the table.

'Oh, you are a dear. I couldn't stand another moment with all those questions. What am I going to do Sarah?' Dorcas sunk in the chair clasping her face in her hands. 'I can't deal with much more of this.'

'Dare I say more tea?' Sarah lifted a quizzical eyebrow and gave a belly laugh as the two women grinned.

When Mr Reece the rent collector came on Thursday, Dorcas had enough to pay him. She had put the money with the book on the parlour shelf as usual and asked him to step inside as she went to the pot. He smiled at her and took the money counting it and putting it in his leather bag. He stroked his moustache then got out his fountain pen, making a lot of fuss marking up the rent book. Head on one side he asked her how she was doing and, smiling, he seemed more chatty than usual.

'I want to say something, Mrs. Haddon … um... Dorcas. If any week you haven't got quite enough ... a bit hard up, I'm sure I can help you out.' He patted her hand. Dorcas was flummoxed.

He had never called her Dorcas before; she had never dreamt he would. 'Well, it's kind of you but I always pay my way Mr Reece, so it really won't be necessary, thank you!'

'As I say, you are a woman on her own so to speak, I'd love to be of service if there is anything you need. You know my dear.' He looked at her with a sideways glance and stroked her hand as she took back the rent book. 'You only have to ask.' He lifted a questioning eyebrow. She flashed him a haughty look which she hoped would kill any ideas he had. How dare he? Was he to be the first of many men who thought they could take liberties? She must be careful. Dorcas felt indignant but a little concerned. Ushering him out, she closed the door behind him with a sharp click as he walked away wearing a sly smile. She would not let him get past the kitchen door again if she could help it. Horrid little man, she thought.

When the children were home that afternoon, Dorcas gazed across the cluttered kitchen at Ethel, who sat beside the hearth on a small wooden stool. It was just her size and one George had made when Tilda was tiny. The rays of sunlight shone on her dark curls as Ethel frowned at the reader in her hand looking at the pen drawing of fairies. The book had the simple words each of their children had learnt from in the past.

I should give her some time though I'm always too busy. Dorcas pounded the dough in frustration, realising how distracted she'd been. Perhaps Olive will help her, or Tilda. Ethel was struggling to decipher the words letter by letter, her finger tracing the line. 'Mam, what's this say?' At seven years old she found it difficult, but Dorcas guessed her daughter would enjoy reading once she got started. Her sixth child had always searched for books, getting her sisters to read to her whenever she could. Dorcas knew stories would be a quiet escape for Ethel in the future, smiling as she remembered enjoying tales of adventure and heroism when she was young.

Ethel had always been timid, and shy with none of her sisters' bounciness. Dorcas often found her tucked in a corner, under a table silently mouthing the words of some story unfolding around the pictures in her mind. As soon as she can really read, she'll be avid for proper books, not just primers, Dorcas thought. Are there libraries in

Canada? Surely there must be. Dorcas pondered on how little she knew about this 'promised land.'

'Come here Ethel, let's see if I can help.' Covering the dough with a tea towel and wiping her floured hands on her apron, Dorcas hitched her daughter onto her knee and started to read from their family's old copy of Blackie's First Reader. For the next few minutes mother and daughter shared a few fun moments hearing the magic words unfold for Ethel's imagination. Her eyes glowed as she entered the mystery of fairy tales, loving the sound of the words.

Warm and secure in her mother's love, Ethel wallowed in the unexpected attention she received. Being neither the baby nor one of the confident older girls, with her undemanding character she rarely had her mother to herself. The pleasure of their close safeness showed in one of her rare smiles. Dorcas's help made the words come alive and, after listening to the whole story, mother and daughter bent their heads as Dorcas's finger followed the words. Ethel found herself saying words she remembered, recognising them with delight, conjuring rainbows in her own images, her tiny body tense with anticipation.

Dorcas hugged Ethel and sat her down on the stool listening to her while sorting clothes into piles, reminding her of difficult words. Soon she returned to the dough in the scullery, delighted at the sight of Ethel interpreting the magic of the story in front of her. She would soon be a reader Dorcas thought. I must tell George in my letter.

Roger, waiting for his fourteenth birthday in a month, when he could leave school and start to earn, noticed his mother's worried frown when she was thinking at the end of each day, pencil and cash book on the table. He guessed it was about money. It was always about money. He had often helped his father with many practical tasks holding tools or helping solder joints in pipes on a Saturday or after school. He had expected to learn more from George, although now his father was no longer there, he wondered what he could do? Roger decided the town must have a new plumber and if he could find him, maybe a new man would give him some work.

A week later when he talked to Fred Price, he felt this could work. He spoke politely to him and Fred, who had recently moved to the village, agreed to give him a try. Roger didn't know how to tell his mother.

Tilda worked alongside Dorcas tidying in the shop one evening when, with no customers in, Dorcas told her to mind the shop while she went into the kitchen to see to the children. 'Mam,' Tilda said putting her hand out to Dorcas, 'can I talk to you for a minute please?' Dorcas looked at her wondering why she was so serious.

'Well of course love. What's the matter?'

'You see, it's Roger. He doesn't want to tell you, but as he's been helping Dadda a lot, learning how to do things in the business, plumbing and everything, well, as that's stopped with Dadda away, he wants to work for someone else, earn a bit to help out.'

'It would depend on what it was Tilda. Has he been looking out for work?'

'Yes, only after school, but he said he might get more work when he can leave school.' Tilda looked hesitant.

'Well, it would be good for him. There is so little work here, any opportunity would be useful. Come on, what is it and why isn't he talking to me about this?' Dorcas knew work was not easy to get at present so she was suspicious. 'It isn't far away, is it?

'No, no nothing like that. It's with young Fred, whose getting some work our Dadda used to get and he needs a hand sometimes. He heard Roger has often been helping Dadda this year, so he guessed he'd know what to do.' Tilda looked intently at her mother. Dorcas took a sharp breath. She should have guessed this would happen.

'I'll think about this, come along. Let's stop gossiping because I've got to go in and see to the girls. I can hear them quarrelling and … tell Roger I'll talk to him about it later. I don't want to discuss this with the others around.' Dorcas took off her shop apron with a flourish and walked into their kitchen, frowning.

Busying herself with the children she thought over what Tilda had said. George knew Roger was a quick and useful worker. They had both planned he would work with George in the future. Now this young Fred, as he was being called in the village although he wasn't so young, was moving in on the gap left by George's absence. What if George came back? Would the village easily return their work to George or did Fred charge less? Was this disloyal to George or was it a way her son would learn the trade and maybe get real work.

Roger was intelligent and, if there had been more money, he might have gone to one of the nearby town's secondary schools, instead of staying at the local Elementary School. She had dearly wished it for her children, but wishes did not pay the fees, didn't buy uniform or books. If they really were going to emigrate, would it matter if the lad had some work in the meantime? Dorcas mulled over the questions. When the younger girls were in bed and quiet, she sat down with Roger at the kitchen table.

'Now son, Tilda said you wanted to speak to me. What's this about?' Roger blushed and started to tell her about Fred.

'Right, well I've thought about what you've said, and I think you can start to help him after school and on Saturdays for the moment and let's see how you get on. If he really offers you more work when you leave school after your birthday, we'll decide then.'

'Won't Dadda think badly of me for doing that? Should you write and ask him?' The lad looked worried.

'No, I think your father would want you to go on learning how to fix things and if we do get to Canada you will be on the way to helping him out again. I think you should do this but make sure he pays you fairly and doesn't give you only the dirty jobs. He must show you what to do properly. Tell him your Dadda always did that and then he'll feel he ought to do it too. Make sure you are safe using those tools and any hot solder. I don't want you hurt. No climbing, you hear me? Perhaps I should speak to him.' Roger hugged his mother. She brushed his tousled head before going through to lock the shop.

So, throughout the autumn as the leaves clogged the gutters and rain dripped through leaking pipes Roger learnt with Fred. For his few hours after school as the evenings shortened, and on his Saturdays spent with Fred, he got a shilling or two each week for his troubles. He trundled the cart with ladders and tools, cleared the debris of their work and seriously tried to learn all Fred told him. He grew to like Fred who seemed much younger than his father and treated Roger like a mate. At times Roger swelled with pride when he managed a new skill and Fred praised him. His father never did that.

Each week, when he had been paid, he proudly took the money to his mother. She tried to refuse it, but he argued with her and said it was his contribution to his keep. Dorcas hated taking it yet was so grateful for the little help it gave, as she hugged her son with a lump in her throat. She would remember his concern for the problems George had left with her for a long time.

CHAPTER 7: George, September 1923

Disembarking, George looked about for something familiar. The skyline was open with a few cranes and high gantries used to service the ships, their shadows cast by the sharp sunlight. He could not see the land past the high walls enclosing the windy dock. Leaves and paper whisked about in eddies. The cobbles underfoot were slippery and crowded with luggage and wooden crates of goods. Dockside smells stirred up by the swish of the foul water with chains and ropes moving through it, caught in his throat. Flotsam and weeds added to the scum on the water. Men were unloading the ship and he heard strange calls in a foreign tongue. He guessed it was French. Something unfamiliar about their clothes, their gestures made him question his previous images of Canada.

They went through some form of customs where questions were asked of the three men and they were checked for signs of disease although they were hurried through their procedures. As he came into the open air he looked around. Wherever was he? Another busy dock with more shouts in foreign languages. The three men had looked at a map on the wall of the ship's lounge to get some sense of direction. George realised he knew little of this large country, but it felt good to get his feet back on firm ground.

He followed the others laden with their kitbags out of the dock area, grateful they had arrived in the daylight. Buildings and wide roads spread out before them, all busy with a newer look than back home. Carts and vehicles cut through the streets, full of bustle and hurry. They sensed a feeling of urgency in the people, a youthfulness which encouraged them. They grinned at each other. The pace was different, sounds and smells sharper. They felt this was the place to be, each one of their senses alert. It was a new beginning.

Dark clouds scuttled across the sky and when the threatened rain started it was bitterly cold, its ice-like needles slapping his face and George's cheeks became stiff. Could it be hail? So early in the autumn? He blinked away the wet and pulled his jacket about him. At least he could see the street signs. He had no idea where he would sleep that night. George went with Bert and Jim to the nearest shop to buy a loaf of bread, some cheese and a bottle of beer to share. They asked about accommodation and were given a couple of directions towards some cheap boarding houses. They must find somewhere to stay while they enquired about work permits and casual employment. It meant it might be some time before they got work but it was the priority for them all. They needed to earn some money fast.

Strolling through the streets looking for street names or numbers all three were animated. Soon they split up, each going to different digs for a couple of nights but promising to meet in the public house each evening to share whatever they discovered. There seemed to be many men like themselves wandering around, strangers to the district. Each ship unloaded more immigrants, some very young and unaccompanied, brought in as cheap labour on one of the government schemes. Canada needed workers.

George got a shared room in a terraced house down a dingy back street with no curtains on the windows or between the beds. It smelt of stale cooking and strong disinfectant. He hardly undressed and lay awake, anxious about his things which he hid beneath his bed at night, hoping to hear if the other man tried to steal anything. When at last he heard him snoring, he felt he could sleep. He checked next morning but nothing seemed to have been moved.

Finally, he wrote a letter to Dorcas talking of what he saw in the streets; of the makeshift stores, the shack-like buildings. He had to lean on a small shelf under the window, as it was hard to find words. George reassured her he would be busy looking for work and would write again when he got settled. Those things he really wanted to say about how he missed her and about the stars he'd watched on the ship seemed silly now. The children were bound to read his letters and he could not share his feelings with them. No, he'd write to her again soon. He queued for a stamp and posted it on the way to the pub.

The landlady was insistent. 'No smoking inside, I'm afraid gentlemen. I have had near misses with fire with my gentlemen before so I'm afraid you'll go out into the yard if you wish to smoke.' George could see why in such a cramped house. He stood in the cold yard late that night to smoke his pipe before climbing into the narrow bed where his wide frame filled every corner. The blankets were thin and smelt of mould and of previous other men as he lay there and tried to sleep, watching the shadows from the street reflected on the ceiling. As he tossed about, he could not help becoming aware of his loneliness. As he drifted, he thought of Dorcas and remembered their first meeting when she was just a girl of eighteen.

George had seen Dorcas for the first time as she played the piano in a village entertainment. He had visited an aunt and cousins in the little Welsh town a few days before Christmas, when he was only twenty-one. They took him to the crowded chapel hall, where he sat squashed between his cousin Ellen and rows of excited parents. Nervous children sang carols and a broad-hipped lady on a small chair played a harp. A few adults performed poems and jokes before a young girl, dressed in an emerald velvet, fancy costume with a crimson bodice, which matched her blushing cheeks, sat at the piano. He stared at her, transfixed. She fascinated him as he watched her upright back, hair coiling down it. Swallowing hard George whispered to Ellen. 'Who's the girl at the piano? '

'It's Dorcas, she's a music teacher here at the school. If you want, I'll introduce you later.' With a mischievous grin she glanced at him guessing his motive. He sat enthralled watching every movement of her neat figure and shy smile as the audience clapped the children. At the end of the entertainment, he watched the girl shepherd children outside where their parents reclaimed them, and he tried to see over all the heads but lost sight of her small figure. His cousin went to talk to a friend and forgot her promise. He went out at the back of the hall, looked around everywhere but couldn't see Dorcas. As they walked home later he felt disappointed at not having been introduced. Throughout the evening he had thought about her, surprised at his own interest, remembering her slim figure and shy smile.

In the past, he had known a few women who were friendly, but no one had intrigued him like this girl. In bed he decided to ask where she lived, find out a bit more. Maybe walk along her road, past her home. He daydreamed they met and chatted, of the witty things he'd say. At last George slept but when he woke she was still on his mind.

Bored with the visit, he had secretly planned to return home early next morning but as the day wore on, the thought of the girl persisted, and he decided to stay till evening. Frustrated as the day passed, in the late afternoon he went for a walk and strolled along the chilly village street, past the lighted windows and glanced in at the few shops scattered between houses. He heard a shop door open, bell pinging and he watched as a girl in a dark green cloak came out, shopping basket in hand. He stopped and could not believe his luck. He had found her. She turned up the hill and he hurried after her breathing hard.

'Excuse me Miss. It's a bit forward of me, but can I say how much I enjoyed your playing at the concert last night?' Dorcas turned and looked up at him and he felt his stomach wrench. From that moment he was lost. Something in his chest leapt and he felt himself blush.

Desperate he wanted to know her more, to talk to her. She fascinated him and he could not think of a thing to say. Dorcas made some comment about the children enjoying it with their parents and he must have replied for she smiled, and they walked towards the grocer's shop together. Afterwards George could not remember a word he had said but every gesture she made was imprinted on his mind. George decided she was the one for him.

It sounds stupid after all this time he thought as he lay in the narrow bed, but he had been right about that he was certain. As he turned over he shivered, got out and pulled his jacket across his feet over the thin blanket.

The pitcher of water in the morning was cold but George had often washed as a lad with his shivering brothers at an outside pump, so he made little of it. Breakfast was bread and beef dripping with a cup of tea which did not satisfy his appetite, but he didn't complain as the lodgings were cheap. He'd buy some food later. Today he must get work.

When he walked outside he saw men trudging into the centre of town where large organisations were based. He followed them, joining the queues for various companies who only wanted labourers but the few at the front got the day's work. George guessed others understood any local opportunities but he stood out as a well-fed foreigner and was ignored. Moving to the next queue he tried again.

As the hours wore on he became frustrated and impatient. When he tried to argue he was met with surly indifference. By mid-afternoon, weary and disheartened, he wandered into the square to look for somewhere to eat. He found a small cafe, ordered bread and cheese eating it in a hurry. From his perch on a high stool by the window he watched the square where a fight had broken out. George imagined it was in part the frustration men felt. The workers brawled, shouting, their French voices spitting abuse. Beer was thrown, the bottle shattering on hardened earth. Pulled apart by others the men swore at each other, adjusting their clothes, reluctantly walking away.

Around him the Canadians chattered in various languages and he noticed a native, with plaits and huddled in blankets, sitting stone-faced on the ground by a wall. It dawned on George he too was a foreigner. He remembered his own caution when dealing with any strangers back home in his own village. He ate some apple pie crushing the pastry, thinking hard. Even they didn't taste the same, not like Dorcas' pies. Things here were different, very different. George brushed away the crumbs on his trousers as he stood up, telling himself he'd be careful. This place certainly was not like home.

For the next few days George tramped the streets queuing for work and becoming more disheartened. Further in from the docks he noticed a change. Workers seemed resigned to joining pointless lines of desperate men. He saw men, frayed and forlorn, waiting for work and some begging in doorways. Hunger made men watchful and irritable. Tired women carried children; skirts plucked at by a gaggle of others. He guessed they were homeless staying in temporary shelters and grateful for church soup kitchens. Children seemed subdued, though babies grizzled while the busy world passed by. This was not the picture he had visualized before he disembarked, not the picture suggested by the posters in the emigration office. Life here for some was as hard as it was at home he realized.

The three men met each night in the local pub. Careful of their money they ordered half pints and made them last. They needed somewhere warmer than the streets to meet.

'There seems nothing 'ere. They don't want us. I've been getting there earlier than many in those queues but still no chance,' Bert said. 'I reckon lots of men queue overnight, 'though it must be freezing. Yer could be dead in the morning.'

George agreed. 'There's less here than at home. I think we'd do better go inland perhaps, somewhere they need men like us. Men in the queue were talking about going to labour camps, places where you lived on site, bunked down with others and helped push into the outback. Might give us a start.'

'I've 'eard it too. Bet it's bloody 'ard work though,' Jim nodded.

'Yea but it's better than starving 'ere. That ain't what we came for. S'pose we could try it for a couple of months. Get ourselves on our feet, like.' Bert took out a cigarette pack, realised it was empty and, with an annoyed tut, threw it away. He stuffed his hands into his pockets. 'Oh damn, I must manage without even a fag I suppose.'

'And I ain't got none left so it's no good looking at me.' Jim shrugged.

George searched in his pockets and offered them both a cigarette. 'That's your last tonight, understand?'

By the end of the evening the three of them agreed they must move inland to find work and soon. They asked the pub landlord about the labour camps which employed men to push further into undeveloped territory. He lowered his eyes but told them some men were working on new mining sites and tunnelling into mountains for railways. 'Go and have a word with the fella with the grey pigtail in the corner, he'll tell you more.'

They went across, bought him a half and he gave them directions. 'I deliver to some of the camps around here. Bloody hard work mate but you get your grub and somewhere to kip at night. Think about it and be outside here at sun-up if you want a ride. It's too far to walk, but it'll cost yer.'

Sitting together they talked it through and decided. They begrudged having to pay for the transport but could hardly walk the many miles to the camps. Here in this town their shabby accommodation was costing them precious cash when there was little promise of work. They'd be glad to leave this depressing place.

The following morning the three gathered their packs and started out. Seated in the open back of his truck they travelled all day jolting along over ruts and rough ground. The dirt tracks led through an occasional township though most of the day was spent bouncing through forests and over rocky hills, past bright rivers and tiny settlements of dark wooden shacks, with smoking chimneys. The smell of vegetation and the sound of bird and animal calls intrigued them as they stared around.

'How much further is this camp, for God's sake? We come miles already.' Jim asked.

By the late afternoon, tiredness made them doze. They were dumped, hungry with limbs cramped and aching, outside a camp, more than thirty miles into the wilderness as the light started to fade. They trudged uphill for half a mile until they reached high fences and gates. Explaining their need for work at the entrance their papers were checked, and they were shown into a wooden hut to be questioned by the foreman.

A scrawny man sat in a battered swivel chair, surveyed them from beneath thick brows. 'English?' He removed his pipe and with a French accent set out his rules of employment. 'And in case you have any clever ideas, the bosses do not allow any unions on site, so, if it bothers you, you can, how you call it, "sling your hook." I don't want any reds here!'

George kept silent though he felt Bert twitch, so he touched his arm. Without unions they could be hired and fired for no reason, their pay withheld, and they had no rights. By now they were hungry and exhausted with no way to go on or back. They must stay for the moment, realizing they were trapped. They would have to settle for this … for now.

George watched the foreman smirk as they each signed the docket for their place in the bunkhouse, a meal ticket and a blanket. The man stank of tobacco and worse, though George guessed the foreman enjoyed having the upper hand on the three men and he had no reason to disguise it. George had met men like this before and decided to say nothing as the foreman coughed and spat into a brass spittoon on the floor. He looked up at them his eyes flashing a challenge. The three men stayed silent, their downward glances admitting nothing. This was the best way to keep the job.

After stowing their bags beneath their bunks in a wooden hut, where the gaps were stuffed with paper and rags around the windows to stop the draughts, they found their way to the canteen. Jim patted George's back.

'Well George, thank God we at last got some work. I 'ope the food's good.'

'I 'ope there's plenty of it. Me guts is rumbling like a steam train. I'm bloody starving,' Bert said as he pushed through the door. The hubbub of voices was mostly French. George felt vulnerable, aware of his lack of understanding and the hooded glances of the men in the queue. The two others seemed unaware, having a smattering of French from their time in France. The meal was a stew, maybe a bit of beef with lots of onion with soggy vegetables, standard food for working men with no other option. Bert chatted at the other two as he ate but with little encouragement he fell silent. George became aware of being watched as the voices in the canteen lowered to a whisper. Obviously, others were curious, measuring them as newcomers, foreigners. As soon as they'd cleaned their plates they left, the feeling of being amongst strangers chilling the air.

Later, after wandering around the beaten earth paths to get their bearings and finding nothing except huts and small groups of other men smoking, they returned to their bunkhouse. They chatted quietly for a while, aware soon others would be joining them in the confined space.

George, tired of Jim's chiding, agreed he must write a letter to Dorcas. He sat and chewed his pencil pondering what to say before scribbling on a notepad which smelt of his kitbag and its contents. Somehow, he could not tell her much about how he felt, so he told them of his journey and talked about obtaining a new job. He wanted them to imagine him working away, despite not yet knowing what the job would entail. George pictured the children, particularly his boys, listening to his words as Dorcas read his letter out. He wanted them to feel proud of him, to be excited by his adventure, so the words were positive. As later he lay back and thought, he wasn't so sure this was such a good idea. This wasn't what he had dreamt.

The light had gone so Jim lit the oil lamp balanced on the shelf to the side of the central stove, and Bert put more wood in from the pile to stoke some heat. Others came in from the cold and prattled on mainly in French, excluding the three men. George squinted in the yellow glow as he reread his letter.

Send to George Haddon, East Camp, Laval, Quebec, c/o Toronot City Postal Office, Ottawa, Canada

'Dear Dorcas and Children,
After a journey on an enormous ship, I have arrived at a work camp where most of the men are French. Your old Dadda may learn some while he is here. It seems there is plenty of work at this place, so it won't be long before I can send for you all. This letter may take quite a time to reach you as we are miles from any post office, so they collect the letters every week and the carter takes them to Toronto for

posting. The houses in the bigger towns have white fences and apple trees. I think it will be a grand life here for us all.

It was a long journey on a truck through wild country with huge trees. I'm not sure if I heard a bear in the forest. I have had some strange stew, not sure what the meat was, probably some wild animal. No good for you, Tilda!

Love to each of you and take care of your Mam, especially you, Roger. Help her as much as you can. Love Dadda.'

He wondered if he should say more, something to Dorcas, or even kisses at the bottom but decided not this time, next time perhaps. He was tired, his back ached, and he was not in the mood to write more. What could he tell them, not the truth of the feeling of unrest he felt? No, there were some things men never said.

CHAPTER 8: Dorcas, October 1923

Dorcas got another letter from George at the end of October. She read it before the children returned home. It was full of encouragement for her to join him speaking little of his work.

Send reply to George Haddon, East Camp, Laval, Quebec c/o Toronto City Postal Office, Ottawa and it will find me.

Dear Dorcas and children,
Hope you are well and being good. You must be wondering about my decision to come here, but there are lots of opportunities in Canada. It is a grand country, wide open and with lots of pretty houses which you girls will love. They want people to emigrate and are helping with the fares. It will be a little while before I can send you the fare to join me, but I am working hard to save up. No toffees here May, but we do get maple syrup sometimes, which they tell me comes from trees and it is good. The post here is very slow as it has to wait for the carter to come to the camp, so you may not hear from me for a while. Take care of your mam for me.
Love to you all, Dadda. XXXX

She held the paper to her cheek hoping she could catch a sense of George but there seemed nothing, just an earthy smell. George was not there, his words only talking about houses he had seen, with white fences and fruit trees in the garden. She guessed these were more of George's dreams, his optimistic ideas when he had barely arrived. She feared for the truth as he said it would be some time before he could send her any money to pay for their fares. He promised he would write again soon, though the mail was difficult and slow as he'd heard but he sounded positive.

'Lots of promises George but you've no idea what it's like here. You don't face those prattling neighbours who are so sure you've gone off with another woman though I won't admit anything, Not a word to me, just the children.' she murmured as she folded the letter into her apron pocket. How soon would this be? She glanced about the kitchen, knowing she must give the mats a beating, and the floor a sweep. There was always so much to do. George had no idea.

The shop provided enough cash to keep things above the breadline, but it was getting tighter every week. She'd not replenished much, a few basics, stuff sold every week and often had to disappoint customers as she ran the existing stock lower. The cart with kindling and paraffin barrels still called weekly, but the vendor would no longer give her credit. Begrudgingly she parted with a handful of coins each Saturday.

Mostly, she realised, Dorcas felt lost without him, without his company, his cheerfulness, as she appreciated more what he brought to the family. Shaking herself, she must cheer up before the children would burst in later in the afternoon, so she could encourage them with their father's loving words for them. His letter hadn't given her anything to cling to, nothing to help her while she struggled with the mounting problems. Dorcas guessed there was a lot unsaid and wished she could read between the lines. She sat in the kitchen worrying, looking it over once more. Reading his words again she finally folded it away behind the clock. Many questions struggled through her thoughts; frowning, they worried her.

Dissatisfied, Dorcas put on her coat and hat before glancing in the tiny mirror hung above the sink in the scullery where George had always shaved. She'd regularly moaned at how long he took when she had chores to complete there but she wished he was standing in his vest with soap about his chin, humming as he stropped his cut-throat razor on the long leather strap. Swallowing hard, she told herself she must put on a good face for the neighbours. She adjusted her hat and sniffed back a tear.

Dorcas hurried to the market square distracted by thoughts of the letter. A strong breeze caught the smell of food and canvas awnings, of paraffin lamps and horses surrounding her but she could not gather her wits. As she stood, gazing at some cooking apples and trying to think about their meal, she became aware of a familiar woman's voice at a cloth stall nearby.

'Well if you ask me there's a lot more to it than she says. He's always been such a charming chap, hasn't he, especially with the younger women? After all she's burdened him with all those children, life can't be very exciting for him, can it, poor chap? Every penny he earns must go to feed them all.'

Murmurs of agreement sounded, and another voice said, ' Well, it puts a strain on a man, when he's got to provide for so many. Any wonder if he strays a bit.'

'I've known them for a long time and I can tell you, she's being very quiet about it all. "Gone to find work in Canada," she says.' The woman laughed. 'I wonder who with and what kind of work?' Sniggers of laughter responded to the first voice.

'I can think of a few things he could do for me too!' a shrill voice added then cackled. Dorcas froze, her fists clenched as she turned and stamped towards them. The voice she recognised was Becky Turner who lived several doors away. Broad and short, she stood arms folded, her back to Dorcas, delighted to lead the women's gossip. Dorcas shot out her hand and grabbed Becky's shoulder, pulling her around to face her. Dorcas' eyes blazed. The look of horror on Becky's face made them pull back. Others gasped. An older woman, frowning, started to shuffle away and the rest began to fidget with their bags, embarrassed but curious what might be revealed by a confrontation.

'If you have anything to say about my George, you'll have the courtesy to say it to my face Becky Turner!' Grabbing her by her coat Dorcas pulled the startled woman nearer, glaring at her, the others melted away and the two women were left red-faced as they stared at each other. 'At least George has the guts to go to another country to find work, not like your lazy good-for-nothing man who spends his days and every penny you can earn down the pub all the time!'

Becky raised her eyebrow in defence. 'It's not what I heard. Everyone thinks your George's found himself a pretty bit of skirt and you're too proud to admit it. You've always thought yourself too good for us, Dorcas Haddon, and look at you. Scrabbling to pay your bills so I hear.'

'How dare you say that? I pay my way always.' Dorcas longed to slap her but didn't want any more of a scene, so she turned and hurried away, breathing hard and grasping her shopping bag tightly. How could those women be so heartless? Weren't they in the same position, struggling with shrinking pay packets, too many children to feed and men on the dole? She wanted to hit out at this spiteful woman. Her face was stiff, as her nails bit into her palms.

Dorcas fought her tears as she marched home, her breath tightening her chest, her lips pursed and shoulders back. Was there any truth in what she had denied? Had he another purpose? Doubts she'd never admit crept into her thoughts and once in the house, she reread George's letter, sobbing. Not a hint of anything but he wouldn't say, would he? She looked again in the tiny mirror above the sink. She stabbed her hat pin into her hat as it lay on the draining board. 'So there Becky Turner!' she snarled. Her eyes were red and her hair awry. She splashed cold water on her face before the children arrived home from school. They must have no doubts about their father. It was the least she could do for them.

Frustrated and bewildered, Dorcas hurried about the kitchen, went to the washing line in the yard then started to fold the dry clothes, smoothing and patting them in time with the silent argument she was having with George in her mind.

'You didn't think did you George? You only thought about yourself, not about how it would look, about how I would feel,' she muttered to herself. Later, answering her children's queries she began to hear herself sounding sharp. I must calm down, she thought, not let them see how I feel.

Dorcas picked up her work basket and fished out her crochet hook. The repairs, the lost buttons, the socks needing darning and some alterations for her growing children, ought to take precedence, though today she needed the rhythm of crochet, the rhythmic flicking of her fingers and cotton with the intricacies of pattern, of hook and lace to calm her mood. Whenever in the past she felt like stamping her feet she had fled to her work basket to relax. The lacy web she spun had every unspoken answer, every query about her life knotted into its design. At present Dorcas was making lace collars for the younger girls to trim the hand-me-downs they were to wear for best at Christmas. Make them feel a bit new.

Gradually she calmed as the rhythm soothed her. Marjorie came in and stood beside her with her plump arm across the back of the chair stroking her mother's shoulder with her hand. Watching Dorcas, she frowned. 'How do you do it Mam? You are so fast.' Dorcas glanced at her innocent face. 'It's pretty.'

'Shall I teach you? Would you like to learn?' Marjorie gets less than her share of my time Dorcas admitted to herself. Her eight-year-old child was often herded in with 'the girls' or 'the younger ones'. She was rarely given individual attention, somehow the family demanded her mam's time. Even her birthday, Christmas Day, had to be shared with the other festivities.

Dorcas lifted her daughter onto her lap deciding to show her the first principles of crochet, to help her make a chain. Discarding the unfinished collar, she found thicker thread and a larger hook. With her arms about her daughter, together they struggled to give Marjorie success, her clumsy young fingers attempting to wield the hook and tangling the thread. The child's palms were sweaty, and the white thread took on a beige colour as she worked trying to use her fingers and thumbs as her mam had, but getting a spider's web of confusion. Dorcas persisted, her impatience of earlier discarded in a few shared moments as an uneven chain hung coiling from the hook. Marjorie was overjoyed, unaware of the skills yet to be learned. Her small success was enough for today. Dorcas kissed the plump cheek and gave her a hug.

'I'll teach you a bit more next time,' Dorcas promised, remembering how rare it was she had time for this. Marjorie sat on the floor happily producing a lengthening chain, which spiralled while her mother went to the scullery. Looking out of the window she remembered back to the night of Marjorie's birth, a crazy Christmas. Daydreaming as the kettle boiled, her images were vivid of the end of 1915.

It had been late on Christmas Eve that year when the familiar pain hit Dorcas in the back.

'Oh, no!' she murmured, 'Not now.' She straightened from beneath their market stall with a box of candles in her hand, drew a sharp breath, and wrapped them in newspaper. Taking the woman's money, without showing her pain to such a gossiping neighbour as Emily Jones, took some concentration on Dorcas's part. Several women had grinned and gossiped once more about her "condition."

Moving nearer to George, Dorcas waited until he finished serving. 'George, I'm sorry bach, but we'll have to pack up. I think I've started.' She looked up at him in the soft light of the oil lamps swinging at the corners of the stall, their familiar smell prickling her nose. They cast shadows on its green tarpaulin but in their light his blond hair shone almost silver. She loved him. It was precisely their love which had caused their change of plans.

George gave her a stern look. 'I'm not packing up on Christmas Eve until I've got to!' he whispered, smiling through clenched teeth at a young man fingering some tools. 'This is one of the best days for sales and we need the money. Can't you go home and take the baby with you in your shawl. I'll have to manage here on my own and I'll bring young Peter on the cart when I've finished.' His stern glance told her he was annoyed, just annoyed.

'No sympathy, not even a kind word.' she thought. 'I'll be damned if I ever let him near me again!' The pain took her breath. She stretched upright and knew she must move herself. She wouldn't have long. 'Here George, can you tie the shawl for me at the back then I'll carry Olive comfortably, I hope.' Dorcas took the baby from her Moses' basket and tucked her in the warm shawl. She tousled Peter's blond hair as he sat in a highchair chuckling, confined but able to play with a string of cotton reels tied to the tray. Smiling at him she thought about each of her children. 'Please George, don't be too late. Mary may need you; you never know.'

'Don't fuss Dorcas. You've always been alright before, don't worry girl. You don't need me for this, do you? I'll pack up as soon as it goes quiet. Looks like a storm's brewing so we'll be home in no time, see if we aren't.' He turned from her to serve an elderly man who smelt of drink, chattering on. Dorcas awkwardly walked away.

When she left the market square the wind whipped at her auburn hair and around the skirts of her old coat. She waddled across the cobbles and onto the pavement on the side of the square, one arm around Olive and the other feeling in the darkness for the railings. Scudding clouds cast moonlit shadows across the narrow streets with their lit windows. She stopped again for a pain to pass holding onto the metal uprights of the school bars and gasped as she caught her breath. She walked on, dreading the next few hours. This baby should have come in January, but it would surely be a Christmas babe.

'Oh dear,' she whispered in the darkness. What about their four little ones? What kind of Christmas would they have? Mary, a village girl who daily helped Dorcas, at fourteen had hoped to go home to her mother for Christmas, not to look after a woman in childbirth. Dorcas felt for her, but hoped the girl would help her, young as she was. Maybe Mary would get her own mam from along the road to help too. She shook her head; it was a lot to ask. Dorcas's own mother was a mile away up the mountain and could not come out at night. A quiet tear slipped from the corner of her eye.

'Come on girl, it's useless weeping,' she thought. 'And oh! These boots pinch too.' She tried to cross the road, but a wave of pain made her hold tight to the spiked railings by the school, pressing her forehead against the cold upright. 'George is a good man really, he wants the best for us all, he doesn't mean to be hard, but he just doesn't understand.'

Dorcas crossed the road to the rusting iron bridge. She staggered, feeling dizzy. Breathing through another pain she grasped the bars, closing her eyes to get her balance. A strong arm came around her as she crumpled.

'Sorry, Mrs Haddon. You looked very unsteady on your feet my girl.' Jonas, an older neighbour, smiled and gently took the baby from her. 'I'll carry the babe, if you can manage the 'ill. We'll take it slowly. Is anyone at 'ome? I mean, who's looking after your other little 'uns?'

Slowly, Dorcas climbed the steep hill, stopping several times as the threatening rain started to lash across their faces. Jonas found a high doorstep, sitting her there while he hurried away to her home with the baby sheltered beneath his jacket. He was soon back half carrying, half supporting Dorcas to her front door. A kind man, he remembered her as a small girl skipping with friends, watching the slim young girl become a proud mother as the family grew, too fast and too many. It was the way of things and no-one decent ever mentioned it.

Dorcas thanked him, went indoors and sank into the chair with relief. Mary looked at her in horror. Not tonight. It was Christmas!

'It's alright, Mary. Put the babe down in her cot first, then go and get your mam please. Ask her to come and help. I'm so sorry! Oh and I'd love a cup of tea.' Dorcas must help Mary with her obvious panic. She hoped Mary's mother would come and maybe her neighbour, Sarah too. She prayed the girl would cope with the children. Dorcas slowly went into the kitchen, lifted a metal bucket onto the range, and started to fill it with jugs of water from their large pump in the yard. The wind was beginning to whistle about the house as the door slammed shut. Filling the kettle, she sat down to rest as another pain shuddered through her. She looked up at the window. A storm was blowing up and she began to worry about George and little Peter.

'They'll get soaked on a night like this. Well at least, everyone will have left the market to get home, so he won't be tempted to stay much longer. Damn the money! He's got a young family to think about.' Mary clattered back through the kitchen door, slamming it against the storm as she shook raindrops from her hair and shawl.

'It's awful out there. Mam says she'll be along in a minute. She must finish the dishes. Shouldn't you be in bed Mrs Haddon?' Mary frowned. She liked Dorcas, enjoyed the young children and she was glad to have work locally. One day she might go away into service. Since the war had started there were not so many big houses taking on untrained girls. Mary did not want to go for a year or two, not right away from home to live. The idea frightened her. She hurried upstairs as a child started to cry. 'I'll settle her, don't worry, I think it's little Tilda, she probably needs the potty,' she called down. By the time Mary came out of the children's room, Dorcas had hauled her tired body up to her bedroom.

'Mary, I'll need those draw sheets and old towels from the middle drawer. And could you help me with my boots? I can't do those.' Dorcas's small frame was swollen by her pregnancy and undressing seemed too much for her. Mary felt very grown-up, helping Mrs Haddon like this but she had little knowledge about babies and all that, for with no brothers and sisters, she had not been around when the mystery of birth was being wordlessly explained. She was frightened by the tales she'd heard and prayed her Mam would help.

'I'd love a drink of water so forget the tea.' Dorcas smiled at Mary to encourage the girl whose face had gone pale, looking scared. Mary rushed downstairs when the kitchen suddenly became crowded as both Mr Haddon with young Peter and Mary's mother arrived, each shaking off the rain and discarding top coats. Mr Haddon handed his sleeping son to Mary and bounded upstairs to see Dorcas. Mary got Peter dry and gave him a warm drink while her mother made tea for Mr Haddon.

'You should have seen that big man pushing his great cart up our hill with his little lad seated on top. I couldn't believe my eyes,' she whispered. 'Fancy him not bringing her home. I can't make them out. I really can't.'

'Shush Mam, they'll hear you.' Mary put her fingers to her lips. For the next hour her mother kept Mary busy and Sarah joined them to help. Things seemed to die down after midnight. Mary nodded off in the kitchen, her head on her hands spread on the table while Dorcas battled on. Over the next hours she suppressed every moan, trying hard to keep noises down though her back screamed and pains were almost constant. She breathed as deeply as she could, closing her eyes with each new wave.

'This child is big,' she thought between the overwhelming pains. 'I've got to be alright.' She closed her eyes as she thought of her other children. If she was bad, how would they manage, how would George manage? 'Oh, I can't think about those things. I've got to get on and get this done.' George came in and held her hand for a few minutes, frowning at the pain his wife was in, before Mary's mother shooed him out, telling him he was under her feet. Sarah boiled more water, feeling for her friend.

Just after four o'clock in the morning as the storm raged, a great gust of wind lifted several tiles off the roof, sliding down with a clatter. George stuffed rags under the eaves from inside where it was likely to leak and cursed the job which awaited him with daylight. As he climbed down from the loft, he heard the familiar sound of mewing, as his next child had entered their world. He swallowed hard, putting his back against the door. Little Marjorie was born on Christmas morning.

Watching her some eight years later, Dorcas loved how her daughter had grown to be the cheerful one in the family, and smiled at her memories, as standing at the sink, she realized had already peeled the potatoes.

Soon a wail came from Marjorie. 'Mam, she's pulling it off!' Olive, jealous of her sister's new skill, had sat beside her and was telling her how to do it. Marjorie and Olive always quarrelled, Olive's latent jealousy frequently leading to cruel remarks to her sisters especially Marjorie.

Dorcas looked at her daughters squatting together. Olive, slim and quick with a clever tongue, Marjorie, plump and kind though given to frequent floods of tears.

'Now come on you two. Olive, leave her alone, she's only learning, and Marjorie I think it's long enough. Put it back in the basket and both of you come and help lay the table. Now, this minute!' Dorcas saw the two girls make faces at each other. Her moments of peace were over.

When the younger children were tucked in bed at night, Roger sat beside Dorcas in George's chair. He would never dare to do that if his father was there, but the lad was doing George's chores, so he felt the man of the house. She hid her grin at the thought.

'Mam, I don't want to upset you, but I think you should hear what they are saying at school. Tilda said I shouldn't mention it. Please, I want to know. Has our Dadda gone off with another woman, gone to Canada to start a new family?' The boy looked so serious. Dorcas laid her hand on his.

'Of course not, Roger. Your Dadda wouldn't do that to me or to all of you. He loves us, and he's doing his best for us. I expect it is a hard life out there without any of you to disturb him whenever he wants to read the paper!' She tried to giggle at him and saw Tilda's questioning look across the room. Aware the gossip had bitten deeper than she had guessed, Dorcas wanted to help her children to stay proud of their father. George had never made her feel in doubt about their marriage and, despite the gossip and her own wavering fears, she must keep up her faith it would work out. Peter looked at her and she smiled to reassure her children, putting out her hand to touch each one of them.

Dorcas worried about Roger. At nearly fourteen he would leave school on his birthday and he wanted to be out to work to help her. He, most of all, felt resentment at George's absence with a negative feeling about his father. He had become quite protective of her since George left.

Lately there was no work in the area except the mines and she was not having her sons go down below. She had seen it destroy men as they never saw the sun and constantly breathed in the coal dust. She had lost one brother and seen another maimed by coal. No, anything but that. But at present there was so much anger, so many talks of strikes, of pay cuts and longer hours for the miners, it was not the place for her sons. She wanted something better for them both.

Roger was good with his hands and intelligent she knew, though without a chance to extend his education, he would only get manual work. How could she help him find some useful job? Maybe 'Young Fred' would have enough work to take him on, but it might not be regular. There would be workless days even for a willing lad.

That night in bed she felt dejected. How would she cope? She had so many things to think about, so many problems. Her tears came in the privacy of her room.

'George, oh George, why did you do this? Why did you leave me with this to sort? You never gave it a thought, did you?' She felt so low, so vulnerable without him. She turned over in her bed and pulled the blankets over her, trying to sleep.

Dorcas woke early and as the dawn filtered through the window she resolved to go forward with George's plan or at least to be seen to do so. The children needed a way forward, some plan for their future, and so did her Mam. Neighbours might stop speculating if she sold things off and moved things on towards their departure to Canada. She didn't even know where to start. When would this be? Where would they go? London and then Canada were big places and she had no idea how much it would cost or how long it would take. Dorcas had no knowledge of what to expect in Canada. She'd never been to London or sailed on a ship. She'd only ever lived in this village.

Dorcas had always obeyed George in the big things as the wives in the village did. It was what everyone expected. In many ways it was the law of the land. She had been lucky because he had always talked to her about decisions, always considered her ideas, unlike many men she knew. Now he said he wanted her to go ahead with something she had no say in. The thought of a new country, full of open spaces, wooden houses and white fences, was exciting but she had grown up amongst these hills, walked down every street and could name most families. She would leave it behind probably for ever and what about her Mam and Ernest? A knot in her stomach tightened. This was where she was born though not George of course. He came from Bristol, used to busy cities and had less attachment to this village.

Later in the morning, once the house was empty, after the usual early bustle as they hurried down to their school, Dorcas sat at the kitchen table with a cup of tea. The post brought a letter, just one sheet, written in pencil from George. At last!

Send to: Mr George Haddon, East Camp, Laval, Quebec, c/o Toronto City Postal Office, Ottawa, Canada as we get letters brought in by the man who brings our supplies, but it takes several weeks.

Dear Dorcas and children,
I hope this finds you well. This is a lovely country, wide, open spaces and lots of trees to climb. I am settling in at a camp, with plenty of work. My muscles will be enormous soon. Do ask teachers what they know about the land, as I am sure they will tell you lots about it. Look it up in an atlas if you can.

Hope you are helping Mam with the chores. I may be able to tell you more next time. Do write and tell me what you are doing.
Love Dadda XXXXX

Dorcas guessed he'd not say anything personal to her, yet she felt hurt that there was no extra sheet, no message to his wife. Did George have any idea of the turmoil he had created? Pursing her lips, she swallowed the sob that rose in her throat, looking at the sunlight peeping behind heavy clouds through the kitchen window. She knew she must do this.

She scratched her head with the end of her pencil. Money was getting tighter each week, though she always managed to pay the rent. Soon she must move to start to take it seriously. Without a man's wage, or his regular weekly income, she knew she had no alternative. If her brothers or her dadda had still been around they might have been able to help, but they were no longer there. She must do this alone. How else could she feed seven children with the lads already having appetites like adults? She must trust George, leave the village, must emigrate. Maybe he was right.

She started to make lists, plans of what they must take and what they must leave. Most of their furniture was well worn and was bought years before as second hand. It would make little in any sale. Their clothing was needed, though some of her own stuff that she had kept out of sentiment must go. Her mother had no spare room to house anything, so Dorcas planned to give away some of her useful things to good friends.

Oh dear! There was so much to think about because she had no idea when they would go. She'd write back to George, hoping the letter would reach him wherever he was. He must understand she'd need time to do this. Dorcas guessed he would plough on allowing no delays. He'd not see the problems. That was George!

Rain drops on the window made her look up. She stood and brought the wooden airer from the yard into the scullery to finish drying. It would clutter her way there all day. She had work to do which was immediate, so her daydreams and worries about the future must wait.

In the shop she looked about, beginning to list the stock, hoping she could sell it off at almost cost price. Locals couldn't afford to keep spare things in their small houses and backyards unless they were cheap, dirt cheap. The tools and hardware were not the kind of thing you needed two of, so most neighbours wouldn't buy them. Probably the sales men, who regularly called to sell them stock, would be more interested in a bargain but they'd not be too pleased when they heard there'd be no more orders from George's shop. Maybe the Kilner jars would sell as it was autumn and there was a glut of fruit locally. She would be too busy to make preserves herself even as gifts, but others might be interested. She piled some of the smaller things into baskets to sell off cheaply, putting them around the shop. She'd tell the children to call her if anyone showed interest in a bargain when they were serving them.

She gazed around the shelves. George had always kept them neat, well organised but they were starting to look muddled. What did it matter if it was being sold? He'd left it without a backwards glance, guessed she'd sort it as she always did. She stroked her forehead, smoothing the frown that frequently seemed to be there. The bell on the shop door rang and she smiled at a young woman, sold her some firewood, some spills and lucifers and took her sixpence. The shop became silent again and she went back into her kitchen.

Much later Dorcas undressed by the light of her candle and brushed her hair, her mind whirring as she glanced into her mottled mirror on the washstand. Was it the beginning of more grey hairs? She peered closer pulling a couple out. Stroking her face, she regarded herself. She was looking older, more like her mother looked when Dorcas was a girl, she remembered. Taking a deep breath, she started to plait her hair. She shivered as she climbed into the cold bed wearing a pair of George's woollen stockings. She hoped he had bought himself some more. He'd need them out there she was sure.

Autumn had begun to bite. She dreaded the battle against the wet and cold each winter. Roger would do his best to deal with George's chores, though she must remember to order in the logs and coal, to watch the paraffin supplies, not just for themselves but for the shop too. People would expect to be able to buy them when the first frosts set in. Maybe they'd be gone by then.

Huddled in the candlelight, telling herself not to worry she began to read, pulling a shawl around her shoulders as she slanted the pages towards the light. She could hear the gentle breathing and soft snores of her children in the other rooms. The house creaked. After a few minutes she put the book down and blew out the candle. She lay hunched up and still in their bed, as she tried to get warm pulling up her feet into her nightdress. She missed George's cuddles and reassurance, his large calves she always put her cold feet on and he would not complain. She squeezed her eyes shut, sighing. In her mind she hugged the bulk of him, the loving body which calmed and always encouraged her. She wanted to cut out the dark she remembered feeling at times as a child.

'George, George,' she whispered to herself as she regretted her anger with him a couple of months before. 'I'm sorry, so sorry.' Her mind returned to Roger, her eldest son filling her thoughts. Soon she started thinking of each of the girls in turn, one by one with whatever problem she imagined. There seemed no answers.

Although very soon it would be Peter who would give her real concern.

CHAPTER 9: George, October 1923

When George first arrived at the camp he was told about the showers alongside the latrines behind each bunkhouse. Wooden shacks, they contained metal sinks for the men to wash their clothes and with only a couple of changes of clothes, and no bath for a fortnight, George needed that. A line of shower heads with drainage, stood at the far end of the shack.

Great, he thought rubbing his hands. Returning from work much later, covered in dust, he grabbed his towel and precious soap and headed across the yard to the shower block. The wooden walls were dark and the concrete floors basic with drains scored through to sluice the water away. Taps dripping echoed around the open shower space. No privacy but with no one there he turned on the faucet. Cold water flowed out, but he waited, imagining the hot water would gradually come through to the shower head. Nothing happened, no success so he had a quick cold shower and questioned an older man when he returned to the bunkhouse. 'Are the showers always cold or had someone run off the hot water?'

'No mate, they are always bloody cold. Never get any hot through ours.' Moving closer the man lowered his voice.' I often sneak into one of the other blocks. They get hot or at least warm water sometimes. Make sure they don't catch you, though!' The old timer curled his lip. 'These damn Frenchies ain't very forgiving, you'll find.'

Each time George tried the showers they were cold. Why didn't the boss sort this? With so many men working in rock dust or clinging mud he felt it should be a priority, though many of the men didn't shower often. Drying himself a few mornings later he looked up at the range of curved pipes which led out from the wooden showers to the back of the roof of their bunkhouse. He followed them back with his eyes working them out. Somewhere beyond was the source of the problem. He guessed there was a cold supply pumped straight off the river so where did a hot supply feed in? George spoke to Jim. 'Where do you reckon the hot water comes from?'

'Obvious ain't it? There must be a tank in the loft of our bunkhouse. I reckon the flue from the stove passes through and it warms the water in the tank when it's working.' Jim replied. 'Not sure why it don't work?' he queried.

'Yes, though we don't get it coming through, do we? There must be a blockage of some kind or it's dripping away somewhere.'

'Could be as simple as rust from the old tank blocking the pump. It'd be fine if we could fix it, but they'll make you get permission and you can guess how damned difficult they'd make it. Forms and dockets.'

'But surely, if we tried to solve this…?'

'No mate. Loads of questions. You know these French rules. They're bound to put up some objection, you can be sure. Worried they'd have to pay out for a replacement tank or summat. Reckon these pipes are so ancient. Not sure how old this camp must be. It's falling apart. Part of some barracks once I heard.'

'But if…' George argued.

'Easiest if you drop it mate. Shave with a saucepan of water from the top of the stove like the rest of us and forget the damn showers. I don't care if you stink a bit!' Jim punched George's arm with a grin. It obviously did not bother Jim. George felt frustrated. He hated the feel of mud and dust accumulating on his skin and in his hair. He'd always prided himself on being clean. No wonder the men looked so dishevelled.

Long after darkness had descended, he lay on his bunk gazing at the rafters, looking at the flue pipe as it disappeared into them. He frowned.

'It's probably quite simple,' he thought the idea irritating him. When the others were out of the bunkhouse the next day George dragged his double bunk until it was below the trap door in the ceiling. Climbing through to the loft and hauling up his tool bag, he fished around for his lamp. Clambering across the beams he found the tank and lifted the cover. It stank. With his fingertip he felt the water which was very hot but smelt foul. Obviously, the down pipe was blocked and only the cold river water was getting through.

George gave the pipe a bash with his wrench and heard vibrations then a clattering sound and loud creaks within the pipe as it expanded. Clambering along to a darker end, following the pipes towards the back of the room below, he found the rusty pump. With his largest spanners he turned off two valves then George disconnected the pump, praying he would be able to reconnect the rusty old pipes.

There in the darkness, kneeling with care on the rafters with only his lamp to help him see, he took apart the pump, unclogged it, greased it, and reconnected it. Packing the joint with red lead he sealed it. Gathering up his tools he crawled backwards across the beams and climbed down out of the loft. He brushed his knees then pushed back the beds. His head was covered with dust and cobwebs, and he shook himself free, his fingers running through his hair.

Feeling satisfied he picked up his towel and soap, crossing his fingers as he hurried for the showers. He unscrewed the shower head and a large scattering of rust and mould fell through followed by a lot of hot but stagnant-smelling water. He waited a few minutes. Then with a smirk of satisfaction, he turned on the steaming hot water. He decided not to tell the others, let them discover this luxury for themselves. His grin became a quiet chuckle. He'd show them. It was good to feel clean for once. He didn't want to stink, whatever Jim said. This would prove to them he was a skilled man, not only a manual worker. George felt good and began to hum a tune.

The men's reaction was mixed. The handful of British men praised him when they discovered he'd made the effort but the French on the camp were disdainful. Their attitude to him was churlish and dismissive, even hinting with a suggestive curl of their lip only women needed hot showers. George was secretly angry. He screwed up his fists trying to resist giving them a sharp reply. He had done this for them expecting some minor recognition for his success.

A few days later George was summoned to the foreman's office after the end-of-work siren. Hurrying across the yard he wondered what it was about and hoped it meant he'd be taken off the labouring tasks and given more plumbing to do. The scowl of the French foreman made him doubt. Jacques stood flexing his shoulders, but George was so much taller than him, he had to look up, screwing up his mouth.

'I hear you have been interfering wiv de pump in your bunkhouse wiv out permission, Haddon. Do you not realize, stupid English, you could have flooded de whole bunk house? You had no permit, no signed form to "tinker" wiv dat pump.' Spittle dribbled down Jacques's chin. 'On this camp we do not permit workers damaging de premises. You should know dat by now!' he shouted; his face puce. 'We should fine you for dat.'

George stepped forward with an angry snarl, fists clenched.

'I repaired the damn shower supply, that's all. No one cared our showers weren't even warm, and it was a simple matter really, one I've dealt with before many times. I am a trained plumber, not a lad still wet behind the ears!'

'Here you are just a labourer, Haddon. To us you are only manual labour!' he spat in the spittoon. 'We don't care how experienced you are and frankly we don't want your clever ideas 'ere. We have many good local men whom we can rely on, so do not interfere again or you will get a warning. We run this camp, not you, do you hear?' The foreman slapped his hands on the desk, making the pencils rattle in their battered tankard. George gritted his teeth and remembered Jim's cautioning when he'd left them both going to the canteen. No, he'd not answer back but it was frustrating. His face flushed red and his hands sweated. He guessed it wouldn't be the last time he suffered from their deliberate attempts to block his skills and to treat him as 'only manual labour.' He strode out banging the door.

For weeks he worked on at the heavy jobs; hauling and digging, trundling barrow loads of earth and rocks to the dumping ground and not complaining. As he worked, he no longer noticed the coarse language of the workers which he understood by the tone of their voices. A curse has its own tone, its unique international bitterness he learnt. At first other men's habits startled him but he soon ignored their rough ways. There were no women here to check them. Over the next weeks the muscles of which he had been so proud back home, screamed and strengthened, strained and ached. He lost fat as he became lean and supple, though his muscles ached when he lay in bed. His hair and beard grew unchecked.

The food from the canteen was barely enough and the men grumbled as they bought extra at high prices at the camp store. There was little variety there, everyone being dependent on the supplies brought in each week.

For a month or so while the autumn sun shone, George noticed an older man disappearing into the forest early on his off-day. Where does he go, he wondered? He spoke to him over dinner. 'Pierre, where do you go on your off-day? I've watched you go out of camp with your bag.' Pierre looked sceptically at him.

'I go to de river for a little rest. Zat's all, George.' Obviously reluctant at first, as the trust grew, Pierre agreed to take him next time. 'Listen, you must be quiet, or it disturbs de fish … and talk, it disturbs me too. I go for de silence.' Quietly in the morning mist, George pulled on his boots, and crept from the bunkhouse where the others snored on. After a good mile of walking through forest, climbing down through giant trees and thorny bushes, they reached the river. The gushing sound of running water falling over rocks carried across the vast valley. The view was spectacular as it wound away through the hillside. The sparkle of moving water and the freshness of the air made George breathe deeply. This was a different world, full of promise.

The valley had its own sounds, ones he had not heard before and pungent smells of vegetation and life. It gave him renewed hope, this could be a new start for them all. It truly was an amazing land.

Pierre set up a net in the water and instructed George to find dry wood for their fire. Showing him how to get a fire going, Pierre then brought fish from his net, staked it over the hot ash and sat on a rock. The smell of the fish was good, and George relaxed in the tranquillity of the morning. He thought about Pierre's warning. Here, in the wilderness, away from the constant noise of the camp, of men shouting, machines and engines churning and thumping … the peace steadied his heartbeat. Other sounds of birds twittering and rushing water falling over rocks, gradually came through to him. Pierre took out his pipe and checked his tobacco pouch. George ate the fish from an enamel plate, pulling the pink flesh with relish.

'Pierre, it's the best thing I've tasted since I've been in this country,' he said.

'Now I think we will sleep,' was his reply as he lay on a tarpaulin that he pulled from his canvas bag and closed his eyes. George lay back, his hands behind his head and contemplated the sky. He breathed deeply and soon slept soundly.

Pierre woke him as shadows crept across the river. Clearing their fire, they tramped back to camp. George strolled alongside Pierre feeling relaxed, refreshed and able to think. He must not rise to the taunts of the French workers he told himself.

'I promise I'll say nothing, Pierre, and thanks. It's been a great day. Done me a power of good.' Bert and Jim were in town until late that night, so it was easy to avoid saying where he had been. He lay on his bunk, remembering the day, feeling at last he could plan the future.

By the end of the month the weather worsened, and Pierre's off days changed so he didn't go often to the river. Their first special day beside the water had become a silent memory for George, a glimpse of life in the wilderness which he dreamt of often, thinking of sharing the outdoor life with his sons particularly.

George rarely felt relaxed in the camp, and his temper was shortening with the daylight, daily. He was too exhausted to question why he tolerated the conditions as the days rolled into weeks. He tried to walk and run his frustrations away around the perimeter of the camp after work when he could muster the energy, but he felt discouraged about everything as the bitter cold began to bite.

'What is the point?' he asked himself as he pounded the rough track.

When he next complained he was capable of engineering tasks, not just manual work, it was after a frustrating Saturday removing rock which had been blasted away the previous day. His team had worked solidly and only had half an hour for a midday meal. The soup was thin and greasy but sheer hunger made them consume it quickly. Trying to use the latrines before returning to their shift, the men had found them flooded and foul. George protested with the others taking it further by appealing to be allowed to sort the faulty plumbing. A French voice from their team was heard.

'So 'ow do you think you can do that? Can you do miracles, English idiot?'

So naturally, George started to explain the intricacies, becoming aware not only his team but the foreman was giving him a derisive grin. George saw red, pulled himself to his full height and yelled at them. Mostly they backed away, as only the foreman and his mate took a step towards him. George stared down at the wrench in Henri's hand and instinct made him put his hand up to defend his head. Jacques turned away deciding not to witness Henri's imminent attack.

'Any more trouble from you Haddon and you'll learn what dis can do!' Henri snarled in a threatening tone through his blackened teeth, shaking the wrench before George's face. George smelt his foul breath and wanted to answer, to use his fists but somehow, he held himself back.

'Don't George mate, don't!' George heard Bert's warning whisper and stepped away. The team dispersed to their work as he took the rough handles of his barrow in his shaking hands. How much more of this could he stand? He guessed there would be trouble soon, sure they would goad him again.

When the siren at the end of the day's shift sounded, Jacques shouted. 'Not you Haddon. You finish dis pile of rocks before you go.' The others dropped their eyes as they went to the canteen. Henri sneered as he collected his tools.

George worked on, every movement venting his frustration, then he imagined he could hear Dorcas's voice whispering. 'Keep calm, George. Don't give them the satisfaction of watching you get into trouble. It's all they are waiting for. Take a deep breath and calm down.' He finished by the light of a lantern and returned his barrow. When he reached the canteen, they had cleared away, but Jim was leaning against the open canteen door.

'Come on mate, we've saved you a dish of stew. We put the enamel dish on the back of the stove to keep warm. It ain't so good, but it'll sure be hot. Don't burn your fingers.'

'Thought yer could do with this George. Keep yer temper mate!' Bert said. George ate it quietly sopping up the gravy with his bread, and wiping every drop around the plate, then later stretching full length on his bunk going over and over the day's events. A lump came in his throat. Back home he was respected. He never had to cope with this level of hatred. The most that might occur could be a minor dispute over an invoice with a tradesman or even Dorcas in one of her moods. No, he could do without this anxiety, always being unsure of what might happen. George began to check someone else was around when he visited the shower block, to be safe. He didn't want to be caught alone. His eyes were constantly searching, aware that trouble could be around every corner.

CHAPTER 10: Dorcas, November 1923

It was after school on a Thursday in November when Dorcas noticed her eleven-year- old Peter was quiet. The others were bustling about as they argued and whispered in the corners of their kitchen, with little May endlessly singing a school chant, as she sat beneath the table with her doll. Dorcas was recording the takings from the shop as she always did on their half-day-closing but the children's noise disturbed her. With no customers it might be her only chance till late on Saturday when they closed. The figures wouldn't balance, and she put down her pencil with a sigh and hoped to get back to it when the younger children were in bed. She must start their meal. Standing up she noticed Peter looked very flushed slumped in a chair. She went across and felt his forehead. He was burning hot.

Tilda stood at the sink in the scullery peeling vegetables. 'Tilda, come here a minute. Was Peter unwell at school today?' Dorcas looked at her son as his eyes drooped and his whole body sagged in the chair.

'Well, he said he had a sore throat and felt sick on the way home, but you were busy when we came in, so he said not to bother you Mam.' Tilda, apologising, looked anxious.

'Open your mouth son.' Dorcas looked down his throat. It was red and swollen. She felt a tremor of fear. 'All of you outside to play, now!' Puzzled the children began to protest.

'Oh Mam, I want to … ' Olive whined.

'Out. You heard me, this minute!' Tilda and Roger glanced at each other as they went silent and began to hustle the younger girls out of the scullery door into the yard. They guessed there was something strange by the tone of their mother's voice.

Dorcas turned back to look at her son. 'Bring me a cup of water Tilda, don't stand there!' Tilda dashed to the tap. Peter could barely swallow the water and then shook his head.

'Tell Aunt Sarah that I need her! 'Dorcas modulated tone hinted at a mixture of desperation along with concern though she must not panic the children. Tilda went silently, with a serious glance at Dorcas, who put her shawl about Peter's shoulders. She whispered, 'Don't worry son, we'll get the doctor. He'll soon make you feel better.' She hurried out to the yard and told Roger to run for the doctor.

Sarah Harris looked serious when Dorcas told her of Peter's sore throat. 'There's talk of diphtheria in the village,' she whispered.

'I know, that's what I suspect this is.'

'They'll send the lad to the fever hospital and you won't be able to see him till he's better if he goes in there.' Her neighbour shook her grey head looking sharply at Dorcas.

'I'm not having him go away. Not many come out of those places Sarah, except in a box,' Dorcas whispered, pursing her lips with a determined look, an alert panic squeezing her eyes.

'You've got to think of the others. You canna let it go through them all!' Sarah frowned; her eyes alarmed.

'It's why I called you. I will need a hand at times and I could do with help getting his bed down into the parlour. Will you help me Sarah? Have you had it? Can you spare a few minutes?'

Sarah looked at her friend saying, 'Ai, of course lovey, you can rely on me. I had it as a girl. Not sure how you're going to do this, but I'll help if I can, you know.' The two women dragged the bed down into the parlour and, as soon as Sarah made it, Peter lay down with relief closing his eyes, slumping into the pillow.

Doctor Jones knocked on the front parlour door and entered putting his bag on the small table in the corner. He was thin with a sombre, stern face, often distracted by the problems of his patients. He frowned as he looked at Peter. He'd known the family for a long time and had delivered May some five years before. Dorcas trusted him, though he was part of the old school, a doctor trained in Victoria's reign. He had experience of what worked for most things she felt but so much had moved on since then she'd read. He beckoned her into the scullery. With a sigh the doctor confirmed it was probably diphtheria and strongly advised Dorcas that Peter should be taken to the fever hospital in the city.

'No thank you Doctor. I will nurse my son at home. My Tilda can look after the others in the rest of the house. She's nearly sixteen and my neighbours are good.'

'I advise you; you are most unwise. I'll not charge you for this visit Mrs. Haddon, though you'll have to pay for the medicine I'm afraid.' He scribbled on a pad tearing off the name of a sore throat remedy Dorcas had used before. 'I'm sorry we don't have much more to help him. It's the fifth case I've seen in the village this week. Not sure if we can keep the school open for much longer, I'll talk to the headmaster, see what he feels. And you'll must keep your shop closed too. This thing is far too contagious for any of you to be serving customers.'

'Thank you, Doctor.'

He glanced at her seeing the impossible situation she faced. He closed his bag with a snap and picked up his hat. 'Let me know if any of the others gets sick,' he called as he went out of the street door, shaking his head. Walking quickly away he stroked his chin, frowning. 'Oh dear, I must send a report to the medical board as there are several local cases,' he mumbled. 'They may have to close the school.'

Back in their parlour Peter murmured as he slept. Dorcas watched him and thought of how proud she was of him, her gentle son. She must get him through this.

Dorcas collected items she thought she would need, putting them in the parlour. She told Tilda to make some supper for them and she'd explain later. Tilda had already put the vegetables on as the children were outside in the evening gloom and complaining of feeling cold. Roger made them run around but May refused and sucked her thumb as she sat on the step.

Dorcas nailed a sheet to hang in the parlour doorway into their kitchen and draped its end into the tin bath part full of water with Izal in it. The disinfectant soaked up the sheet making the kitchen smell strongly.

'Now Tilda, anything that comes out of this room must go into this water to clean it. I will put it in when I've finished with it and you must leave it to soak. Everything, you hear me? I don't want any of you catching this. Leave it for Sarah to take it out and make sure it's clean. I rely on you my girl to keep the others safe. We are going to beat this thing.' Dorcas didn't feel as confident as she tried to sound, and Tilda imagined her mother behind the damp sheet, both scared by what the future might hold.

'Should we tell our Dadda, write him a letter or something?'

'No, come on Tilda, a letter?' Dorcas silently cursed George's absence. If ever she needed him, it would be now. This was her worst nightmare. She didn't dare think what might lie ahead. 'You can put things on a tray on this stool by the door and I will open it and get anything when you are out of the kitchen. This thing is very infectious, so you must make sure the others understand Tilda.'

'Yes Mam,' she whispered frowning as she heard her mother's voice through the smelly sheet. 'How long will it be?'

'Several weeks I'm afraid, but I rely on you and Roger to help the others. Aunt Sarah's promised to help you if you need anything I can't tell you, so use your sense. Don't bother her too much, there's a good girl.'

While Dorcas washed Peter's flushed neck and arms with a cool flannel, she watched her son's face. His skin was mottled pink but already dark around his sunken eyes.

He was no longer the cheerful son she knew, unaware the whole family were on the other side of the door thoughtfully eating their supper, not sounding like their usual noisy meal. Peter was too exhausted to think why. He mumbled his throat hurt, and he could not swallow. Closing his drooping eyes, he fell back to sleep.

Tilda got the others to bed early as no-one complained. They sensed the serious situation. The little girls whispered in bed together, Olive and Marjorie trying to reassure Ethel and May.

'Peter will be alright soon, you see,' said Olive.

'Yes, Mam will surely make him better!' Marjorie lisped. 'He's got some medicine from the doctor.'

On the other side of the parlour door Dorcas made a list; working out the instructions, thinking what she would need. She called it out to Tilda adding bits as she remembered. Tilda wrote it down.

'Where will you sleep then Mam?'

'Oh, I'll manage in the chair. I'll be fine. Don't worry about me.'

'What if you get it, what should I do?' Tilda's voice choked.

'No don't worry. I've had it as a child long ago. You take care of the others, love.'

'What about the shop?'

'It must stay closed. People know we have sickness, they won't want to come here, not for the next few weeks, my lovely. Just help with the little ones, that's all you need to do.'

Tilda felt a little queasy, unsure if she could do this. Roger, soon to be fourteen, drew himself upright and took her arm. 'I'll help, we've got to do this Tild, we've just got to! Mam will do her best for Peter, you know she will, so we must help as much as we can.'

Sarah peeped in around the scullery door a little later. 'You all right Tilda? Does your mam want anything more tonight? Tell her to knock on the wall if she needs anything in the night. Well, if you're sure I'll away to my bed. I'll look in early to give you a hand with getting them off to school. Oh, and lock up carefully after I've gone, there's a good lass.'

As Sarah closed the door Tilda felt very alone. Later she lay in bed while she chewed her finger in the dark and tried not to cry. She wished her father was snoring in his bed. She would feel so much better if he was here.

Roger missed being annoyed with his brother as he lay alone in his cramped bedroom. He felt frightened but determined to be responsible and really help Tilda. His mother's absence made life serious, and frowning, he realised his role as the man of the house with his father absent. He pulled himself upright.

Dorcas was as careful as she could be and put their cutlery and china along with any rags and draw sheets into the disinfectant in the bath outside the parlour door. The sheet which hung into it was soaked in fresh disinfectant each day on her instructions. Dorcas used the front door to visit the privy at the back and to empty their water in and she blessed George for giving them a flushing outdoor lavatory, which was still a rarity in their street. Her thoughts of George came, sometimes wishing he was with them and sometimes cursing he wasn't.

Over the first week, Peter got worse, his temperature rose, while the fever made him thrash about and mumble, often delirious at times. Dorcas stroked his forehead, whispered to him, her frown a constant attempt to hold back her tears. She watched him day and night, terrified of what was happening. She dozed at night, waking in the darkness, feeling guilty and then checking him. 'Please, please let him live. I'll do anything if he can get through this,' she whispered to herself.

The long days and longer nights became weeks, and the doctor visited several times. Dorcas knitted, sewed and tried to read, to pass the long hours when there was little else she could do. She made lists of things for Tilda and Roger to do and fussed about the others as she called instructions through the door. She reminded them of the precautions with the gas mantles, the lamps and the fire. Each of the children talked to her in hushed tones from the other side of the hateful sheet across the door, as she asked how their school day was and what they were doing. They seemed quieter and missed her hugs. She longed for their smiles and noisy chatter.

The days dragged, but Dorcas never felt relaxed. The winter nights were endless and full of fear. She watched her child and worried. Sometimes in the small hours, she would stand outside the parlour door in the silent street breathing the chilly air, her red eyes wet and with a solid lump in her chest as she tried to gather her courage to face another day of doubt.

The shop stayed closed and neighbours asked Sarah how things were with Peter. Some condemned Dorcas for not sending him to the fever hospital but others, who'd heard the odds, whispered they understood why she chose to keep him there. A few donations of vegetables from their allotments were left on the doorstep. No money came in, though Tilda and Sarah managed to put food on the table and the doctor said he would wait for the cost of medicine.

The gossip also included the idea of how unfortunate it was that George was so far away, always delivered with a raised eyebrow. The local women had no realisation of how far Canada really was or how impossible it was for him to come back to help Dorcas. It seemed like unusual behaviour to them and must hint at some rift, some unknown misdemeanour Dorcas or George had perpetrated. Stories were rife over the garden fences and in the market, punctuated by a raised eyebrow and a suspicious look. Dorcas didn't hear but she guessed. She was too worried, too busy to care. She had her son to nurse. Let 'em talk!

The first nights had dragged as she slept in the chair until, after several problems and a great deal of backache, Sarah dragged her own spare mattress in for Dorcas to make a bed on the floor beside Peter. Rising several times each night to check his temperature, she warmed him, cooled him, washed him and changed him. Much of the time he had little awareness and was limp. Although nearly twelve he was as tall as Roger who was a couple of years older and Dorcas struggled at times with the supine figure.

Years of hard work had strengthened her muscles and, although small herself, she must beat this. She prayed she was doing the right thing. Tears threatened often but she brushed them away. They would not help Peter. He must not give up the struggle, it was their only hope.

Each evening after the smaller girls were tucked up in their beds, she asked in whispers through the door if they were all well, either of Sarah or Tilda. Terrified one of the children would become ill, with no idea how she would cope then, she worried for them all.

She spent hours fretting about the troubles she felt had descended on them in the past year. Why, oh why had George gone? Despite her insistence it was for work, she wondered in her heart if there were more reasons. Women often blamed themselves and others were too quick to speculate against their neighbours. Dorcas guessed the men would side with George out of some male loyalty. Dorcas felt many women would do so too, with no real understanding of the situation. For the next few weeks, she was unable to tackle their gossip but she mustn't fret she told herself. Doubtless rumours would sprout and grow. Let them. She must concentrate on Peter as he was her priority.

Tilda talked to Sarah when she overheard some prattling women condemning her mother. 'How could they say that? Mam is struggling to keep Peter here and to tell me how to cope with the others. And we're managing aren't we, Aunty Sarah?'

'Yes lovey, of course you are, and you've done a grand job of it too. Take no notice of them silly biddies. They've now't better to do than gossip.'

'You see Aunty, Mam would be so angry if she knew.' Tears were reflected in the girl's eyes.

'True and you're not to tell her, you hear me? You've got to be a bonny girl and manage a bit longer. Your Mam says young Peter's getting a little better and soon I'm sure you'll be back together again. Don't worry!' Sarah took Tilda's hand and stroked it. 'Your Mam is so proud of you, hinny.' Sarah hoped she was right, for nearly three weeks had passed, and the lad was still alive.

Talking through the closed door when the children were in school, Dorcas had told her how weak Peter had become. Finally, his temperature was coming down, almost normal, though he was wasted and pale. The doctor had come again and told Dorcas, 'Perhaps another week will do it if the lad doesn't take a sudden turn for the worst.'

As she saw him from the parlour door, she pulled her shawl closer around her. It was much colder. At least it hadn't snowed. No-one wanted that.

Tilda and Roger felt like adults when they looked after their sisters. Sometimes the girls objected to their orders, but Roger raised his voice blustering through to them. Dorcas heard him, realising that at least they had taken good care of her family. She smiled as she heard echoes of George in her son, as Roger too cared a lot for the smaller ones. He'd not be rough with them; it was all noise. That was like George too.

Dorcas tried to write a letter to George, wanting to make him share her suffering and the fear of what might happen to Peter or to any of their children. She wanted him to feel guilty he had left her with these problems, that he hadn't shared his decision with her to go away to some foreign country. The terror of the possible outcome of these weeks had grown with her isolation, unable to do anything, only watching her son appear to waste away nightly. Dorcas scribbled angry words which, when she reread them although perhaps justified, were bitter, haughty and unfair.

As dawn broke, she screwed up the paper and decided this was for her to sort. George could do nothing. By the time he got the letter life would have made the decision. Peter would be better…or not. The children were her responsibility, at least until George came back or they met whenever that might be. She would write later.

She prayed soon this would be over. Peter was sitting up and wanting to walk about though Dorcas was shocked at his paleness and how much weight he had lost. His muscles were weakened, and his long legs were thin and unsteady. She told Tilda to cook gruel and puddings to tempt him but she was heartened by his tremulous smile. Always her special boy, she hugged him and said she thought they could soon be back with the others. The doctor would confirm what her instincts told her. At last it was nearly over.

The children were in school and Peter was snoring when Sarah helped Dorcas take down the sheet which had imprisoned her for so long. As she bundled some bedding into the yard Sarah told Dorcas to get undressed. Dorcas frowned.

'Come on my lass, I mean it. I've lit the fire under the copper and the water's good and hot so the first thing you are going to do is have a bath. A good soak will help with those aches and pains. It might take your frown away too.' Sarah hung towels over the airer by the stove.

'Oh, Sarah, you are a dear. It's just what I need.'

'Right, young Peter will sleep a little longer and you can soak it all away.' As she spoke Sarah tipped buckets of steaming water into the scrubbed tin bath and swirled in a handful of soda to soften the water. Out of her pocket came some of the precious scented soap she had taken from their shop and the perfume made Dorcas inhale.

'Oh Sarah, will I ever get the smell of disinfectant out of this house? Everything smells of carbolic. I've probably got the least bed bugs in the whole street!'

'Never mind Pet. You've done a grand thing for your Peter and for the others too. Don't even think about what could have happened. Enough to say you've beaten it.'

'Well this time yes but please God I don't ever have to do this again.' Dorcas found herself sobbing at last. Her friend hugged her, as the two women cried and laughed together. She climbed in and sat with relief. She closed her eyes and dunked her head beneath the water. Peter was safe. At last she could relax. Sarah rubbed her hair with a towel and gently combed it through. Dorcas smiled at last.

It was the next day when Peter, after a long sleep, was presented with a tub full of hot water and warm towels when he emerged from the parlour. Dorcas and Sarah, respecting his privacy, meanwhile cleaned and scrubbed the parlour, opening the small window for a few chilly moments. Clean clothes were piled on a chair and when he was bathed and dressed, both the women complimented him on how smart he looked, despite their secret thoughts on his pallor and weight loss. At least he was alive.

It was later she found the time to write to George. She told him of Peter's illness and of the two other children who had sadly died of diphtheria in the village. She hoped he would share her thankful prayers, and she wrote that with the children's and Sarah's help she had managed. It sounded measured, resigned, if a little smug. Not emphasising the fear but telling him there was no urgency now. She felt secretly proud she didn't need him to look after their children. She could cope.

CHAPTER 11: George, November 1923

On their off-days, most men slept late and then made their way to the local town with the carter. Some, including Bert and Jim, started to drink as soon as they arrived. George wandered around and tried to make sense of this town in the wilderness. The amazing light, which reflected its brightness off forgotten pockets of snow held there by the bitter winds, dazzled him. The town consisted of a main street and clusters of buildings; neat houses, wooden shacks and a small school, used by the handful of residents, with a constant flow of camp workers swelling the town's coffers. George wandered around trying to get his bearings.

He saw, for all those workers, men like him, there was nothing but bars and a general store selling food, clothes and hardware. Racks of fur caps and working boots stood amongst a mixture of thick jackets and stiff canvas overcoats, hanging on string lines in the rafters giving off a distinctive animal smell. Large jars and tinned food littered the counter with tools hung high from hooks into the beams. The wooden floor echoed with the sound of men's boots.

Next to the store was the sheriff's office built of wood with dull metal grids across its windows where he locked up the rowdy men for a night releasing them next day with a stern warning. The sheriff was short but built like a barrel and known to be light on his feet. In the bar men told tales of his exploits, how he had won his badge. He certainly seemed to have the town folks' respect.

All the money in the town came from the camp workers; lonely, desperate men living a rough life who had no alternative but to pay the prices. They had to replace items that had been stolen or ruined; boots, jackets and, as the weather worsened, woollen socks and warmer underwear which they wore night and day. In the camp, the fireside chatter was that no one wanted to be in this town except those who could overcharge for the meagre pleasures on offer. Most of the men saved to get away, to get a new life, a new start, some escaping past lives or maybe the law. George heard them, some moaning constantly at the working conditions, some choosing to remain silent.

George had always worked for himself, though he remembered working as a lad for his father in Bristol, when he'd told his father how he intended to work for himself one day. The old man had grinned and said, 'You've still got a lot to learn my lad so you'd better get on with the job in hand, pretty sharpish, before you feel my boot on your backside.'

George had been right, as he had worked alone for most of his married life, although young Roger was useful too. Up until the last year or so he always earned enough. Determined, he made it work but that bloody war had left another cruel legacy, not only men lost. Everyone had tightened their belts.

George pouted but he resolved to save. Gradually as the weeks passed he realised it wasn't happening, as he needed a few warm clothes himself. The money he earned was less than he'd imagined, and he frowned at his pay packet after the reductions for small items essential to the work were charged at ridiculous prices by the camp. Jim cursed each week too. 'What the hell are they charging me for now? Any more damn stoppages and I'll be paying 'em for the pleasure of being here!'

George was sure it wasn't fair, and Bert agreed. 'They got the upper hand, ain't they? We got no unions, no-one to fight for our rights. What can we do? Argue and you're out on your ear.' Any visit to the town took most of the rest yet George promised himself he would tighten his belt.

One Sunday he decided not to go into town, planning to explore the frozen woodlands outside the camp. He wandered amongst the tall trees for a while, climbed down a bank, watched the river for signs of beavers and fish jumping. The clouds blew across and sleet stung his skin. Soon, getting too cold, he returned to his bunk. He shed his wet things to steam on the lines across the rafters and spent much of a bitter wet day sprawled on his bunk, tired with little to distract him. He missed his family. The hours dragged. Their bunk house was empty with most men on shifts or in town, with no one to chat to and nothing to do but polish his boots. As he rubbed dubbin into the leather, working it into the cracks and creases he thought about his boys, teaching them to clean their boots when they were small. He pictured them at home, sitting at the table and his stomach turned. He missed them so much.

He tried to write to Dorcas and his children, but the words didn't come. What could he tell them? Not about this miserable place.

He struggled through the following week feeling the work was endless. On the next off-day he spent even more money than usual in town and realised the futility of it all. How could he save for their future? What he needed was a plan.

The grip of winter held them in its bite. Ice made many tasks impossible. Deep snow often prevented progress with the track and many men moaned they were not needed, often laid off for days, sometimes a week. The sky was heavy with snow clouds, piled one above another, waiting to fall whenever they had cleared a path between the bunkhouse and the canteen. The men, huddled in all their clothing, cursed and quarrelled, most with heavy beards. With nowhere to go but the most promise of work being at the camp, they hung around with no pay, still having to find money for their food. A few gave up or went away though most played cards and slept, waiting for a day's work.

Men shovelled snow into high walls either side of the track where they could. At least the work kept them warmer, but then they were hungry. Everyone was on day rates, hired and laid off at the whim of the overseer and the cruel weather. Their bunkhouse continuously smelt of damp socks draped over makeshift lines above the bunks. George was lucky at times to be chosen to be part of the maintenance team which made him feel involved. Pipes and machinery above ground often froze overnight and needed gentle persuasion and repeated repair to keep water or oil flowing. This preserved both the slow progress with the project and some basic needs of the camp to function and his skills were needed though not always paid at the better rate.

He worked from dawn till long after the meagre sun disappeared. His hands often froze in his thick gloves as he battled with the pipes. He was not alone. Several others with the knowledge worked in the same team. The four plumbers were led by Jacques, the short French Canadian who resented George's Bristol accent, his British manner, and his height. George worked hard and tried every trick to maintain the work's progress but any success he showed to the team was resented he realised. 'Damned if you do, damned if you don't,' he told Bert. Day after day he fell out of bed before dawn, grabbed his work clothes, wrapped up warmly and, after watery canteen porridge and black coffee, he reported on time to join the team at the work hut.

As the only English-speaking man in their team, he had to discover the meaning of the Frenchman's orders growled for the day. Pierre, who was older than George, translated as best he could, though George noticed Jacques's contempt as they whispered together. George tried to keep his wits about him for any details; often unsure how recently a pipe had frozen or seized, whether it had expanded or cracked, if it could be coaxed and cleared, or was an essential replacement. His pride often prevented him asking Pierre to explain again. Sometimes they were working a distance apart and, if he approached Pierre, the foreman would spit a stream of tobacco juice towards his boots with a scornful glance. Then he would put his hand on George's arm as he repeated instructions in colloquial French gesturing with his hands and shoulders as he showed his dislike. George narrowed his eyes as he watched the muscles beside the Frenchman's mouth bunch in disdain at his lack of understanding.

He tried to comprehend the gestures, but Jacques didn't want to make it easy. George railed against the unfairness of their attitude towards him but tried to say nothing. He simmered beneath the surface. 'This bloody winter,' he muttered, 'and these damned Frenchmen!' Everything seemed against him and as he pouted, his stubborn glance caused the friction to mount. George had learnt not to complain. It would cause him to be sent packing. He had seen it with others where the tension had broken in curses. It was only his long hours of hard work in freezing conditions, which prevented him from being sacked. At present he was a valuable member of the team and he knew it, although no comment was made, no praise offered.

Paid each Saturday afternoon, he queued for his pay packet, which never was a full wage, always with stoppages for minor infringements dreamt up by the foreman. George squirrelled it away in his body belt. Bert had moaned, 'Yer daren't leave a shirt button in your locker or some Frenchy will pinch it, sell it for a beer.'

Jim, always wanting to agree with his mate, said 'Yea, they do a roaring trade at night between these huts selling our stuff, yer know!'

George treasured his watch because Dorcas had bought it for his twenty-first birthday when they were courting. She'd saved hard for it and, although it was not valuable, to him it was precious. She'd had it engraved on the back of the case, 'Love to G. from D.' There wasn't room for more, but he guessed she couldn't afford a longer message. Whenever he rubbed his thumb across its smooth back, he felt the love she'd intended and remembered her young face as she'd given it to him, eyes shining with their new-found love. Nothing would ever part him from the watch or from her he had told her. It kept good time, always tucked deep in his waistcoat pocket with the chain ending in a tee bar fixed from his buttonhole.

He remembered how his younger children loved to look at it. Back home he'd take it out and show them how he wound it, setting it right each Sunday by the chapel clock. They attended chapel out of habit and their useful weekly meeting with other villagers often brought him some business, until this last year. Most of those who were his potential customers kept up their chapel attendance, so he rarely walked home without a promise to fix someone's problem. Dorcas said it built up trust being a chapelgoer though the children fidgeted more these days. George smiled at the thought, remembering five-year old May's pins and needles because her feet didn't touch the floor as she sat in the pew. He often rubbed her toes on his lap when that happened, and she'd screwed up her blue eyes at the sensation.

He sighed as he thought of his wife and family and wondered how they were managing back home, as the ruthless Canadian winter froze everything about him.

Weeks passed, days blending into one another in a muddle of the same tasks repeated, while the relentless cold proved its persistence. Sitting on his bunk one night looking across the bunk house at other men, bored and frustrated, he thought about the life he'd imagined on the ship coming here. Hard work yes, that had never bothered him, but he had dreamt of a life, a home here in this land of opportunity, of fresh fields, of new challenges. Yet his savings were meagre, his days anxious and resentful spent always covering his back. This was not what he had promised himself. There seemed no chance of having dreams. This gruelling regime was fading his hopes. George, who had always been positive, questioned his ideas of making a new life for his beloved family. He was too far away from opportunities and guessed, when he could, he must get to a proper town.

'It will be years at this rate before I can send for Dorcas and my children,' he mumbled as he looked at today's pay packet, scribbled details on a tatty brown envelope. He tried to check the calculations for the stoppages, unsure of the details, wishing for Dorcas with her sure checking to verify a fair wage. Not that he'd dare protest.

Then George noticed the date. Could it be the end of the year? Often so tired he fell into bed without thinking of which day it was, he had no idea of the passing of the months. He realised he had arrived in August so it must be … he hesitated as he counted on his fingers … nearly five months. He was truly surprised to see it was almost Christmas, shocked into guilt he hadn't written, he hadn't sent greetings to his family. Would they imagine him at some feast, at someone else's table and hearth without remembering them? The truth was relentless work and tiredness with bitter arguments held silently in his thoughts. He had never had this before, always enjoying the satisfaction of success back home. He remembered his Sunday School teacher telling him of the parable of the Prodigal Son and questioned his future. No, he'd not go home with his tail between his legs. He would struggle on.

His friends saw the battle he was having each day. 'George ole fella, yer must keep your temper. They are trying to goad yer but don't let 'em win. If you fight any of these bastards, they'll slaughter yer and dump yer down one of them pits under a lot of rubble.' Bert said as they sat huddled by the stove.

'Yea, I've heard it whispered it wouldn't be the first time a man had vanished. Out here no one would know. Don't give the buggers a chance, mate,' Jim nodded. It was true. The hatred he'd seen told him they'd give him no quarter. He might just disappear.

Earlier there was an announcement on the notice board in the canteen. Pierre had translated. 'Only essential workers needed for Christmas Day.' George's heart sank. It included him, finding his name on the essential list, no extra pay either. The men mumbled.

Bert spread his hands in disbelief. 'Damn me. Would you believe it? How mean can they get?' All other work suspended for one day only, except for them.

George couldn't believe it either. 'I thought this was a Christian country,' he muttered. 'Even the mines back home give you Christmas Day off with basic pay.' Of course, It was the union's doing but unions in this camp were forbidden. Resigned he dared not ask why but he had heard of the contentions.

'So, when exactly is Christmas Day?' he asked. He had no calendar with only pay days and non-pay days marking his weeks. The three men sat by the stove in their hut trying to thaw out, smoking their pipes: their only comfort. Wet jackets and socks steamed on a string above, their smell unnoticed.

'Day after tomorrow, but it'll make no difference to us lest there's a bloody miracle to thaw things overnight, mate. We're essential to keep this place ticking. Might be some extra grub though. Love a bit of plum duff. Supposed to be no drinking in the camp of course. Some of them will be heading into town to get a skin-full tomorrow night, you can be sure.' Bert rubbed his stomach.

'Beer and women for some,' George thought resenting his hum-drum life. Many of the men rode to town each Saturday evening on the wagon returning late on Sunday to sleep off the ravages of their lonely lives. George had felt tempted seeing the women in the saloons. He had not yet succumbed, the thought of Dorcas holding him in check, though the pressure was mounting. 'I live like a bloody monk and barely a word from her!' he whispered. He no longer reread her first indignant letter sent weeks before in response to his telegram. It had found him eventually, her words biting him even at this distance.

20th September '23
Dear George,
How could you do this to us? Where are you? How am I supposed to manage alone with so little money? Have you thought of this?

You say you will send for us but when? I'm not sure if I can do what you want. We are settled here and, although it has been tough these past few years, I never wanted to go to a big city let alone a new country. I think you should at least have asked me what I thought before going. I am sure someone has sold you a grand idea. I rather doubt it will work.

People in the village are going to young Fred for their plumbing repairs, of course. He is delighted, though I heard from Miss Featherstone that he's not as good as you. Her drains are getting blocked again apparently. If you decide to come back soon you may be able to get the work though he's got a big grin on his face!

The children are well and the weather is warm. Please think about all this.

Dorcas.

By now she will have calmed down he thought. I hope she's getting rid of that stock, making a clean sweep of it all. Time had dimmed his image of the shop, giving him illusions as how much would be left, sure his Dorcas would manage to sell his stock. He turned his thoughts back to Bert who continued to explain, seated as always by the stove drinking scalding coffee.

'Don't worry mate. We'll have a night out soon. We've got to get someone to cover for you on your day off. Let's plan it and we can show them fellas in town what Englishmen can do!' Bert laughed as he shoved another log into the stove. George grinned back.

Christmas Day dawned bright and clear. George worked through with others from the emergency team in a quiet camp vacated by most men. They hoped there wouldn't be a blow, or some disaster. The bosses told them of any contingency plans, but the team secretly guessed they would be in extreme trouble being so short-handed if things went wrong. As the working hours shifted from the sharp rays of early daylight to the longer rays of lengthening afternoon shadows, and on to bleak darkness broken by lanterns and reflected snow, nothing happened. They worked through, quieter than usual with no blasting or whistles. It felt strange. After extra food at lunchtime and second helpings of maple syrup dumplings as a token feast for men left behind, they worked a long day. He tried not to think of home. Already snoring in bed that night, they were disturbed by rowdy men arriving back on various forms of carts. Most of them were in no state to walk straight, let alone help with any emergency at the tunnels.

CHAPTER 12: Dorcas, December 1923

Dorcas thought it was strange how each of the children felt about the move. The little girls, all four of them, were in awe of the adventure, only Olive really having heard of Canada in geography lessons. May and Ethel seemed to imagine London and Canada were next to each other. Marjorie just frowned. The two boys were keen. It seemed like new opportunities opening before them. They had visited the town's lending library on their occasional shopping visits and seen pictures in a book about forests and lakes, railways and highways. They studied the maps and dreamt of adventures. Their excitement encouraged Dorcas.

Tilda frequently looked down, busying herself with chores. She wouldn't explain why she was reluctant. Her mother guessed she'd miss her girlfriend Muriel, but Dorcas was too distracted to spot the obvious signs that there were other things on Tilda's mind.

Nearly sixteen, Tilda had not grown tall. 'Thank goodness,' she thought, 'I don't grow out of clothes like Muriel, who wears dresses with those extra frills she sews around the hem and cuffs to lengthen them. My dresses may be plain but at least decent.'

It was important for Tilda to look neat. Joseph liked neat things she'd noticed, and she hoped he'd notice her soon too. Joseph had been in the school when they were younger but now he worked as a post boy cycling around the village helping their postmaster with deliveries. He'd brought George's recent letter shuffling on the doorstep while Dorcas read it and Tilda looked over her shoulder and blushed. She dared not look at him directly, her eyes glancing down as she noticed his every move. He was so … so gorgeous. He had grown tall, with soft brown eyes and a mischievous smile. She began to daydream again. No, Tilda didn't want to leave the village at all. She had other dreams.

Tilda's hair was long and brown, just brown. It wasn't luxurious and wavy, only straight and stubborn. She had tried putting it into rags overnight, longing for ringlets like Muriel but it had looked fussed next morning, and she'd combed it through with some water, tied it back and bundled it in a snood, before setting off for the school where she earnt a little as a pupil teacher.

If she saw Joseph cycling past she would pretend she hadn't seen him, blushing like her father, but all day she would carry his image in her head. Several times the headmaster had noticed her absent mindedness and reproved her. Tilda did not want to go away. She couldn't tell anyone, especially her mother. If she was older perhaps she could stay with her grandma, but her mother would never allow that. She dreamt of impossible meetings, soft lips, sweet words and found excuses to visit the post office.

One afternoon Dorcas had rolled out some pastry on the board as Sarah sat in the corner, her knitting on her lap, their chat returning to George.

'It's not easy lass, you've a hell of a lot to do, so don't worry. I'll help you. I will miss you so much if you go, but George is right really. There's no work hereabouts at present. He's doing his best and so must you. We women have little choice. We must get on with it. Look at me. I had to come to Wales when my man came for the work in the mine.'

'Yes, but why didn't you go back after he'd died? Didn't you want to return to your own folks?' Dorcas balanced the dish high on her fingertips as she cut around the pie dish shedding strips of soft pastry.

'Well, there was only an elderly aunt left in Tyneside by then. I had nothing to go back to, and I'd learnt to love you and your bairns. I suppose I've kinda grown used to this place.'

'And now we're going to leave you. Oh, I will miss you Sarah.' A frown crossed Dorcas's face. 'What will I do without you? You're such a comfort.' She took Sarah's hand. 'You did so much to help when Peter was ill.'

'You'll be fine lass, once you get your George back. And because you've already started selling off stuff and getting ready, and you'll have so much to do in the next few months, you won't have time to think on all that.' Sarah swallowed the thought of her own loneliness when the family went. She had been their neighbour since Dorcas came as a bride and had seen each child arrive, helping Dorcas when asked.

'How are the little ones coping with the idea of a move?'

'Well, the boys seem to be keen. They think there's more opportunities for them and the little ones don't really understand about it all. But have you noticed Tilda's constantly got a face like a wet week? She says it's leaving her friends but I'm not so sure.' Popping the pies in the oven, Dorcas folded a cloth on the table and started ironing the pile waiting in the basket.

'I expect there's someone she's got her eye on, lovely young girl.' Sarah looked down.

'No. I don't think so Sarah. She'd have told me, I'm sure.' Dorcas glanced at her friend beginning to query Tilda's motives.

'My dear, you're the last person she'd tell. Don't you remember how we were as girls?' Sighing she packed her knitting in her bag. 'Well, it's time I was getting along. Thanks for the tea.' Sarah stood awkwardly and waddled to the scullery door.

Dorcas knew Olive loved the shop too much to want to move. She had seen her daughter glow whenever she was 'in charge' of their shop. Wednesday was Olive's night for sitting in the shop. Each of the older ones took turns to mind the shop while the others ate their meal.

Now she was nearly eleven, Olive was very proud that Dorcas allowed her to do this alone. She had practised alongside her mother for a long time before she was trusted to serve customers, but Olive was sharp. She soon learnt what to say and where things were. She felt important and grown up wearing Mam's shop apron tied securely around her skinny waist. She loved the homely smell of the shop; of chopped wood and washing soda, soap and lamp oil.

Not many customers came in at tea-time when she would serve them with a polite word and a prim look. If what they wanted was too difficult, she would say in clipped tones, 'Just one moment please, I'll get some assistance for you,' scampering away into the kitchen and either Tilda or Roger would come with a reluctant shrug. Olive tried hard not to do this often, climbing on the wooden steps her father had made to reach the higher drawers, remembering where most things were. Some things were too heavy or dangerous for her to tackle. Only then would she get help.

When the shop was empty, she tidied things away, wiping the serving counter and sweeping the black and white tiles around the boxes and baskets on the floor. She hummed a tune for she loved their shop. A single lamp gave a warm light glancing off the shelves and the tall cabinets which lined the walls, built by George to last. They sold tools and bundles of kindling, paraffin poured through a funnel into a customer's bottle by the pint and wood glue by the stick. Olive counted out the hinges and screws along with candles and delicate gas mantles. She remembered most prices, running an efficient finger down the handwritten price list. Holding her head at an angle in imitation of her mother she added the items on paper, checking as she went, licking her indelible pencil. She took the coins, put them in the drawer and gave change, closing the drawer with a satisfying click. When she was grown up she would have her own shop and make lots of money, she thought.

When it got dark her mother locked the door and only opened it when some customer rang the bell. In the winter village children were often sent for more kindling or a gas mantle after school. Olive loved her classmates seeing her transformed into a shopkeeper, though when it got late one of the older ones took over, Olive having to go to bed. Mam insisted they get their sleep, so they could be up in time to do their chores before school. School was important. Mam said so.

In bed Olive chided Marjorie. 'You won't be allowed to do it even when you get to eleven!' she whispered smirking.

Marjorie hunched her shoulders saying, 'I don't want to anyway so there. Silly old shop!' as she buried herself under the blankets and burst into tears.

Peter imagined opportunities outside this village. Canada seemed like a modern idea. He loved his art, but he also wanted a new life. Roger and he had discussed it in bed. The boys had read of the way men were carving out new lives for their families and the pictures of lumberjacks, of logging and construction teams seemed so much livelier than the dull village they had always lived in with its narrow, cobbled streets. Here the purple mountains in the background foreshadowed each dawn and sunset, casting a gloom to the day. The constant growth of slag heaps above the village reminded them of the mine. After his illness, he had grown closer to his mother wanting the best for her and dreaming he'd help build her a larger house with a real garden bursting with exotic flowers and blossoming trees. She loved beautiful things as he did. Her eyes shone when they shared his drawings. They understood one another in a secret way. Perhaps in Canada it would be possible.

Roger felt a new place would be good, but he had started to think about girls and to imagine different opportunities. His voice had become annoyingly unreliable, deepening in mid speech, and his shoulders stretched his jackets. He hated the way his brother chided him for checking his hair and peering in the scullery mirror before he went to school. The two boys were good mates at school, though they rowed frequently at home.

Dorcas watched them both and guessed the changes were because they were both growing up, but George would have had a lot to say to them, not in a diplomatic way but George wasn't there, she reminded herself, it was up to her. She wondered what she might need to tell them.

The weather was wet and wild on the day Roger came home with bruises and a black eye. He went straight up to his bed and threw himself down ignoring his brother's anxious glances. Peter whispered, 'You've got to tell Mam, she can't help seeing the state you are in. She's going to be furious when she sees.'

'It's none of your business, Peter. I'm not saying anything, and don't you stir it up either. I can look after myself. It's over, so there, busybody.' Roger buried his face in the pillow.

Peter slouched downstairs and was told by Tilda to get more coal in for the fire. Their mother was serving in the shop. Later, when the meal was on the table and Dorcas called the children to the kitchen, she noticed Roger was not there. Usually amongst the hungriest, she called upstairs and when he didn't appear, she went up to the boys' tiny room. Her gasp of horror when she saw his face made the children sitting silently around the table, stiffen. Their Mam would be angry as well as worried. Her words echoed down the stairs. 'I've told you before about fighting Roger. It never solved any problems. Whoever made you do it?' Her words went on and they couldn't hear Roger's whispered replies until his voice became louder and the frustration, mingled with tears, was obvious as he started to shout back at her.

'I hate what they say about you and Dadda. Jenkins wouldn't stop so I closed his mouth for him!' Dorcas looked shocked as she realised the cause of his bruises. Wanting to apologise, she gave him a secret hug then said nothing more.

Tilda told the others to start to eat but it was a very silent meal. They had heard Roger being subjected to endless taunts about his mother and their family situation in the playground and he had eventually snapped. They had seen the punches and the scuffles and witnessed the school master's disgust. Dorcas made Tilda and Peter tell the truth and again she blamed George for causing this. She took Roger up some food, but she dared not tell him of her secret pride he'd defended her and their family. Dorcas recognised George's bluff way of reacting which Roger had inherited. Bathing his eye later she put an arm around him and Roger didn't shrink away. For once he was glad to be her child.

Dorcas dreaded Christmas this year. It was usually a welcome break from the shop and work. Each year the anticipation of both receiving and giving of little gifts by the children gave a glow to the day. Most people made it a two-day holiday, trying to get home, joining with family and friends, perhaps hosting a guest for Christmas dinner. The children would spend hours making decorations from bits, adding greenery to sills and keeping secrets. For adults it was a chance to sit, maybe a glass of port or beer, even a daytime snooze if the children were occupied.

This year would be different. No good-humoured George to add to their outrageous jokes. They would notice George's empty chair at Christmas. There'd be a large hole in their kitchen, a gap in the laughter. Dorcas had always been able to get on with the dinner with some help, hearing the little girls clambering over their father, knowing they could tease him today especially, be tickled and he would make faces at them with odd noises and co-operate with their childish fun. Their festive meal was always orchestrated by his presence … but not this year.

Marjorie's birthday added an extra poignancy to the day. Every year the day passed in the celebration of Christmas and she got very little extra attention. Birthdays were not greatly celebrated although there was always a cake for tea, which Dorcas iced with Christmas and Birthday cheer. This year it would seem different and at nine Marjorie might feel disappointed in a quiet puzzled way.

Dorcas did her best, her own mam and Sarah contributing a little to help them. Gran and Ernest visited for Christmas day as the weather wasn't too severe, but it seemed much quieter. Several squabbles broke out amongst the younger ones and, when Roger saw Dorcas's frustrated look, he chided his sisters. The day seemed deflated; its atmosphere subdued. She was relieved when the evening darkened, and the curtains drawn, after Gran and Ernest had left in the shared trap with some neighbours to return up the hill to home. Dorcas sat with Peter and looked fondly at his new drawings admiring the portrait of Ernest he'd drawn that afternoon. She sighed. Tilda came in wiping her hands.

'Before we go to bed Mam, can I play your piano, a few carols perhaps?' Soon the chilly parlour echoed to the children's voices and Tilda's attempts at familiar tunes. Sarah was away visiting her friend, so their music would not disturb her through the walls. A few jokey songs were attempted before Dorcas noticed their yawns.

'Time for bed and if you are quick maybe … maybe a short story from your new book perhaps?' Dorcas read to them and tucked them in, kissing each one. No-one mentioned George till they prayed for him, when Dorcas reassured them he was having a good time though he would miss them all. She hid her personal doubts. What sort of Christmas was he really having she wondered? She hoped he'd truly missed them all!

CHAPTER 13: George, January 1924

20th Dec '23
Dear George,
The past months have been so difficult. Peter has had diphtheria and was so ill. I managed to keep him at home, in the parlour while Tilda with Sarah's help looked after the others. Our girl had to take a lot of responsibility when she is still so young. It was quite a trial for the whole family, but thank God, we managed, and Peter is recovering. He has lost a lot of weight but is his usual cheerful self. The children have been great, hardly squabbling at all. I was so proud of them all. We had to close the shop of course and that meant no money coming in at all for weeks.

One question. Did you get paid for the Cromwell Street work you did before Easter, only when I reminded him, the landlord said he'd paid in July but the money wasn't marked in the book. Did you take it with you?

It is almost Christmas, and I wonder what kind of day it will be for you. We all send our best wishes.
Love Dorcas and your family. X
P.S. Now I have your address I am sending it to your mother so she may write.

When George got her next letter, in late January, he worried. He guessed Peter's illness before Christmas had been hard and was relieved and grateful his son had survived and, according to Dorcas, the rest of his family were safe. He could not imagine how she had managed, but it was more the tone of her letter that annoyed him. Controlled, almost dismissive. He hadn't even known it was happening, hadn’t any idea his boy was in danger. He’d not been told. Concern for them all worried him, but it sounded as though he wasn't even needed. Maybe they didn't realise how difficult his life was, how many times he secretly longed to return. Dorcas asked how he was doing though her tone suggested she didn't have any idea of the trials he faced.

George knew he couldn't go back. He would not admit defeat. He must make a life here to offer them all. There was no work back home. He had to make some progress here. As his father had said, 'This time you've burnt your boats, George, my boy.'

George screwed up her letter, dumping it on his bunk as he stuck out his jaw and pulled back his shoulders. Angry with himself, unfairly blaming her for his woes, yet wishing he could turn back the clock, could wake up and find it all a bad dream, he kicked the leg of the bed. He determined to show her!

A week later they got their day off. 'See, I told you it would come. Now this is our party, our Christmas. Let's be ready as soon as the wagon arrives.' Bert clapped him on the shoulder.

'Fine, I'll be there before you, I bet,' George felt pleased. He deserved a bit of fun. Her letter had made him question his efforts. He hadn't felt like laughing for so long. He was determined to have a good time. He'd spend a bit of this week's wages, for once. ‘After all this is my Christmas,’ he thought. Sprucing himself up, he gave a bit of extra spit and polish to his boots, brushing the worn leather to some semblance of a shine. A clean collar, scrubbed fingernails and George was ready.

When they arrived in town, they rubbed their cold hands and clapped at their biceps after jumping from the cart anticipating a good time. A strange silence greeted them as a few people hurried about in the cold, distracted by bills and minor illnesses. Any village children were back at school and the world was having a working Wednesday. Women in heavy cloaks and hoods, wearing snowshoes struggled with bags of provisions, heads bent against the wind. Recent snowfalls had melted to dirty slush then refrozen on the streets making the ground treacherous. None of the cheer the men had imagined, seemed there, as this town had forgotten last month's Christmas jollity in the reality of working January.

The men decided to have a good meal for once but the menu in the cafe was depressing. It was the usual cook's day off and the proprietor's wife was in charge, so no piled plates today. However, when Jim smiled at her, she made them some pancakes with maple syrup, something the men had never had before but enjoyed. Feeling nicely full, they kissed her cheek as they all three left the cafe, causing her to give them a shy smile. They wandered out into the deserted street. No one else was celebrating. Determined, the men didn't let this stop them. They meant to enjoy themselves. As they sauntered to the saloon George straightened his collar and smoothed his hair.

Some hours later in early evening the men were merry from the several rough beers they had consumed, whilst playing cards. Other men from the town joined them with jokes and wild tales filling the air. Then music from the tinny piano caused them to sing and at last George felt warm inside. He took his watch from inside his waistcoat pocket. Nearly nine, plenty of time before Theo with the wagon returned at midnight for the last stragglers. All the men had paid the burly wagon driver in advance for the return journey, so he'd round them up from either of the two saloons before he started back. Each time he threatened to leave those men who weren't ready, but they climbed or were shoved into the open back of the wooden wagon. If they missed him, they would face an eight mile walk in complete darkness or be late for their shift next morning. Theo would not forget them for no one could afford that, not after a night of drinking.

George was singing loudly, standing around with others when a buxom woman sidled up to him and stood at his side. All the women in the bar were of a certain kind, either easy types or a few older single women who drank together. Most women who lived in the town would avoid drinking saloons where late-night trouble was renowned. Women who were seen there gained a reputation as 'saloon girls.'

George looked down at the saloon girl who stood beside him and smiled. Normally he avoided the temptations but tonight he felt good, tipsy but after all it was his Christmas. He took a deep breath, expanding his chest and she whispered in his ear as she stood on tiptoe, almost overbalancing and putting her plump hand on his chest. His arm went about her waist to prevent her toppling and it stayed there, feeling her warm body. He felt good to hear a husky female voice singing next to him and when the song finished, he asked her if she'd like a drink. In the dim light of the saloon lanterns she seemed glamorous, in her swirling skirt with a hem of red silky petticoat which hinted at a dancer to his eyes. She flicked her lashes as he gazed at her tempting smile. In a whisper she asked, 'What are you called when you are at home, big boy?' her hand on his arm.

'George,' he mumbled into her ear, breathing in her strong perfume splashed on her auburn curls.

'Like the king I suppose,' she teased. 'I'm Kate. I haven't noticed you in here before. I would know if you were a regular; a tall man like you. So where have you been hiding all this time?' She looked up at him, her blue eyes hinting at so much.

George bent and whispered back, and she flicked her eyebrows at him in response. His hand stroked her back and lowered past her waist. This was a woman who understood men, he felt. She saw what they needed. He liked Kate. They sang together with the crowd, and he grew taller, flushed with a warm sensation as both the beer and her perfume heightened his mood. He watched, as she tossed her bright curls in the lamplight of the bar, with his dreams racing ahead of him.

Several drinks later she was leading him by the hand upstairs and into one of the few bedrooms. He felt confused but aroused. He really needed a woman, he told himself. He was only human, wasn't he? He dug into his pocket for some coins. He took another swig of beer from the bottle beside the bed.

'After all,' he thought, 'she's a good laugh, a good mover too!' She backed away from him and he lumbered towards her across the room. He grabbed her, and she smiled coyly up at him, the dimples in her plump cheeks intriguing him. He always loved a challenge, he thought and that's what she was, a load of fun. No spring chicken but what the hell. He picked her up and laid her down on the bed, then knelt beside her. Together they pulled at their clothing as they became locked in each other's arms. Passionately he buried himself in her soft embrace. Her warmed body gave off perfume and he forgot everything in the excitement of the moment. Muddled by the drink he felt this wasn't quite what he had intended, though very soon he found himself lying naked beside her, exhausted. He slept.

She watched him and ran her hand across his broad back. There was something almost innocent about this one, a family man unlike most. 'I rather like you George,' she whispered as he snored loudly. 'I reckon I'll remember you for a while.'

The next thing he knew was the door crashing open as Theo hauled him to his feet. 'Come on mate, we got to get you home,' he yelled in George's ear thrusting his clothes at him before they stumbled down the stairs and into the wagon. George clambered up onto the wooden boards carrying his boots.

Some of the others grinned. 'Didn't reckon you had it in you George!' they spat. George's head buzzed. He slept all the way until the wagon drew to a halt at the entrance to the camp. The men staggered to their beds for a few hours' sleep before the next shift. In the morning George woke with a guilty conscience and a cruel hangover. He hadn't meant it to happen. He'd have to watch out. Things were getting out of hand.

By the end of February, he'd had two warnings. Two minor events which had been blown out of proportion. He'd left a lump hammer which belonged to the company at the site and, when he returned ten minutes later, it had disappeared. If he reported the loss it would cost him, but he was sure Henri had taken it, hiding it in the cart which he collected each day. George confronted him and argued loudly with a good deal of pushing and shoving. Jacques heard their raised voices and his first warning was given. The second came when they searched and discovered the stolen hammer beneath his bunk behind its upright leg. George protested it had been planted there, but the warnings stuck. That night he sat disgruntled by the stove, his fists clenched as he went over the events. Jim sat with him saying little. Bert picked his teeth. They felt trapped.

George had never gambled before. As a lad he'd watched his brothers play cards and occasionally joined them but only for farthings or even just matchsticks, always losing as Billy seemed to hold all the aces. Throughout his married life he was certain Dorcas would have been loud with her views on him gambling.

For several weeks he had ignored the taunts of others at the saloon and refused to enter their card games. Until Bert returned to the cart one Saturday midnight with talk of high stakes and success in the back room of the saloon, George had never been tempted. The men boasted each time of their success.

The following Saturday night he watched as Jim and Bert won several days' wages in under an hour. Surely a win or two would be possible. He would only risk a little and see. He dreamed of something good happening at last, of making up for those months of work. By midnight he was wealthier by three days' pay. He felt good, smiling to himself in the darkness on the way back to camp, breathing deeply. Maybe this would be his breakthrough, his way of getting enough for his new start.

When the landlord sold tickets for a sweepstake he was running on some local derby, the build-up of the excitement over the possible outcome and the talk of high stakes made George put his hand into his pocket and buy a single ticket. Bert and Jim bought several and the men talked constantly about the future races whenever they were in the saloon. George wasn't hopeful as he soon noticed the odds changing on different horses as the days passed. Gradually the talk was of little else and of the wild nights men dreamt about if they won. George imagined getting away, of returning to the city and travelling into America to find the illusive start to his new future. He also guessed the odds of winning were very slim. The day of the race came, and some men took themselves off to see the races. Others stood with George at the mail office listening to the tapping of the wires recording the horses' progress. They were silent as the stenographer read the tape word by word to the waiting crowd. With each win, the men looked again at their tickets wishing them to be winners. Sudden whoops followed by 'Shush!' and fierce frowns broke the silence between races.

As the results came through, each one on his ticket seemed a winner, slowly he began to concentrate. His heart was racing. As the final one came true, he yelled punching the air with his fist. When George realised that he had won ten times his stake his whole body seemed to wake up, a thrill going through him. Maybe this was his way to a new life, so he could find a quicker way out of this drudgery. For the next few weeks, he joined their back-room poker games, winning at times, accruing coins in his small leather purse. Others looked on; glances of hope mixed with flashes of silent jealousy. Others too longed for a way out of this life.

Three Saturdays passed, and before Easter he'd won more than he'd lost. He wrote enthusiastically to Dorcas not telling her how the money was accumulating but he hoped to send for them soon. He never mentioned gambling, she'd not approve. He had no idea how long his letter would take before she read it.

He saw the frowns and scowls on the faces of the other team, the French group in the back room. They were not pleased whenever they had lost vital cash to the Englishmen over the card table. After a successful night and several drinks, George decided to risk his savings in one throw of the dice. The possible odds would make him a fortune.

The poker players lowered their eyes. And Lady Luck turned away from him. He lost it all. He stared in disbelief at his cards. Others at the table scooped up his precious money. George was silent and felt sick.

Lying in his bed later he was bitter. What a fool he had been? Why had he listened to Jim and Bert and got involved in this? Why had he only heard their encouraging words? 'Go on George, just a flutter, you're always lucky, just a bit of fun. Lucky George!' Somehow, he had forgotten his life back home in the fever of gambling, forgotten Dorcas and the children for a while. His hopes of a new life, a white porch for her, his children's smiles of admiration, all his dreams had crashed. The truth was hard. After more than half a year he must start again. When darkness hid a tear or two in his pillow, he silently vowed, 'Never again George. Never again!'

His undated, encouraging letter didn't reach Dorcas for more than two months and she assumed she must soon pack up the house and go. She would never hear about his losses, or of his efforts.

By the following Saturday, George was still disheartened. He shouldn't go with the others to town. He shouldn't really spend his wages in the saloon there but, as he sat slumped on his bunk while the men around him spruced themselves up for their night out, he closed his eyes. A heady, perfumed memory tempted him. He frowned clamping his jaw shut when Bert asked if he was coming.

'Come on George, a couple of beers. A man deserves a drink after a week like this one!' Jim said. Several men chided him, and he tried hard not to think of the last time. His resolve began to fade, and at almost the last minute, he gave in. Slipping on his only clean shirt and waistcoat and tying his boots in a hurry, he ran after the cart and swung up with the others. Everyone laughed, and a few crude jokes were shouted. George grinned and gave in.

The saloon was crowded after the various crews had arrived, with only a few women in tonight. The jokes got bawdy and more lamps were brought out. The inviting atmosphere closed about him like a warm blanket. George found himself looking for her, his eyes searching about the wooden saloon, checking the dimly lit corners where couples sat heads close together. He wanted to see her though his feelings of guilt told him he shouldn't. It would be best if he went he knew, but it was cold and dark outside. Once more he glanced around for her. Somehow, he stayed.

The smell of beer and men cut into George's throat. He started to cough. 'Need another drink,' he told himself. Several beers later, when most of the men had spent nearly all their pay at the bar, the women arrived. Their delay was part of the landlord's ploy to boost takings at the bar while they waited, though the men had no idea this was how it worked. Now it was the ladies' turn. The swelling of voices when the doors swung open, as a pretty boot stepped delicately through, reflected the men's need on a Saturday night.

George looked for her and felt surprised she seemed to ignore him. He sung louder. He hoped that was only her way of showing him he wasn't special but as his pulse raced, he moved towards her. She continued to chat and laugh with Henri and he didn't like that. Standing behind her he put his hand on her sleeve possessively, waiting till she turned. Henri narrowed his eyes and shot him a glance which promised revenge, but George ignored it. He didn't want to waste more time. Kate saw from his bloodshot eyes that he'd been drinking for long enough. She smiled, took his hand, and led him to the stairs.

When he finally closed the bedroom door and turned to take her in his arms, she laughed at him. 'Let's not rush this, George. What do you like? Tell me.' Her wicked look excited him. She held up her hand as she then started to slowly unlace her bodice. He watched, breathing heavily. She moved seductively, her body promising mysteries he had only imagined. Flushed, George finally moved. He buried his face in her silky breast and covered her body with his. Passion overwhelmed him and she responded.

Sometime later Kate lay looking up at the ceiling, his body slumped across her, his bare leg trapping her. She watched him sleep. He had been one of her better men, one of the best. She had enjoyed their time together, and it didn't often happen, hardly ever. She smiled, her arm across his back. She knew she would remember him. She looked at his blond hair flopped onto the pillow. Most of the men she met here were hardened types, but George had a certain naive way about him, obviously used to only one woman. She reckoned she had been a new experience for him. He was less demanding than most, and she'd enjoyed his strong body, it had seemed right. Daydreaming she imagined them together as a couple, in a home with fancy curtains and a family. 'Come on Katie,' she said to herself. 'Get realistic, these things never work.' As she moved his leg she thought she wouldn't mind seeing him again, though she was tiring of this life. She was getting older and recognised she had no future.

She slipped out of the bed and dressed quickly. He had not left any money for her, so she fished in his pockets.

No, there were only a couple of coins there. She found his watch and after a moment's thought she unlinked the tee bar in the buttonhole and slipped the watch into her petticoat pocket. That would pay for it, she thought, or she'd give it back to him if there was a next time. She hoped there would be. There were not many who made her feel like that. She crept back towards the bed. Something made her stretch out her hand to softly stroke his head. George smiled in his sleep, and she gently kissed his hair. Yes, she would remember this one for certain. She left as he shuddered with a giant snore.

At midnight the usual wake-up cry alerted him, and he dashed half dressed, grabbing his clothes as he hurtled down the stairs and ran to the cart. It wasn't till the next morning that George realised he'd lost his precious watch which Dorcas had given him. If he couldn't find it, he'd tell her somehow. That worried him. It had meant a lot to them both. He'd ask when he next went to town, though he doubted he'd get it back, it'd be sold by then, load of bloody thieves. Perhaps he'd say he had to sell it for food. Dorcas would accept that idea he knew.

He felt guilty about the way his life was going. How would he ever face Dorcas, would she guess? When they were in bed together, would she notice a few changes in his love, more openness perhaps? Kate had taught him a lot.

CHAPTER 14: Dorcas, March 1924

Tilda secretly watched from across the street, feeling shy, turning away lest others noticed her blushes. She tossed back her hair and played with it, biting her lips to a rosy red she hoped. Joseph finished his work in the post office soon and if she dawdled, pretending she was interested in a shop window, she might see him come out with his bicycle to go home. Maybe he'd notice her, even wave perhaps. For so long she had felt this thrill whenever she saw him, loving his tall, slim figure. No-one else knew, although she had hinted to Muriel, who had only shrugged. This was Tilda's secret, her dream. It was why she protested at her parents' plan, which seemed to be sliding towards them all moving away. Tilda didn't want to go to Canada, to give up the things she loved here, especially her glimpses of Joseph. Her mam didn't understand, but Tilda wouldn't tell her ever. Her mam questioned her silences, but she never answered. There wasn't anything to tell … yet. How could she leave Joseph? Did he guess how she felt? Did he think about her? She dreamed of him taking her hand, their eyes meeting ... though he rarely looked in her direction. In bed at night curled up in a ball, she fell asleep with thoughts of him looking at her, with his beautiful warm smile.

Tilda heard the door opposite close and glanced across. Yes, there he was, coming out with another lad, chatting and joking. Her heart was pounding in her throat. She blushed as her cheeks warmed at the sight of him, so tall and handsome in his uniform. A smile started to spread across her lips.

Then she noticed Muriel in a lilac dress, her curls bouncing as she walked towards the two young men, smiling as usual, her head on one side. Tilda wished she could smile like that and not look silly. Muriel stopped, laughed and put out a hand touching Joseph as he took hers. Tilda's smile froze. After exchanging a few words, Joseph pushed his bicycle along with one hand as he and Muriel walked together holding hands towards the bridge. Tilda stared. Their smile suggested secrets, as she looked up at him, and he pulled her closer as they walked.

How could she? How dare Muriel take her Joseph away? Tilda could not believe it. Shocked she turned back to the shop window, tears streaming down her face. She blinked them away, her eyes following the reflection of the pair as they talked and laughed, her shock turning to jealousy and real anger. Her whole body shook.

Tilda set down her mother's shopping basket on the pavement and she fished in her pocket for a handkerchief. Her fingernails bit into her palms as she swallowed hard to control the outward signs of her feeling. She hated Muriel. She stood still for a long time, then meandered back home the long way, avoiding people. The pain inside was unbearable. She wanted to hide away, lie in her bed with no one near, to cry and to fume. Anger made her shake, as she walked. There was nothing for her here. Nothing.

As she reached the bottom of their street she decided. If Mam wanted them to go, she'd be delighted, she would help. Yes, it'd serve him right. She'd go to an exciting new place where there were doubtless lots of handsome young men. She flicked her hair determined not to think about Joseph. How dare they? She would never talk to Muriel again. Never. She'd tell Mam she wanted to go soon. She crept in the back door and went straight up to her bedroom to be alone, away from any curious eyes.

Dorcas sat late at night, looking at the meagre takings from the till. Everyone expected bargains now they'd heard she was closing the shop. She wanted to be curt with some of them, but knew she needed their trade to succeed. She counted the coins again. She had sold a lot of stock, some at a loss, to the salesmen who secretly talked about her being 'over a barrel' when Dorcas reckoned they'd make a handsome profit out of these bargains. She argued hard and got the best she could, a few people even being fair when they realised her situation.

Some of the men offered her a decent price while they gave her strange looks as though she owed them something. Dorcas gave a quick mention of their wives, which usually calmed them down and sent them scuttling out of the shop.

Recently she could hardly manage, stretching the meat further and filling up the family's plates with potatoes and dumplings. If this move really happened, if she was ever going to do this, she knew she must keep some money for train fares to London and their lodgings. She prayed George would send the tickets for their passage soon.

She sat thinking about them all, her pencil doodling on the edge of the cash book. Lately she felt bad about Peter. The lad had grown so much in these past months, a lot taller than Roger. She had lengthened his sleeves and his trousers, taking down the turn-ups. She felt a surge of pride that he had survived and would soon be as tall as his father. Thinking, she saw he really needed bigger boots, maybe even two sizes bigger. She had watched him wince at times when he put the old ones on. Peter would never complain. What could she do? She hated the idea he might wear his father's shoes. She worried about it a lot. What else could she sell?

Dorcas looked about her home. Everything had its use and would be missed even if she could sell it. With a big family, over the years the couple had only been able to purchase essentials. Very few were luxuries, treasures, but she had no alternative. She dreaded what she had to do, wandering into the parlour. Her few wedding presents sat proudly in the cabinet in the corner, displayed though never used. She picked up some small items, a pretty jug, a delicate jam dish and spoon which lived on the shelf. They were a hint of a life, wished for her by long dead aunts, a life that had never materialised. Would such things be necessary in Canada? Would they even survive the move? She had precious memories from loved ones and friends who imagined her entertaining of an afternoon. Her rosy tea set, delicate and complete having never been used; silver sugar tongs with roses embossed on them, and the lace tablecloth she'd crocheted as part of her bottom drawer. All waited in vain for her to use them. She guessed she never would.

Taking the pieces out she stroked them lovingly and decided to take them to sell on market day next week and see what she could get for them. These must go, she told herself. I can't take them with me and they may make some money for the growing bills. Although she was practical, she felt guilty and disheartened she must sell her treasures. Dorcas would never tell her mother, though she knew her children's needs must come first. She wrapped each one of them in newspaper. The following week on half day she shut the shop, packed her treasures carefully in her basket covering them with a cloth and walked briskly to the marketplace.

As she crossed the bustling square she saw one of the market traders who had occasionally given her a fair price for bits she had sewn or crocheted.

'Gwennie,' she called, 'Gwennie, I've a few pieces you might be interested in. Would you like to see them?'

'Come to my stall and I'll take a look.' The woman raised an eyebrow when she saw what Dorcas was selling, examining each item closely. 'Not exactly modern are they, my dear?' She thumbed through the basket. ''These might be difficult to get rid of. Money's been tight since the war.' Gwennie pursed her lips and Dorcas guessed she'd make a low offer. Dorcas tried not to look too eager. After they agreed on a price, disappointed but resigned, she took her empty basket to the vegetable stall and spent some of her profits on their next meal.

Before they moved away, she knew she must sell some of her furniture including her beloved piano. She hated the idea of watching it go. It would break her last link with her own Dadda. Memories of his loving smiles haunted her. All this for George. He had no idea what this was costing her. She wished she could tell him how much this hurt. She hurried home, frowning crossly.

Dorcas was distracted working in the busy shop the next afternoon, her thoughts still returning to the sale of her treasures. She was serving a customer while two more were chatting away as they stood at the counter. Dorcas noticed her girls out of the corner of her eye as they entered through the shop. She smiled and winked at Marjorie and Ethel as they came past the counter.

'Hallo Mam,' they said before going through to the kitchen to raid the biscuit tin, dumping bags on the table.

'Where's May then?' Dorcas called after Marjorie.

'Oh, she's with Olive,' was the reply as the girls shed their coats and hats. This customer needed some change and Dorcas sorted through the till for a thrupenny bit. She dealt with the other customers and the shop was empty when she heard Olive's voice raised in the kitchen. She had come in the back door after school as they often did. Dorcas looked into the kitchen and heard the girls arguing.

'She was with you.' Marjorie's voice was panicking.

'No, I told her to go with you.' Olive shouted.

'You shouldn't have been skipping with Winnie. You are always whispering with her!' Marjorie looked sullen and screwed up her face at Olive.

Dorcas came in. 'Now girls, come on. What's the matter? Stop this. Where's May?' Her look sharpening, she barked. 'Olive, where's our May?'

'She was with those two, Mam.'

'No, she was with you. She wouldn't come with us, she always wants you.' Marjorie looked cross, her face red, tears threatening.

'So? Where is she?' Dorcas quickly took off her shop apron and shouted at the girls. 'Olive, Marjorie you go back down to the school yard and find her this minute. Go on, run girls.'

Fear the five-year old had gone elsewhere grew in Dorcas's mind. She closed and locked the doors and hurried after her daughters down the narrow pavement. Ethel scampered behind. Thoughts of the dangers; the river, horses and motors, even cruel strangers, built in Dorcas's imagination tightening her stomach. Where was her small defiant daughter? Where was she? Maybe Tilda, who should be in the school clearing the classroom for the next day, had still got her. That must be it. How had Olive not noticed her? May adored Olive, so why hadn't she stayed? Dorcas remembered a tiny coffin and a trail of mourners on the mountainside less than a year before. A cold sick feeling spread through her.

Dorcas couldn't hurry any faster because Ethel clung to her skirts. She flapped at the child and told her to run. As she neared the school the yard was silent and empty.

'Olive, you go down to the bridge in case she's gone there. Then go to the sweetshop and ask if they've seen her.' As Olive ran away, Dorcas yelled. 'Then come back quickly.' She felt sick as she remembered other child tragedies in recent years locally. Children lost or stolen, each loss a mystery, a tragedy.

She looked at the horizon where thunder clouds rolled across darkening the valley. What if they couldn’t find May before it was dark? Visualising the small child shivering and alone on the mountain, Dorcas swallowed hard. She dared not imagine what George would say, his beloved May, her baby, the little madam. No, she mustn't think like that. She's probably hiding somewhere or surely gone home with someone else.

'Marjorie, run around the back of the school, check everywhere, and see if Tilda's inside. Knock on the door and ask her. I'll go to the market in case she's there. Come on Ethel, keep up.' The market square was almost empty, and no small child wandered there across the dusty cobbles. Where else could she look? How long had the child been gone? She stood still, her eyes searching the scene, the darkened water flowing slowly beneath the bridge, the local streets where doors stood open. Dorcas was frantic, her throat stiff, wanting to scream. She turned not knowing which way to go. As she came back towards the bridge, she saw a woman holding hands with two small girls, hurrying towards her. One was May. Wide-eyed, Dorcas stared at the woman.

'Thank goodness Mrs Haddon. I'm so sorry. I didn't know she was at our place. Come on May, say goodbye to Molly. I brought her back the moment I saw them playing in our yard. She must have followed Molly. May said she'd come to play with Molly's dolls. See, they are such good friends in class. I'm sorry. I didn't notice them sooner.' Dorcas grabbed May's hand and thanked Molly's mother, who nodded, then turned for home. She spoke sharply to May, shaking her arm, her anxiety making her voice fierce. May sulked, looking face angry, screwing up her nose and pouting then making a face at Ethel who stood silently against her mother's skirts.

One by one they hurried back to the house, anxious Tilda, breathless Marjorie and a guilty Olive. May was completely unconcerned and Ethel retreated to her favourite place under the table humming quietly. Dorcas gave them a 'good talking to,' as she later told Sarah. She was so relieved her youngest was safe. She sat heavily at the table resting her head on her hands. If she couldn't keep them safe here, where she knew everyone, how would she manage in London … or Canada? She dreaded to think. It had been a useful lesson for them all.

The following Thursday, Dorcas shut the shop at one o'clock and settled to deal with the bills and takings. The hours stretched. A worried frown set on her face when the girls bounced in and she shushed them and told them to play outside for a while as she couldn't get the bills to balance. The girls joined others in the back alley and time ticked by. When she looked up she realised not only was it nearly dark outside, but she had not seen the older three. As a pupil teacher, Tilda often stayed to clear the classroom and Roger was probably working with Young Fred, but where was Peter? He hadn't come home from school.

When he finally came in, breathing heavily and with flushed cheeks, Dorcas was annoyed. 'Where have you been Peter? I was worried about you.'

'Sorry Mam but look. I've earnt a shilling. Here, it's my wages. See Roger isn't the only one to help out.'

'What did you do? Rob the bank?' Dorcas laughed then realizing her son was serious, she straightened her face.

'No, I helped Mr Howard with his stall in the market. Well, sweeping up the vegetable bits and packing away the fruit. And he asked if I could help on Saturday. Can I Mam?'

'How did you manage that?' Dorcas had calmed and looked lovingly at his enthusiastic face.

'Well I asked in the market if anyone needed help and he said since he hurt his back last year he finds it painful to do the heavy stuff so maybe he'd try me out. He said I had to ask you Mam. Say yes ... please. I can earn more on a Saturday. He will try me for a whole day, he says.'

Dorcas held her hands out to Peter and laughed aloud. Her son's earnest look made her smother her amusement. She hadn't laughed for so long, she thought. His eager eyes showed her she must let him try this.

'You mustn't lift anything too heavy Peter. I don't want you with a bad back too. And remember, bend your knees and keep them together when you lift anything. It'll help.'

Roger came in at that moment and heard her comment. He laughed from the other side of the kitchen. 'He knows Mam, don't worry he knows!' The boys gave an impish grin. Dorcas hated taking the coins from three of the older ones, but she had to admit it was very useful. They felt proud and justified as their contribution to the family. She wished George could see them; he would be so pleased they were helping her.

Olive, always listening, piped up. 'Does it mean I can do more hours in the shop now?'

'We'll see Olive, we'll see.' Dorcas guessed she'd need Olive's help if both the boys were working elsewhere. She admitted to herself Olive was the most enthusiastic of them all to work in the shop and she usually took more money than the others though Dorcas couldn't think how. Perhaps her daughter had a knack. She was a businesswoman in the making, her mother thought.

When she dished up their meal later, she added an extra dumpling to Peter's plate. He was still thin from his illness but growing taller than them all. She decided she would watch him closely to ensure he didn't get too tired. Memories of his illness haunted her, though together her family had got through it, making her proud of them, especially Peter. Somehow, she had done it.

The next Saturday Peter was up early, clean shirt and smart appearance for his vegetable stall. Dorcas felt proud and was secretly sure he would cope. Her son was quiet and obliging so he should not cause any problems for Davey Howard. She had packed him some bread and cheese and he ran down towards the square swinging his canvas bag and whistling. She thought of him all day. When he returned in the late afternoon he was grubby and crumpled but so proud of his earnings. Dorcas didn’t want to take them but knew he needed to feel the small amount helped the family. She hugged him quietly.

CHAPTER 15: George, March 1924

The sky warned of a darkening storm. Each man knew they must tie down everything they could when a gale whipped relentlessly through the camp one afternoon. George had learnt that winter storms could last for days. The men put on extra layers and struggled with the tarpaulins, ropes and the chains until it became impossible with men unable to stay upright, bowled along like empty cans. The wind tore their various voices away as they shouted instructions to each other. The strange, livid light sharpened, cutting through the dark cloud with shafts of purple. Rain lashed them and turned the freezing ground to ice as flashes of lightning struck the trees in the surrounding forest and their crashes echoed through the electric air, blue-white light splitting the sky. Trees splintered through, crunching and bouncing as they hit the ground. Branches whirled and fell. Bushes and loose scrub blew everywhere into the camp.

As darkness descended the rain became hail, large as marbles. Everyone stayed inside the canteen which echoed to the howl of the wind. The three men sat long after they'd finished their meal, seeing they would get soaked if they made their way to the bunkhouse. Time ticked by in the noisy room and eventually they decided to risk it hoping the stove in the centre of their small hut was well stoked. They braced themselves before opening the canteen door which was immediately grabbed by the wind and torn from their grasp.

'Shut that damn door,' men yelled, echoed by the others' foreign curses and once outside all three had to put their backs against it to get it closed before slamming across the clasp.

Each man was almost flattened by the blizzard that raged. Desperately they clung to each other putting their combined weight against the wind. The bitter chill burned their faces and they strove to stay upright and move forward. The thirty yards to the bunkhouse took them ten minutes, enough time to soak through their canvas capes, which became sodden and heavy.

Finally, they battled with the door of the bunkhouse and struggled into the heated room. A cloying wet fug surrounded them. Wet clothes of others were draped about the fire adding a sharp warm smell to the steam in the lamplight. They stripped off and strung more lines across the high wooden beams, hanging their clothing everywhere. Taking their blankets to wrap themselves in, they huddled by the fire hoping the clattering storm shutters and stout door would hold against the storm which raged until the early hours. Fearful of the violent weather, George dreamed of his own fireside. After a long time lying in his bunk he slept, tossing as the sound of the buffeting wind disturbed him.

Next day it dawned calm and bright. They spent much of the day clearing the devastation the storm had left. Lifting poles that had toppled, repairing and renewing the damage to the wide roadway they were building, took all that day.

George wrote to Dorcas telling of the storm. He wanted the children to be excited by the tale, but he found it hard to write much. He tried to describe his feelings about the harsh winter and the forest, yet the letter didn't seem to have the atmosphere he wanted to send. This life was certainly different from his memories of their enclosed village, surrounded by mountains, but he couldn't write of his fears. He wondered what they were doing back home. Was the weather bad? Was she struggling with snow and rain? He thought of the cramped houses with those dull days of winter when the light dwindled, and dusk crept in early, making them close curtains and light the lamps. At least he knew they would get coal and huddle about the stove. Here it felt different, more open, more space. He dreamt of a future for them and once again he renewed his secret promise to build them a new life.

Although the harsh conditions often made the men ruthless in their attitude to life's events, George was not alone in feeling sad at the next day's news. Early over porridge men told of an old timer, respected by everyone, who had been found dead that morning in his bunk. The man had died, no warning, no reason, they said. When he heard it was Pierre, who had helped him, teaching him how to build an open fire by the river, and sharing his fish, a lump came to George's throat. He remembered Pierre showing him the beauty of the wilderness as they relaxed together, renewing his hopes of a future. Their quiet friendship had helped him see another life, not in the camps, not in the shanty towns, but in the wild beside a tranquil river.

When they asked for volunteers to dig the grave in the rock-hard frozen earth, George stepped forward. Towards dusk he helped others carry the simple coffin. Pierre was no weight at all, doubtless worn out, exhausted. Nothing much was said over the mound of earth, as no-one knew much more than his name. A thoughtfulness quietened the usual chatter of the canteen throughout the evening. George turned in early, thinking how fast things could change at times. He decided to post his letter soon. He must not lose touch with his family as Pierre had warned him.

A week later, on a working evening George watched as Bert got his jacket and Jim pulled his boots back on. Once again, the young men were hurrying into town midweek. Gambling and drinking had them hooked. The two men would return in the early hours, get very little sleep, and suffer the following day from their hangover, short tempered and careless. Sometimes they were lucky, and they could beg a late ride for part of the way back to camp on a cart as far as the crossroads, though midweek they frequently had to walk several miles, often supporting each other in the darkness.

Jim held his liquor well, but Bert became belligerent. George no longer went with them so they chided him. 'You're getting too old, too staid and set in your ways, George.'

But he had learnt his lesson. Gambling was no longer for him, still regretting his losses and drink held no attractions when he couldn't sleep it off. Hangovers clouded his thinking and could lead to dangerous mistakes. He'd seen it already with others.

George slept soundly that night, dreaming of home, when he found himself being shaken by Jim. 'George, George. Come on, wake up. We need help. Get yer arse out of bed mate. Bert needs yer quick,' Jim whispered harshly.

'What? What the hell's the matter?' George pushed him away frowning in his fuddled state.

'Come on, get yer things on. Here's yer boots. We need some help.' Jim held them out to him as George pulled on his trousers.

''This had better be important Jim. You might not value your sleep, but I do mine and sorting out your mate puking all over the place, isn't my problem.'

'Quietly George. We don't want a bloody audience.' Jim mumbled.

George glanced at the other bunks as he put on his jacket. All the men seemed to be snoring. As soon as they got outside in the cold wind, George turned to Jim. 'What time is it? What is it? Where's Bert?' he asked.

'He's in the woods. He's hurt.' They both ran along the path through the gates and Jim hurtled off among the trees. Shaking himself to wake up, George followed him, clambering down towards the river. On a fallen tree Bert sat with blood seeping through his sleeve, shivering violently in the moonlight.

'How the hell did you do that?' George stared.

Bert yelled back. ''The bugger stabbed me. He tried to kill me. He's a sly one always watching me with his shifty eyes. I've seen him.' A man was sprawled on the earth amongst the scrub and the jagged rocks.

Jim pulled at George's arm. 'Look, this cove jumped us, flashing his knife about and swearing at Bert. It's that Spaniard, the one what moans about everything, the surly one from the lifting gang. No one likes him, he always fights. Bad-tempered bugger. Yer see, 'e was in the saloon with a girl then Bert chatted to her, bought her a drink.'

'And 'e lost at cards tonight as well. So it made him curse and when I grinned of course he threatened me. I reckon he followed us, vicious type!'

'What's this got to do with me?' George frowned.

'Well yer see, Bert was injured, and this sod was going to try and finish him off, so I grabbed this branch and swung it at him. I thought it would lay him out, so we could get back to camp. The bloody truth is George... I've … I've killed him. He's dead. The bugger's dead!'

'Oh God no!' George gazed at the prone figure on the forest floor and felt cold inside. He went and shook the man. They were right. George had seen dead before.

'What you going to do? Hell. They'll string you up for this Jim.' George stared at them both. Bert began to weep as the beer, the situation and his injury proved too much for him.

'Look, if we can lift him down to the ravine and tip him over, no one will ever know. Why should they? He'll 'ave disappeared. We'll forget we ever saw him.' Jim said grasping George's arm.

'You can't do that. What about his family? Somebody needs to know he's dead.' George stood back and stared at Jim in disbelief. Jim gestured with his hands.

'Oh, no they don't, not out 'ere. He's been in prison for so long they say, there's no one left alive who'll miss 'im. I reckon he's only out on parole. Besides I ain't taking the rap for this. He started it, murdering bastard. This is the best way out. Come on George, 'elp a mate out. I'd do the same if it was yer what was hurt. Yer can't let me down.' Jim pleaded.

'No, sorry no. It's murder, you can't do it.' George was horrified. 'You can tell them, show Bert's arm, explain.' He dared not think what would happen if they found out he'd helped them cover this up. Bert looked at George, flashing a glance at Jim, who nodded before speaking softly.

'We could always say yer did it. Where would yer be then? Yer've got enough enemies back there who'd be only too glad to believe the two of us.'

George stared. He didn't believe this. The two men said nothing more, Jim standing beside Bert, both looking accusingly at George. Shocked George could not believe they would do that. He sat heavily on the tree-trunk. Their faces showed no remorse, just self-preservation. George could feel his heart beating in his chest. He had never been so frightened. He felt trapped.

'Come on mate, let's get it over with and we can get back to our beds.' Jim moved towards the body, so turning his eyes away George held the man's feet as Jim and he carried the Spaniard down the bank to the edge of the rocks. Confused, he tried not to look at the man's damaged flesh. Together they swung the body out wide, let go and the Spaniard crashed bouncing onto the rocks below with a thud. Water gushed over him and they watched as the dim moonlight reflected off the turmoil, while gradually the body slid into the river and disappeared. Wiping their hands on their trousers they returned to Bert who looked faint from loss of blood.

'We've got to get yer back to the camp mate. Sort yer out.' Jim said examining Bert's cuts.

'Best wash off as much as possible of the blood. Let's look at it. Is it still bleeding?' George said, his hands shaking.

'No, I don't think so. He was lucky. Come on mate let's get yer back while there's no one around.' Jim helped Bert to his feet.

'You realise it'll be murder if they ever discover the body. You two won't stand a chance.' George began to think, wishing he had never helped.

'Well, I reckon they'll top the three of us if they ever get a hint of this. Not sure they'll wait for the law either. They hate our guts anyway.' Bert said. 'Get rid of that branch, it might have blood on it or summat!' George threw the wood over the ravine and it bounced off the rocks before disappearing below.

They helped Bert back and managed to creep into the bunk house without anyone waking, praying they hadn't been seen. George left Jim to sort Bert and lay on his bunk trying to calm down. Surely, they couldn't connect him with the Spaniard vanishing? Maybe no one cared enough to bother to question whether he had just gone off.

The French here hated the Spaniard as much as they did the English. They were just foreigners to them. The man had no mates, his temper causing others to back away. Maybe there wouldn't be too many questions providing no one saw the body. George had heard this stretch of the river was deserted for miles. He knew this night would worry him for months, maybe years. What had he got himself into? This crazy life. He wished he had never met these two. His life had somehow become cruel, twisted, since he first listened to them. He couldn't sleep. He lay awake and watched the dawn break as light crept across the boards on the ceiling.

He thought of his brother Billy, so often in fights, so often escaping problems in the dead of night. George had never liked being involved, sorting Billy's disasters. At least he was a brother, and often George had taken risks when they were young to save his mother's tears. He owed nothing to these two. They were mates yes, but not worth swinging for.

'I've got a family and responsibilities. I can't take risks at my age.' George vowed never to go to town with the two men ever again. He realised what a strong influence they had been on him. He regretted his rash decision to come to Canada, with his gambling debts and this fear which could cost him his liberty, maybe his life. How did he get to this point? No, they were both bad news. He'd be friendly, but it was all. He longed for the simple life back home.

CHAPTER 16: Dorcas, April 1924

Dear Dorcas and family,
I hope you are well and taking care of your mam.

I am not sure when you will receive this as the snow here has been higher than the door frames, as tall as me in fact, and we have had to clear a path several times to be able to work. Lots of pipes have frozen, bringing more work for your old dadda. I have had chilblains everywhere, just like our May. I had to work Christmas day though we did have a day off later. I have helped catch a salmon, and cook it over a fire. It tasted grand.

I hear you are being good. I hope the weather is starting to warm up. It is still very cold here. Hope to see you soon.
Love to each one of you, Dadda XXXX

George's letter gave no indication of when he had written it, and Dorcas shook her head. She felt increasingly that she had lost touch with him, that the man she had known for so long had disappeared in some strange land far away. Even his letters made no real connection. The children read them but they were quickly shoved behind the clock, no longer poured over for an evening. She couldn't conjure up his face. Yet she must write back.

Down the hill in the deserted school room, Peter's elderly art teacher, a tired Miss Berry, shuffled the pile of sketches on her desk. All the children had gone home, and the wind buffeted the windows. Looking out at the deserted playground, she stretched her aching neck. She'd soon go home to her lonely room. She tucked her grey hair into her bun and pushed the hairpins back in.

It had been a good day generally and that made her feel better about her teaching. Art was a joy to her and to a few of her students too. Others hated it, she knew, restricted for an hour to draw a chosen object on the teacher's table. Broken pencil leads, and grubby erasers had punctuated the silences. Beatrice Berry tried to help each pupil but for some the whole idea seemed pointless. Why draw it if you could never get it right? Their sullen faces responded as some sighed in the otherwise silent classroom. A few children were disappointed by their own efforts, some truculent at the task, others were plainly disheartened when they saw the efforts of the more gifted ones beside them. She tried to encourage them, but it was an up-hill struggle.

No-one but Beatrice in this village earned their living reading or drawing and years before, she had studied long and hard to teach. It had been her whole life. Unless you lived in the few big houses scattered about, you stood no chance. As a girl this had been her only respectable option and she would spend the rest of her days marking grubby exercise books of already demoralized children. She gazed up at the high window of the empty classroom where the light showed dust motes floating in the air, and thought of her lost future with a man in uniform who had not come back from France.

Though ... thought Beatrice, Peter makes up for all of it. Watching his beaming face, his confident hand and the movement of his pencil over the paper in sweeping strokes, with his eyes glancing at the object, then back to his image on the paper, was a secret pleasure making her smile. She loved hearing his comments. Peter instinctively saw how to capture, not the fact of the jam jar full of wilting wild flowers but the shape, the movement of their stalks, their splayed leaves.

Yes, she thought, Peter makes my Fridays worthwhile. It was an improbable idea that he'd ever be able to work with his pencil, more likely a pick axe in this village. Such a shame. It was a miracle he got well again after his awful time when he was so ill.

'None of these children are likely to have a chance to choose how they earn their living. All the boys will go underground. Mining supports their families, supports this whole village in fact,' the headmaster had told her when she first came to the school and he was right. Beatrice felt disheartened to think of Peter, deep in a dark mine day after day, never seeing the daylight glancing off beautiful things throughout the winter months. She imagined him damaging those long slim fingers, with sharp coal dust rimming his blue eyes.

'I must see his parents, mention his talent,' she murmured, 'see if they can do something before he leaves school.' Shaking her head, she knew they were a big family with young mouths to feed, when so many were going hungry since the war. Miners' wage rates had been cut for same hours, with men in dole queues in Newport. She told herself she must try. She flicked through the pile for his sketch. Taking it out, she held it at a distance. She feasted her eyes on his rare talent, tucking her collar back inside her jacket and buttoning it.

'Yes,' she mumbled nodding to herself as she stood, her voice a soft echo in the high empty room, 'I must at least make sure they realise Peter's talent. It would be such a shame…'

It was two weeks before Beatrice Berry met Dorcas as they were both shopping on Saturday. The market was busy despite the cold wind, stall holders' hoarse voices calling to attract any business. People were spending Saturday pay packets on essential food, while stalls tempted them with other goods. Beatrice hesitated, looking anxious, tilting her head to hear amidst the clamour. After politely greeting each other, Beatrice felt the need to mention her thoughts.

'I know you're busy at the present, Mrs Haddon. I wondered if you could spare a few moments. I'd like to talk to you about Peter.'

Dorcas raised her eyebrows in a query and stepped closer, grasping her basket. 'I hope he isn't being a nuisance. He's usually such a good boy at home,' Dorcas frowned and looked at Beatrice noticing her neat coat and simple hat.

'No, Mrs Haddon, no he's very well behaved, most polite in fact. No, it's not that. I am so glad he got well again; thanks to you I hear. He's very proud of your efforts. He's mentioned it a lot. No, no. It's his art, the boy has real talent Mrs Haddon, real feeling in his drawing. I don't say that about many boys, I can tell you.'

'Oh, right. Thank you for telling me, Miss Berry.' Dorcas had lost her defensive look, listening closely.

'Well, I was wondering if either you or your husband had thought about Art College for him later? I know it's not easy for families, but he deserves a chance. Somewhere he could learn more skills, possibly be able to get employment in that field. Of course, he'd live away, board somewhere.' She left her voice in a questioning tone and Dorcas felt compelled to answer.

'I'm not sure. You see his father's in Canada on business at present and I'm not sure exactly when he'll be home. We may go out there too. Of course, it means we can't make plans for our future, not at present. I promise I'll bear it in mind and mention it to my husband. I do understand Peter deserves some chance other than just any employment.' She didn't want to mention the mine, though she guessed this is what was in both their minds.

'Well, if I can write a letter or something to help, please don't hesitate to ask. I'm sure the headmaster would agree too. Peter's always such a pleasure to teach.' Blushing, Beatrice said her goodbyes and hurried away. Dorcas watched her go, wondering. Would Canada offer her son any chance? She had no idea. Where would the money come from? Would it be fair on the other children even if they could afford it? George's scheme of a new start filled her with anxiety tinged with a little hope. Life here in the village would never change. Perhaps her husband was right, though she couldn't think of her young son leaving home, living in some college. At twelve he was far too young!

Turning back to her constant task of stretching the coins in her purse for their meals, Dorcas was thoughtful. All her children deserved a better chance, but would they get it in Canada she questioned. She wished she could ask George, though maybe he wouldn't understand. No good worrying today. She must get back to their shop, Tilda might have some customers who were difficult. She hurried Ethel and May back home, both dawdlers. She would think about this later.

By the following Thursday, Dorcas was in the kitchen, when she closed her eyes and frowned, as she heard Olive's shout when she came rushing in from school.

'Biddy told me Mam. She said Grandma Haddon has come from Bristol to see Biddy's mam and she's going to visit us tomorrow.' Olive was excited to deliver news she guessed would be contentious. Dorcas stopped midway through pinning up the hem of a dress on Ethel, pins between her lips. For a moment she closed her eyes not wanting to contemplate the imminent visit. Another problem to deal with. Ethel stood on the table, trying not to fidget so as not to get pricked. She was bored, but she did want this dress. Dorcas took the pins out of her mouth and held Ethel's small hand.

'Stay there Ethel, just a minute. Olive calm down, tell me again. When is Grandma coming?'

'Tomorrow. She told me Mam, tomorrow.'

Dorcas finished pinning the hem and took the dress carefully off her daughter lifting her down.

'Right, you can go back to laying the supper now.' She looked about the untidy kitchen which suddenly seemed worse than usual. Of course, she knew this would happen eventually. Of course, after her letter, her mother-in-law had wondered about George's absence after all these months. She was coming to find out more and why. Dorcas felt guilty she hadn't written more. At first, she hadn't believed he would stay away, then Peter's illness and Christmas, all excuses but her mother-in-law wasn't easy to talk to and letters seemed to always cause issues between them.

George normally visited his mother at least once a year when he had business in Bristol and, when Grandma Haddon came to see her sister and niece's family in late spring, she would call most years. This was the cousin who had once promised to introduce Dorcas and George when they first met and they still lived in the village. The old lady was coming tomorrow, and the place looked a mess. Dorcas must get the children to help clear up. She always silently dreaded these visits. They understood their grandma and her "everything ship-shape and Bristol fashion," phrase. Little wonder George was so orderly thought Dorcas. Everyone spent the evening tidying some corner, bickering about their responsibilities, before Dorcas shared the news with Sarah.

'I've a fruit cake I made yesterday if it will help. You're welcome to that. It might sweeten her up!' Sarah winked.

All the next morning Dorcas was busy in the shop giving the empty shelves a quick dust and sweeping the tiled floor between customers. She found herself sharp with time-wasting customers, who wanted to chat, not buy. As lunchtime approached Dorcas got more nervous. She should have written again but had George? What had he told her? Had he told his mother of their row? If she'd heard anything more, would the old lady say? Dorcas thought of the gossip and rumours.

The bell on the door jangled and in swept Enid Haddon. Tall and square like her son, with a large bulging handbag and a solid brown hat, she strode towards her daughter-in-law who gave her a weak smile.

'Hello, Dorcas. Children at school I suppose?'

'I'm so glad you came,' Dorcas said. She turned the notice to CLOSED and locked the shop door before taking her through to the parlour where for once she had lit a fire.

'We'll go through here so we won't be disturbed,' she muttered. Enid's face seemed closed, not yet ready to attack. With a prepared glance Enid brushed her skirt and after examining the chair, sat heavily. She didn't remove her hat. Dorcas crossed her fingers in her pocket and offered tea and the cake.

Finally, Enid spoke. 'What is this I hear about you and my George? Some trouble I gather, and he's … gone off abroad? No one even bothered to tell me why, his mother!'

Dorcas took a deep breath and plunged in. 'No, it's not like that, you see …' Dorcas stuttered on, trying to make it sound normal, but they both knew it was not. Ten minutes later, while the tea stewed, they were negotiating their fragile relationship where politeness in respect of their mutual love for George and the children meant they dared not actually fight. Dorcas was flustered, and Enid felt vindicated. She was sure it was Dorcas's fault. Now she had as good as lost her George as years before, she had lost her Billy.

Sarah knocked, came in apologetically, smiled and generally took the heat out of the situation. Dorcas escaped to the kitchen to make fresh tea gratefully looking at the cake which had appeared. She silently blessed Sarah as she heard her diplomatically praise George for his dedication to Dorcas and his children with his attempt to give them a better life. By the time the school bell echoing across the village signalled the children's return, the three women were chatting amicably, Enid proudly telling of her sons' exploits when they were three schoolboys.

Olive excitedly rushed into the parlour. She loved her grandma, who softened with the children's hugs. The next hour dragged for Dorcas though the children hugged their granny who found them sweets from her handbag. Later the boys said they would walk Grandma Haddon back on their way to their evening work. Roger gave Dorcas a sly wink and taking his grandma's arm he guided her out into the street. Enid favoured Roger, he was so like his father she told him. Dorcas sat with relief. That was over. Thank goodness!

Dorcas had felt low for several days with a bad cold. Even the spring warmth didn't help as she was hot and coughing. Sarah told her she should look after herself but when on an early morning she got herself out of bed and the world tilted, she had to sit back on the eiderdown. Tilda saw her and put an arm around her. 'Mam get back to bed. You shouldn't be up. You aren't well at all.'

'No, I must get breakfast started. I … Oh dear!' Dorcas sighed as the room swirled around her.

'No Mam, I insist, we can manage. I can get the girls to school, and Roger can look after the shop for this morning with Sarah's help. We talked about it last night. You haven't been well for days. Please do as I say and get yourself back between those covers and have a good sleep.'

'I'm sure I'll be alright after I have a drink of tea, Tilda,' Dorcas croaked, her sore throat rasping.

'Roger, Roger come up and tell Mam to be sensible. She won't listen to me,' she called downstairs.

Roger's footsteps bounded up the wooden stairs and he stood trying to look big and filling the doorway. 'Mam, even Dadda would insist you spend the day in bed. It's for the best. We certainly can't manage without you, so you have got to get well, and you need the rest.' Dorcas looked at her son, so like George in his determination, and feeling weak, she let Tilda help her back between the sheets. Tilda brought her mother a hot wrapped stone for her feet and a warm drink.

'Mam, you are precious to us. We need you to be well. Please stop worrying. We will manage.' Dorcas relished her warm bed sleeping fitfully for most of the day. At the end of the afternoon she was disturbed by the exaggerated whispers as the children returned from school. She lay there luxuriating in the middle of their sagging bed and drank the tea Tilda brought up. The day's rest had done her good and the cold symptoms had lessened. Tilda said she should sleep, so warm and relaxed, she did.

When Dorcas woke again it was dark so, wrapping her shawl about her, she pulled on a pair of George's stockings, deciding to go down and reassure her children. She came to the bottom of the stairs and was hugged by the two youngest. She felt loved. She looked at each one asking questions and answering queries.

'Yes. I'm a lot better thank you. I feel really lazy!' Marjorie and Peter were busy brushing boots in the scullery and Tilda was in the shop, so the little girls led her to the table to sit where Olive was laying the supper. Everyone was chattering. Roger came in the scullery door with a full coal scuttle taking it across to the hearth. And then Dorcas noticed it.

'Where's your father's chair? Where have you put it?' The gap by the fire was noticeable. The girls looked at each other avoiding her gaze and Dorcas called to Roger, her suspicion growing.

Peter blushed, and Roger's face tightened. 'I've sold it. I sold it for a pound to old Mr Jones. Well, Dadda doesn't need it anymore!' Roger looked defiant.

'You did what? You sold it? How dare you, young man? How dare you sell your father's special chair? You will go this minute and get it back. How could you sell something he loved so much? He made that chair, extra tall and big to fit him. He was so proud of it. Roger, you take the pound and get the chair back from Mr Jones, you hear me?' Her eyes flashed.

Standing squarely Roger spoke in a quiet voice. 'No Mam, I can't. We've spent the money.'

Dorcas glared at him. 'You've spent it? On what for heaven's sake?'

'We spent it on new boots for Peter and me. Peter really needs them, even you said so. You haven't looked lately how small his were with loads of holes. Our Dadda will never come back here. You can't take the chair all the way to London and on the ship. He didn't care about us so why should we care about him?' Roger's face reddened and, adamant as he was, she saw his tears threatened.

Dorcas looked in horror at her two sons. What did they think about their father? She sat at the table her hands smoothing the cloth watching the four girls seated silently on their bench, May on Olive's lap. Dorcas was overwhelmed by her sons' actions and questioned herself. Had she been so distracted, so bound up in her own efforts to sell items, to sort lists, and worried by problems, that she had not thought of her growing boys? To lose George's chair felt like losing him once more. His presence seemed truly gone almost as if he had never been. The room looked different, not empty, too many bodies for that but she felt bereft, alone amidst them all. She choked back a tear.

Peter came and touched her shoulder. She looked up at him with swollen eyes.

'We saved his cushion for you Mam. We didn't sell it.' The red cushion was clutched in his arms, the one she had made for George's birthday. She took it and buried her face in it.

'Perhaps you could take the boots back,' lisped Marjorie.

'No of course not. You definitely need them. It's a … surprise I suppose.' Dorcas smiled around at them all.

'You were right. Good salesmen really. How did you deliver it to Mr Jones?'

'On the wheelbarrow of course, Mam.' The boys looked relieved and grinning, winked at each other. For the rest of the evening Dorcas puzzled over how this change was felt by each of her children as she watched them chattering together. They were each growing in their own way and she felt shocked at how little she had noticed.

CHAPTER 17: George, April 1924

The last week in April, George queued in line for his food in the canteen. Men shuffled forward, muttering surly words when they saw more stew again, as George daydreamed of warmer weather and summer. He hoped to find the river again, to have a quiet day away. The midday sun shone through the single window reflected off the light snow which had fallen throughout the previous night. It would soon melt.

Planning how he might get small gifts for his children and Dorcas when they eventually met up, he hadn't noticed he'd been served his stew. He nodded his thanks to the man with the ladle and hurriedly turned from the queue to find a place at the rough bench tables. From behind, Henri knocked the tray George held, jolting his arm, spilling much of his stew. George reacted by instinct and pushed back at the embittered man, hatred in his eyes. Henri made the pretence of falling to the floor, with a loud groan. Other Frenchmen supported their team mate helping him up and making a scene. Anything for a distraction.

'Not you again, Haddon? You know what this means, English!' The foreman came across as George started to argue and he was left with another warning and the loss of a day's pay for fighting. His protests were met with a disdainful smirk.

As George walked from the canteen he felt he was on dangerous ground. If he got another warning it meant instant dismissal. For the rest of the week he was quiet and cautious. Trying to avoid Jacques, Henri and their cronies wherever he went became harder as they seemed to search him out. Often standing in groups near to where he worked, they laughed at him or sent meaningful glances. He knew they wanted him gone.

'How long can I stand this?' he asked himself. He found he was given the worst conditions to work in, though dare not complain. Often working knee-deep in melting snow and drenched with rain, he struggled on while others got work above him benefiting from the earliest sun of the year. To protect himself he decided to always be at the end of the dinner queue, so Henri had already left the canteen. By then most days he found the stew had run out and only consisted of some watered gravy with a few dubious vegetables.

Even in his bunk at night he felt vulnerable, turning towards the door, cautious of closing his eyes, never trusting the dark. Anxiously putting his tools in bed with him, to keep them safe, and checking them daily, made him nervous. Suppressing his anger day after day tested his patience and he was anxious he'd soon explode. The nights seemed endless as he couldn't relax, the tension in every muscle. The least sound startled him awake. Each morning when he woke he felt muddled, alert for more problems.

One morning, when he found his boots full of wet mud, he snapped. He seethed as he scrabbled across the damp yard in his stocking feet, fists clenched. He searched out Henri and accused him of the trick, only to see him smirk as he lifted a questioning eyebrow and then shrug, his palms upright in a hopeless gesture. George exploded, smashed his fist into Henri's grin and the two fought one another to the floor. Henri kicked, and George wrestled. George's anger prevented him registering the pain from the bruises he'd later find as he pounded Henri. When Jacques hauled George away from Henri and threw him across the ground, George knew it was the end.

'Get your things English and go. Get yourself off zis site before I kick you off. Do you hear what I'm saying?' Jacques quivered with hate. Shaking and seething with anger George stamped back to his bunk, grabbed his few possessions and picked up his tool bag. He snatched his drying socks hanging from the rafters.

Bert patted his back. 'I'm sorry mate, really, I am. We'll miss you. What the hell are you going to do now?'

'Not sure but I'll be glad to be out of this dump I can tell you!' George spat as he scooped the mud from his boots and, wiping them inside with an old rag, pulled them on. 'So long, Bert, and tell Jim goodbye when you see him and thanks to both of you. You be careful too. Just mind yourselves,' he warned as he trudged away heading in his soggy boots towards the pay office.

The clerk made him wait, seeing the swelling eye and guessing the truth from George's angry stance. He tried to breathe deeply to calm himself while the clerk went to the back office and George heard angry, gruff voices.

When the rough Cockney came through, he closed the door.

'Well Haddon, they ain't going to give you a bean today,' the clerk said sucking on his pipe. 'Not my doing. There'll be fines and stoppages to sort, so I can't pay yer a penny yet. If you leave me yer address somewhere that'll find yer, the company says it'll mail on any money due to yer at the end of the week.' The man grinned, his hands spread questioningly. George asked him to send it to the Toronto City mail office. He would send them an address as soon as he was fixed up with a new job in some town. It meant no money for today and he doubted he'd see much when it arrived. The total injustice bit deep but he was relieved to be going. Slamming the door, George strode away down the path carrying his tools with his blanket and clothes slung over his shoulder. His anger at the Frenchmen's prejudice made him more determined, yet he'd find it hard to get another job.

Walking towards the gates he passed a clump of bushes which hid him from view. Out of the greenery three men rushed him knocking him to the ground. They kicked him, and his tool bag and lifted it high. His terror had turned his anger white hot, his nostrils flared, his teeth clenched. His instinct forced him to defend himself from the imminent danger without a thought, as he swung the heavy wrench through the air. They backed off, sneering though wary. Henri curled his lip muttering in English with a snarl. 'Go on then English. Go on. You wouldn't dare!'

George yelled back and lunged at him bringing the wrench down towards the man's head, but Henri ducked and dodged as it glanced his shoulder, hands gesturing crudely as all three men, chastened though undaunted, slunk away.

George stopped, panting as he watched them go. Shocked by how far they had succeeded in riling him and how near he had come to killing the man. He stood sweating as they sauntered back towards the foreman's office. He trembled all over. Never in his life had he been given to violence. He could be loud, he could shout and bang his fist, but he'd never hurt anyone. George questioned himself. What was he becoming? How far had he let them push him? There had been seconds there when he felt so threatened, so vulnerable that his primitive reaction was to kill or be killed.

With legs which quivered, he picked up his gear and hurried through the gates. He had walked more than a mile before he calmed down. He feared he would relive the moment again and again. As he strode along the rough track he banged his fist into his leg, mumbling to himself.

Only as George started to calm down did he begin to think, first things first. How the hell was he going to get anywhere by walking? He remembered the tough journey they had made to this camp. It had been long with rough paths and little sign of humans along the way. The cold bit into him and he realised once the short afternoon light faded he would be in for a long night in freezing conditions with only the clothes he stood up in. He must look for shelter or a lift. If he didn't succeed, he might be dead or near to it, by the morning.

Thoughts of his own land, soft spring weather and blossom on the trees haunted him. Here the winter grip was still fast, dragging on. He longed to be home but he dreaded his failure. 'No, George,' he said to himself, 'you mustn't give up, you can't go back home with so little to show for it all. You must have another try.' He tried to convince himself this had only been bad luck.

Puzzled, he planned to head southeast but that would take him off the path. Trying to keep his bearings was not easy. He might stagger about for days in the thick undergrowth of the wilderness he guessed. There, tall trees overshadowed his path and cruel thorns barred his way. The scents of the forest about him told of verdant decay and animal haunts. He thought of tales of bears, even grizzlies. No, he must keep near to the path. Somewhere he could hear trickling water. The sound made him thirsty and he found a small opening in the bushes which led downwards to a stream. Scrabbling down the bank he saw sparkling water bubbling out of the rocks. Kneeling there he scooped up some to drink and dabbed with his kerchief at his swelling eye. The water was icy, although it refreshed him.

Memories of the Spaniard made him shudder. Stumbling back to the path through the undergrowth without retracing his steps, he realised what a dangerous journey this could become. Taking up much of the daylight left, it was a long time before he got back on the main path, cursing his folly. Thoughts of what could happen made him edgy and feeling anxious, his stomach tight, though hungry. He hurried for a mile or so before having to slacken pace as he started again to cough.

By late afternoon when the shadows of the trees were long, his legs ached, his stomach was empty, and he cursed the day he had got on that ship. At least he thought, Dorcas doesn't know about this and I'll never tell her. He felt so ashamed he had not succeeded. Then above the forest sounds he heard the whinny of a horse and stopped. There were a few muffled sounds ahead and he ran towards them along the rough path and heard a man whistling a tune. 'Hey, wait, wait!' George called out and crashed towards the sounds. As the way opened out he came to a rough crossroads where a cart stood with the driver about to remount. He called again and ran to the horse harnessed to a wagon, which held crates and baskets of provisions. He started to cough again.

'Any chance of a lift, mate?' he spluttered and was relieved when he heard English spoken back.

'Where yer going? Didn't expect to see anyone out here.' The man fingered a gun at his belt. George realised he could have been a thief or worse, understanding the man's note of caution as he looked him over.

'It's alright mate. I've just left East Camp. Had a row with the foreman and got the sack. They'd filled my boots with wet mud, lousy sods, so I let fly.' George pointed to his boots with his hand. He looked scruffy with streaks of mud on his clothes from the scuffle he had outside the camp and his eye told a story, so he'd better be honest and up-front for anything less would make the man suspicious. Besides Dorcas had always said she could tell from his face when he was lying.

'You're English, ain't yer?' the man asked. George nodded. 'Thought so. East Camp's run entirely by the French and yer'd never get a chance there if you weren't used to their bloody rules. Where yer heading?'

'Got no idea. I need a job. I'm not frightened of hard work and I can mend most stuff. Any ideas?'

'Well, Campbell's Camp needs men for open cast mining, though 'tis tough work with rotten conditions they say. I don't rightly know 'cause I only collect and deliver with Nellie here. I had me fill of the camps long ago, too much bloody anger. All those men cooped up together, what can yer expect? I'm on me way there if yer want a ride. Got to get there afore the light fades and Nellie here'll need some food soon. I'll stay there for the night then make me way back to town for more provisions for the camps.' He adjusted his fur hat.

George took no time to consider. If he could get work everything would be fine.

'They'll let us bunk down for a night for a quid each and yer can buy food in their canteen. If there's no work, yer can come back to town with me in the morning. Yer can pay for me meal mate, for the ride. Cost yer ten bob.' The driver held out his hand to help him up.

'Thanks,' George clambered up beside him on the box. 'I'm George by the way.'

'Yea, Chuck's the name,' he said shaking George's hand with his own gloved one. George watched as the driver picked up the rough reins and clicked his tongue to Nellie to walk on. Chuck wore an old thick leather coat which smelt of sweat and horse, but George guessed was necessary for times when he couldn't shelter from the cold and rain.

For a while they talked a little. George told him about home and family and his plans for a new life for them all.

Chuck said he had been married once back in Birmingham but it was long ago.

'Now I got me Nellie here. She's enough for me. She don't answer back. As long as she's got some grub and somewhere warm at night, she don't complain!'

Then for several miles Chuck hummed and whistled. George dozed until he felt himself sliding and automatically righted himself on the box seat. When the path widened George could see another camp down in the hollow. He knew he must be more cautious here. Chuck said little, chewing his moustache. Thanking him and giving Chuck enough for his meal they parted. George jumped down and walked across to a wooden hut, knocked and took a deep breath as he pushed open the door which said 'Foreman.' A small lad was sitting at a desk and said the foreman would only be a short while. George stood and looked about.

The office was plain with tables, chairs and a wood burner. The lad stoked it opening the metal door with a glove and putting in some small logs. The room was stifling, and George coughed with the dry air as he stood, his aching legs beginning to shake. It had been a long day already.

When the door opened a large man entered, put keys on a rack and after removing his jacket and sitting at the big table he looked up as if he had just noticed George waiting, who sensed it was only part of the man's act, to tell him who was boss. The man's Scottish accent made the first sentences difficult, but George managed and was signed-on to work from the next day and was assigned a bunk. Once again it was a camp where no unions were tolerated. Sounds familiar, thought George as he walked away thinking what a day it had been.

By the time he got to the canteen, Chuck had gone to his bunkhouse. George realised he was alone, no Bert nor Jim. He must mind his back. At least the men sort-of spoke English, though he had to listen hard to get the gist of conversations. The camp was different, but much was familiar. He introduced himself to a couple of men but felt they were reluctant to converse. George realised this was not any different really from the French camp. Men only trusted you after some time. It would not be easy to make friends.

He raked his fingers through his hair noticing it had grown longer than he normally wore it. Others seemed to only hack at theirs when it got in the way, some braiding it like many locals. He took a deep breath. Maybe this place would be better. He needed money to eat. He must make it work.

Later, as he sat on his bunk at night he wrote to Dorcas. He needed to tell her he was here, sure the French Camp wouldn't send on any letters to him even when they heard where he was. He glossed over the fight and the dismissal. Said the new camp was a kind of a promotion. Well, he thought, I can't worry her, though I don't want to lose face or admit defeat. He mentioned he would soon be able to send her tickets and to go ahead with his plan. He wanted to encourage them after her depressing letter telling him of all that was making her life difficult. Normally she didn't moan but George could sense her worries. His letter was brief, and he finished saying he had to catch the post and posted it in the box in the office. He guessed Chuck would deliver mail to a post office somewhere several days later. He didn't know Chuck would not be able to get through the mud to the camp again for several weeks. His letter lay with a few others, in a damp box for a long time, long enough for the indelible-pencil writing to smudge, the facts to distort.

Back at the saloon in the Quebec town of Lalal, Kate noticed George did not visit there anymore. She was reluctant at first to ask others about him but after a couple of months, it became an urgent matter in her mind. Should she try to convince him it might be his? Would he want to know? She had never asked him about his home, or any possible wife. A girl like her, never mentioned such things usually. Men did not want to be reminded of responsibilities back home in the heat of the moment. Sometimes these things happen she thought, and she hoped it was George had caused it. Somehow that would make it bearable. She guessed the men kept the whereabouts of their mates secret, playing dumb as women often wanted to trace them for money, or more. She put her hand on Bert's arm when she saw him in the saloon. 'Where's your mate George these nights? He doesn't seem around much.'

'No, he got sacked, poor bloke. Some Frenchy had it in for him and he went away to get work. We ain't heard from him since. No idea where he is. If I do hear I'll mention yer asked.' Bert picked up his pint and wandered away. Later he said 'Jim, some woman wants to know about George. She gave me that look, yer know? I reckon we should keep quiet about him.'

'Well, I ain't heard a word about him since he left. Hope the blighter's alright and none of those damn Frenchies have done for him some dark night. We've a devil of a lot to be grateful to old George for,' Jim said quietly. They both nodded remembering.

Kate travelled to see her sister needing to talk about her situation. She couldn't get rid of another child, the last time had been so awful. She secretly hoped it was his, wanted it to be George's child, one of the few men she had liked, that she had enjoyed.

Frowning, her sister, after a lot of tears, agreed to help her through the birth and if necessary keep the child herself. 'So, give up your crazy life Katherine. No-one here knows what you do, so you could come and live with Father and me. We can tell them you are a widow with a young child. Dad will never notice. He doesn't know what day of the week it is, so your secret's safe with me. Please, I would love us to be together. Have a new start, We could give a child a proper life, a family.' She looked pleadingly at her younger sister. Kate doubted if the plan would work, but events the following month made her change her mind, when her father had a stroke. Feeling guilty, Kate could no longer leave her sister to care for him alone, she knew she must help. Packing up her life, Kate moved back home where she was needed, where she felt safe. She kept George's watch for old times' sake, secretly sure she knew the father of her son born later that Thanksgiving.

CHAPTER 18: Dorcas, May 1924

When she thought back over the year, Dorcas was never sure how it happened, though she would always remember how it began. Tilda always wanted piano lessons and there'd been a visiting music teacher who'd seen her trying to accompany the pupils' Easter hymns. One day after the morning service a tall, distinguished man had spoken to Dorcas in chapel.

'Good morning, Mrs Haddon. My name is Adam Brook.' They shook hands, standing on the gravel path. 'Excuse me for approaching you but I have been watching Matilda playing the piano. She has potential I believe, and I wondered if you would allow me to help her progress. She deserves some tutoring I feel.'

Dorcas looked up at him, noticing his greying sideburns and a jagged scar running along his jaw. He looked a little older than George. She was aware her innocent daughter was a good-looking girl, so she was cautious of his motives, and frowned. 'How do you propose to do that? In the school?'

'Well, it's why I am asking you. I have no idea but if you have a piano at home, I would be willing to come there if it was convenient. Before you ask there would be no cost. I just like to help youngsters with potential when I can. Others gave me chances when I was young and I like to pass it on.' He gently insisted that he felt Tilda should be given the opportunity to learn more. 'I'm to work some days at this school for the next term and I also tutor a student in Cardiff.'

Dorcas looked at him, studying his face. Why did she feel a recognition, something arresting? A silence hung between them for a fraction of time as he gazed back. She was convinced he felt it too. She was cautious yet hoped she could trust him.

'I have just taken a room in the village for the summer until I have to move home to help with family.' Mr Brook glanced from Tilda to Dorcas, challenging her concern. Dorcas looked at her daughter's eager face, hesitating, then agreed.

Dorcas still had her piano. It had been a precious gift from her dadda when she was sixteen. He had worked a lot of overtime at the mine to get this for his beloved daughter who hoped to study music at a college. Dorcas's mother had considered it a waste of money, but his young daughter had been delighted.

'Life held promise in those days,' she remembered, whenever she dusted the glossy top as it stood in the parlour. It seemed a long time ago, several years before she met George but only two years before her father dropped dead at work from his weak heart. Without warning, without their breadwinner, her family's life changed for ever, and her ideas of college were forgotten. She had needed to earn and learnt to clean houses and serve in shops. Somehow the whole time had seemed like a downhill slide whirling through mists of grief. Her beloved Dadda gone.

By the time she was twenty-two Dorcas had left work in a hurry, was married and little Tilda was on the way. George found their first home to rent as more children came. They both had built their life together by hard work and long hours, but they were happy. She'd give him that, he'd always been a good husband.

Her piano took up valuable space in the parlour although she rarely opened or played it. Tilda wanted to learn, and she had taught herself the basics but somehow Dorcas could never find the time to help her daughter. It felt too painful, so she made excuses even to herself. Yet this tall man, Adam Brook, the teacher, had offered to give Tilda lessons. Dorcas, distressed by George's absence, felt she should give her eldest child this chance. Tilda had been so responsible when Peter had been ill. Dorcas decided. ''That is very kind of you Mr. Brook. I will allow her to learn with your help, but it must always be in my house. She is very young you see. I have a piano so, if you can spare the time, we would both be grateful. I fear it may be a little out of tune. But please, I must pay you whatever you say. How much do you charge please?'

'Mrs Haddon, I have no intention of charging anyone and I can get it tuned. I want to help her. And you can be assured she will be safe with me, though I understand your caution. I am only staying locally until the summer holiday when I must return to my own home. I have a niece about Tilda's age who is returning in August to Britain from India where her parents are stationed. She will be starting at a small private school for deaf children and staying with me. I promised my sister I would care for her until they can return.' Dorcas watched him, looking into his honest eyes and felt reassured.

She agreed, and Mr. Brook came at first for two afternoons a week when Tilda returned from her pupil teaching at the village school and their parlour became an unexpected source of music. At first Dorcas worried, feeling uncomfortable and made young Olive sit in the parlour to finish her needlework throughout her sister's lesson.

Later, as Dorcas heard her daughter's progress, she relaxed with this man and offered him a cup of tea each afternoon when he arrived. Gradually he came a little earlier some days when he wasn't working, and he would share Dorcas's special five minutes when she could sit and relax before opening the shop for the afternoon, until her children burst in.

Dorcas had always kept herself neat, changing her apron every day before entering the shop. She appreciated shops which were clean and well organised, in fact she did not enter those that were sloppy with grubby entrances and shopkeepers with unwashed hands. Their constant battle against germs divided the village women into those who carefully washed and those who didn't believe in others' comments, muttering in response, 'A peck of dirt never killed anyone!'

'But it did!' thought Dorcas, remembering what she had read and shaking her head.

Since Adam Brook's visits, she found herself going to her bedroom on those afternoons, glancing in the mirror on her chest of drawers, slipping off her blouse and, after a dab of Ashes of Roses scent, putting on a clean one. She hadn't always time to unpin and retie her hair, but she smoothed the wayward strands back into place as she watched her reflection. She told herself it was because she had more time as May was at school too, though deep down she admitted it was not the reason. This tall, gentle man with a shy smile was the reason. Looking at her reflection, she smiled holding her head high, questioning how he saw her. 'What are you doing girl?' she silently asked herself.

When Dorcas realised how much time he gave to Tilda, and the fact he refused her offer to pay him, she gave him a fruit cake she'd made. The next time he brought two rabbits his friend had caught, and he shyly asked, 'Could you cook these and perhaps you would like them for your evening meal?'

'Of course, thank you,' she said taking them into the scullery calling over her shoulder, 'and I hope you will stay and join us. The children will be delighted to have a bit of company.'

'Many thanks, Mrs Haddon,' he smiled at her and they shared a rich meal with a good deal of laughter that evening. This became a regular feature of their afternoons together and eventually one day, when it was the two of them sharing a pot of tea, he asked her about the piano which she'd said belonged to her.

'Do you ever play Mrs Haddon?' he asked.

'Please call me Dorcas. No, no, I'm not sure why but since my dadda died I have not felt the urge to play. Too many memories I suppose.'

'Pity. I'm sure he would be very distressed to hear that,' Adam said and feeling confused she turned away. Dorcas looked down at her hands and swallowing hard, went into the parlour and lifted the lid. Getting a favourite piece of music out of the piano stool she sat at the keyboard. She rubbed her fingers, flexed them then cautiously she started to play. He stood in the doorway watching her and, after several minutes, he stood close behind her.

As she struggled with a piece of fingering his slim right hand took over the intricate keys. Slowly she let him play as the left hand came forward by her left shoulder and he reminded her how it should be phrased. It was not only the gentle music she was experiencing. Her mind froze as she felt his warmth with the nearness of his chest behind her shoulders. His long arms surrounded her while he played. She could feel his breath on her hair, and she shrunk within herself, unable to move, a primitive longing confusing her. She felt surrounded, protected. She closed her eyes and tried to collect her thoughts, knowing her cheeks were flushed as she felt her heart beating. She was sure he would hear it.

He said nothing as the music ended. He stood, breathed deeply and strode back to the doorway. She fussed with her skirt, brushing it with her hand as she stood. When she looked towards him, his glance told her he had felt it too. Something was growing between them, a feeling which had a lot to do with romantic music and little to do with being a wife and mother. She blushed, looking down and he stood aside as she bustled out of the parlour. Within minutes the children burst in and the moment was over.

As Dorcas lay awake savouring her thoughts that night, guilty at her growing feelings, she saw him again in the darkness, tall and refined, with his long, slim fingers caressing the piano keys. As she felt his breath on her hair again, she closed her eyes. He had smelt clean and masculine. She had noticed a little chalk dust on his jacket which showed creases where it had been hung on a peg. She longed to brush and press it, to care for it, perhaps for him too. Adam seemed distracted by his music and had spoken to her of the poetry he loved. Not a practical man perhaps but a kind one. She worried why he should affect her so much. It was his eyes, quiet and calming, with a sense of longing. She turned over determined to sleep for she had to be up early next day, though she dreamt of him even then.

For several visits nothing revealing was said before one day when he arrived very early, and they talked about their mutual love of poetry and music. He told her of his time at university, of concerts he had attended and quoted from his favourite poems while she watched his face as it showed delight at his memories. They laughed together, her eyes shining with merriment. She breathed deeply and felt happy if slightly guilty.

Later Adam talked briefly of his time at the Somme and a girl he had loved who'd died of influenza. Dorcas's hands wanted to touch him in sympathy, but she felt it was not what he needed then. He talked of his home and a loving childhood, laughing at memories. She felt a glow of pleasure at sharing a little of his past, inhaling the moment like delicious perfume. Its warmth tinged her cheeks and made her smile. Adam looked at her, with a sad pleasure before smiling. She glanced at him then dropped her eyes in confusion. They both felt younger.

May crashed into the kitchen crying, clutching a grazed knee. Once again the spell was broken.

A week later Tilda came home overjoyed. 'I've been asked to accompany the choir at chapel on the piano for a special concert for the new Minister. Can I do it, Mam? Please?' Dorcas looked at her daughter proudly and smiled.

'Of course, though I think you should speak to Mr Brook about it. He may be able to help you with the practice. We must all come and listen. When is it?'

'Oh, I don't think the little ones would want to sit through it all. They would start to fidget and make a noise Mam. Besides it'll go on quite late.' Tilda looked alarmed. Dorcas glanced at her daughter's face and guessed she didn't want any family embarrassment. No, maybe she would ask Sarah to sit with the smaller girls at least.

Of course, Tilda hoped Joseph would be there, but she was determined she would ignore him. She mustn't make a single mistake. When she told Adam Brook, he was delighted and promised to give her extra practice. Now he was there each evening and the sound of the piano became a regular feature in their home. Tilda was improving Dorcas felt and she enjoyed Adam's company at the family meal listening to his quiet laughter at the boys' jokes. May always chose to sit near him whenever the others would let her, though they liked to share his side of the table but Roger pointedly sat in his father's place. Dorcas was sure there must be gossip but she felt with all the children around what could be wrong about his regular help for Tilda.

Dorcas helped Tilda dress before the concert in an emerald dress which she had altered from one of her own, a dress she'd last worn when she was as slim as Tilda. Dorcas had crocheted a lacy collar and cuffs and shortened the skirt to make it more approved by her fussy daughter. Tilda's brown hair was neatly bunched with a green ribbon and the curls about her face were produced by the tongs heated on the top of the stove. Dorcas, wearing her best blouse, admired her pretty daughter. Twirling around in their parlour Tilda looked excited. 'Thank you, Mam. This is much better than my old skirt and blouse.'

'You look lovely, doesn't she girls?' The smaller girls, in nightdresses, stood with Sarah on the stairs, smiling at Tilda. Sarah winked at her.

'Come on Cinderella, it's time we were on our way to the ball!' Dorcas laughed. The two boys accompanied Dorcas and Tilda, as they made their way through the darkening streets, smirking at Tilda's nerves. Peter was really interested, though Roger had been reluctant, not really understanding their enthusiasm, but pleased and determined to chaperone his mother.

When they arrived, they found their seats and Tilda was sitting at the piano. Adam joined them, watching Tilda closely as she played. He whispered to Dorcas, 'She has talent. When I am gone and wherever you are, do encourage her to continue. She loves it so much.' Dorcas watched his proud smile and felt confused by strange feelings in her chest. When Tilda received applause at the end of her piece Adam instinctively put his hand on Dorcas's arm, squeezing it in the darkness with their mutual pride at Tilda's success. Dorcas blushed, becoming aware of the beating of her heart. She breathed deeply bringing her emotions under control. She wasn't a silly young girl so why was she allowing herself these feelings, when she should be concentrating on her daughter's achievement?

At the end of the concert as the big lamps were lit and brought into the chapel, they stood. She covered her feelings by fussing around the boys and collecting her gloves and bag. When Tilda joined them, Dorcas noticed her smile of surprise when Joseph approached them from the audience and congratulated her.

'You were really good Tilda. I didn't know you could play like that.' The young man looked eager. Tilda's blush hinted to Dorcas of her daughter's secret, though she said nothing. Roger and Peter grinned of course, so Dorcas told them both to hurry up and help with stacking the chairs. A secret look passed between Dorcas and Adam, beginning as an understanding about Tilda's blushes but lingering as something more. Blushing too, Dorcas looked down.

On the way home, they strolled together as far as the corner, Adam and the boys ahead, enthusing about the Olympics in Paris and about how two British athletes, Liddell and Abraham had won gold. Adam told them of other sporting successes in the newspapers and the boys looked up at him with glowing faces. Living in a family of females, the boys seemed animated by Adam's talk about sport. Even Roger sounded enthusiastic, casting off his reserved attitude for a while.

They parted at Adam's lodgings, raised hands in farewells and the small family went on up the hill. Dorcas praised Tilda walking beside the boys, as she meanwhile remembered Adam's touch. She was thinking about him too often and reminded herself she was not a young girl like Tilda; she had a husband and children. As she later undressed, she realised George had not crossed her mind all evening.

Feeling guilty, she promised she would write to him soon to tell him how well Tilda had done at the concert, but no, not mentioning Adam Brook. Tell him of May starting school and the things about the children, young Fred and Roger and how Peter had started to help out with Davey Howard on his vegetable stall. Ask him again when they could join him. She knew they must go soon, before next winter. Yet he would never read her letter as his life moved on and he struggled through the next few months.

CHAPTER 19: George, May 1924

George looked about him in the first glimmers of sunshine at dawn, as he went around his new camp getting his bearings and hoping the warmth would help his cough. Weeds were sprouting in the cracks and corners of the earth paths. There was a fresh scent in the air, despite the mining smells. He could see the whole place had suffered the throes of the harsh winter, but he also recognised a certain basic lack of care. The wooden shacks had ill-fitting doors with make-shift latrines, cheaply constructed. Patched roofs spoke of leaks and draughts. He was bemused why, with many skilled men on camp, they didn't have more comfortable bunk houses, didn't make life more agreeable for themselves. No-one had put in any effort it seemed, or maybe they were not permitted. Slumped on the wooden steps of his hut, raising his face to the thin warmth of the sun, he asked one of his hut members why no one spent time on the place. 'Well, ye see George my wee laddie, tha put this place up in a hurry and since then nay one's stayed longer than tha needed. None of us wanna make any effort on tha places where others slept or supped!'

'But didn't the bosses and the owners feel they should do something? Look at the state of the place!' George argued.

'Tha Campbells nay want ta spend money or men's time on unnecessary extras. All the men here lang ago lost interest in trying to improve thar lives. We just manage from day ta day.' George looked about him noticing the disheartened look of the men who hurried about their shift. muttering against injustices and cursing problems. They seemed hardy men, shrewd and tight lipped. 'Spare,' his old ma would have called them, counting their pennies and reluctant to make friends.

At this Scottish camp the conditions seemed no better. Life for them was an endless round of work and frugal living. Meals were basic and monotonous though not as meagre as East Camp's canteen. George kept his head down and never answered back, though the anger and frustration bit into him daily. The constant noise of heavy machinery and men calling, coughing and cursing also irritated him but he had no special mates to moan with. He must keep it inside himself.

The weather had improved but, as slush and mud gave way to dust, he hated the dirt in his hair, his eyes and even in his mouth. He felt constantly hungry and, except when the work made him sweat, he felt chilled to the bone. His cough plagued him and without any remedies or even rest, it got worse. With no Bert or Jim, he rarely joked with anyone, feeling lonely though never safely alone.

Often he lay in the lighter evenings thinking of Dorcas, imagining her as a girl, of the joyous feeling when she accepted his love. Sometimes he thought of tiny May, of her pranks and her saucy grin, or his warm pride when Roger had completed a job well, though he'd never tell his son. They were why he must battle on, he told himself, why he must try to make this work, though he knew it would be a long time before he could send for them. He felt moments of concern for how they were managing and promised himself he would write soon.

Even in his bunk he was alert and on edge, sleeping fitfully and becoming more tired each day. He no longer fell asleep exhausted after a long shift. His habit had been broken and he suffered for it. Always tired, rarely laughing. Never in his adult life had George been this aware of his vulnerability, blaming his cough. He'd not admit it, but he felt worried for his future.

He discovered the Scots who worked there, had their own language, at times as incomprehensible as the French-Canadians he had left behind, and many of them resented him as much, his confident manner spilling over. Here men were not interested in each other. Many workers were suspicious of newcomers with barely hidden animosity, and showed their prejudice over racial issues. George learnt of only a few indigenous natives who were trusted because they understood local conditions, and their knowledge was invaluable to the miners, but they were rarely tolerated when the men were not working. Each group kept to itself.

News of the outside world only came as a few small items were gleaned from the out-of-date newspapers brought to the camp by Chuck on his fortnightly deliveries. Word of political changes and challenges emblazoned the headlines, but stories of sports and scandal were devoured by others from the back pages. Chuck sold them at a profit despite their age, or tattered condition. Groups of men could be seen sharing articles, those who could read informing others. For several days the gossip would be enlivened, men talking avidly, for they longed to exist in a real world, something beyond the monotony of the camp regime. George always scanned the pages though only to find news of the missing Spaniard and any hint of his involvement.

The scene which most intrigued George was the evening of Chuck's arrival. Chuck, who visited every few weeks, was always treated to extra grub by the canteen workers, men chosen for their strength but not their experience of cooking, as the camp managers knew of the currency of food and so canteen men must not be intimidated.

Though Chuck was special. He would arrive tired and hungry, seated in the canteen in his great leather coat, spooning mouthfuls into himself. By the time he had finished his dinner, double portions of a solid pudding with currants, syrup and custard would sit before him. The carrier would take a few bites, then start to answer their questions, punctuated by more pudding. Gradually he would slow his eating, bringing fascinating glimpses of the outside world, as he saw it, to these news-starved men. The sudden animation within the canteen showed many different opinions, aired a wide range of ideas. Chuck's spoon would almost conduct the talk as he pointed it at various men, who for that hour would shed their sullen skin worn every day, showing a whole new side to their natures. George looked about and saw downcast glances, tiny smiles and raised eyebrows amongst these usually surly men. Stories of home for some men brought glances of silent reflection; gambling and gossip excited others. George guessed that they could buy illicit whisky from Chuck, made at secret stills in the forests, at places on his route around the camps, but the cost was high. George would sometimes smell the hint of whisky as he walked into the hut, knowing they had been drinking, but he was never offered any. Chuck had his hour of glory and they went to their bunks with private thoughts. It would take several days before quiet descended again.

Chuck caught up with George late one evening. 'You're George Haddon ain't you? I thought so. I've a note from East Camp for you here somewhere.' He foraged in his bag. 'Mates of yourn there sent it, got a letter from home too, what they sent.' George grabbed them and took them straight to his bunk where he could read in peace.

Bert's scribbled note was brief:

'George,

Me and Jim hope you are sorted. Chuck said you were at Campbell's, but we ain't telling no one. Some woman called Kate's been asking after you, but we didn't let on. Good Luck mate. From Bert.'

George wondered about that and smirked. Did Kate miss him? What was that about? He remembered her smile, tucking the note away in his pocket.

He dismissed those thoughts as he opened Dorcas's letter which was longer and had been written two months before. It told him of the goings-on in the family and the village, asking how he was doing and how soon they would be able to come and join him. It made him sad and frustrated. What could he tell her? For all these months, he had made little progress, the cash he'd earnt was meagre, and he knew he was no further towards his goal of a new life. He could not write until things were more settled. Besides, she had sent him no hint she was missing him, the letter did not even sound like her.

A short note from Tilda was enclosed with the children's love. She had got each of them to add their names. He looked hard at their pencilled marks remembering their faces. No Roger there, he must have been at work, George thought. The little ones made him catch his breath, especially his little May with her clumsy letters. He rubbed his thumb across them trying to bring back memories, trying hard to see each one. He frowned realising he was losing them.

At times a cutting wind blew between the buildings, carrying any leaves and scraps into little eddies flattened against the rough-hewn walls. It blew under the doors and through cracked and leaky window panes. Other days his skin baked, working in harsh sunlight. He could not get used to the Canadian climate.

The canteen had uneven benches repaired with bent nails. George guessed he'd frequently need to sew his trousers from their rips in future. Every man carried his own cutlery but, if he lost it or had it stolen, he ate with his hands until he could buy more. Rules were harsh.

Beds in the huts were narrow and cramped into bunkhouses with six men to each, with a few hot-bedding ones by the door. These were used for emergencies and new-comers sleeping shifts, turn and turn-about.

Everyone looked suspiciously at any strangers when they first arrived. George found himself doing that too.

When the sun shone the men would leave the door open to lessen the human stench which pervaded the bunks, before others would complain of the draught or the dust and shut it with a curse. Even these smells became less noticeable as their noses no longer reacted.

The bunks were basic with coarse striped ticking covering their mattresses and pillows stuffed with straw. George thought of the care with which Dorcas made pillowcases from old sheets and turned sides to middles on worn sheets, sewing in tiny stitches along its length. At night he lay, picturing her battling in their tiny yard with clean wet bedlinen which wrapped itself about her as it blew on the line. He remembered their fresh smell and smiled. He relished his thoughts of home trying to recreate his memories. Good thing she could not see how he was living.

George discovered that work at Campbell's Mining Camp was sometimes worse than the French camp. Some weeks when there was vital work, or they needed to catch up with quotas, it was seven full days with no extra pay. The men moaned but dared not say too much. Few men stayed long unless they were a Campbell or their cronies, he heard. So many men needed work to survive, with no alternatives, but for some it became too much. They left, disappearing one dawn with their kit-bags, often mysteriously, sometimes bullied to move on or frightened for their life if they stayed. Some still dreamt of success in this land. Often nothing more was heard of them.

George felt he should not be one of them. He told himself he had skills and in a different world he would be respected. In the past he prided himself he'd never broken the law, which doubtless many of the men here had. He'd not run from debt. No woman was chasing him, yet he laboured alongside men who chose to be known only by their initials. His pride was dented, and he held tight to his tools. He learnt to only talk when he was asked questions and to answer with caution. Alone now, even missing Bert and Jim and their ridiculous jokes, he felt low.

Hauling and cutting, hacking and slashing through the forest to make a road for the mine, many men had accidents, some serious. Others were blasting through rocks to establish footings for new buildings. The sound of blasting often made him jump. Working at the mine he saw men flip coins for which one must check when the blast had not gone off. That could be fatal. They dreaded the dangers when a blowout occurred because it popped rather than exploded. Men would curse and clench their fists because the unexploded charge was still a danger to those who must check it. He heard that the victims of an accident were taken by horse cart to their mortuary, which made everyone take more care for the next few days. Blasting with dynamite was unpredictable and even with the best skilled miner sometimes it did not blow as planned. The foreman instructed them that storing any quantity of it must be done well away from the camp and distributed under strict supervision. Despite this, men took chances, carried it too close and at times their mates also paid the price for their carelessness. George tried hard to avoid those he discovered taking risks. He worried daily. His hands were his lifeline.

George hoped each day to be given a plumbing job, because his palms, though strong, were blistered from the tool handles of pickaxe and spade. He bought more gloves in the camp shop with his precious pay as soon as he could. His back ached, and his legs swelled. The constant noise of steam hammers and rasping saws drilled into his head with the piercing whistles of foremen and warning sirens for blasting alarms. He noticed other mature workers, men of only his age, struggling to keep up with the young. Each night he slumped on his bed, exhausted. His chest tightened when he lay down as he coughed disturbing everyone's sleep. He heard their muttered curses mingled with their snores. He turned to face the wall burying his rasping cough in the pillow.

Normally there were no outside lights except daylight and the men's small campfires. There was a constant concern by the bosses about the potential of forest fires, so pipes and smoking were officially banned. Fire could decimate miles of forest and catch their dynamite stores making an inferno. So, the men drank rough beer at night with nothing else to do sitting in groups, huddled with others of their own kind.

George never told Dorcas in his letter how tough he found it, how lonely. He wrote that all was well, promising himself to put a positive incident in the letter to encourage her. He did not want her to worry. That would not help him. He still clung to the promise of a new start.

George sent a letter to his ma in Bristol to tell her where he was, avoiding the whole truth. She might have heard from Dorcas by now. Whatever his ma thought about it was only guesswork, he dreaded to think. When he got a letter back, Ma was fussing about dry socks and the like, but she mentioned that his elder brother Billy had written a month before from the prison he was in.

'Prison?' he murmured. 'That's a lot for our Ma to swallow. Why the hell's he there? What's he done this time?' He wrote a short note to him at the Ottawa address she gave and was surprised to get a reply. Billy's news sounded dismal, so George wondered how he could visit him, as he'd promised to his ma. Talking to a roommate, George found the prison was at the end of a local line, some twenty miles further on. On his next day off he caught Chuck when he was delivering goods. 'Chuck, I need to visit an old mate in prison. Can I get a lift to the train with you? What'll you charge?'

Chuck grinned. 'Well mate, if you help me with loading at the rail road, I'll take you for free. Got a big load waiting for me and I could do with a hand. I'll be leaving straight after I've had m' grub though.'

So together they unloaded several crates and George caught the train. He owed it to Billy and to his ma to make the effort he thought. He felt bad he had made no attempt to contact his brother before because somehow, he had presumed all these years that Billy was doing well, too busy to write. The brothers had never been great letter writers and only their mother kept them in contact.

As the train slowed he stood and looked from the window at a single track with a few yards of platform.

Large whirls of brush blew along unhindered, bowling across the empty dust. Early weeds had started in the cracks of the disused paving. No other concessions to a station, not even a name plate left, if there ever had been one, he noticed. This was the end of the deserted line and after he climbed down, the train shunted back out from between the platforms to return to some town.

'It will be back in two hours,' the guard told him blowing his whistle, so George knew he had little time to waste. Several others hurried beside him, destined for the prison he reckoned. No one spoke. He walked from the isolated station to the prison, a dry and dusty track in a wilderness leading only there. The gaunt building was stark in the clearing, fences rusty, silent and eerie. The wind whistled through the desolated yards making him pull his jacket tighter. He waited with a few others at the gates hoping they would let him in. After a long time watching more dry brush blow pointlessly around the perimeter, a warder checked him over, peering at him, then said, 'I can see whose brother you are. Just like him, ain't you?'

When he got inside he cringed at the smell of Lysol and urinals in echoing concrete corridors which led him through a fenced and guarded yard to a separate block and a doorway with bars and rusting grills. He waited, appalled at the prison conditions. Shackled men, handcuffed with bowed heads, shuffled about behind fences with watchtowers. Whatever had Billy done for this? George had expected it to be basic, bare walls, rough seats with smells of humanity but it was the latent cruelty, the ruthlessness of the warders reflected in their dismissive eyes that struck him. No wonder the prisoners in the yard seemed dejected, some surly, some desperate though many looking lost and empty.

When Billy was led into the visiting space, his feet and hands clanking with chains, George swallowed hard and blinked away an unexpected tear. They talked through the grill which prevented any contact between them. George frowned, what a hell of a place this was! His brother looked so old and scrawny, his back bent, and his thinning hair was grey. Where was the tall Jack-the-lad Billy had once been, that a young George had looked up to, had worshipped?

'Do you get enough food?' George asked.

'As much as the next man, I s'pose. It ain't like our ma's grub though.'

George studied his brother through the grill. Where was the prosperous home owner George had imagined?

'Don't yer worry about me. It's you what matters and that family of yours. Just get back home mate, I tell yer George, go back. This bloody country has nothing for us foreigners, our George!'

'What did you do? How'd you get in here Bill?'

'Well, yer see, I had a fight with two buggers. They had staves see? Bloody heavy staves. I floored one and he ended up in hospital. He survived but only just, our George. He'd goaded me for a devil of a long time. In the end I saw red. I was lucky I didn't kill him, or I'd have swung for it. It's what I tells meself every day, George. That's what I remembers.' George thought of Henri and how near he had been to that.

'How long's your sentence, Bill? When are you coming out?'

'Oh, I got five years, done three last Christmas and, if I keep me eyes skinned, stay alive, I got nearly two more to do. Then I'm getting meself back home as soon as I can work me passage. I ain't staying here and you shouldn't either George me old son. We'll always be the hated foreigner to these men.'

George was silent, his eyes searching Billy's face noticing the broken teeth, the thinning hair.

'Promise me one thing George,' Billy clutched at the bars between them. 'Promise me you'll not tell Ma, not about all this. Say I'm fine, that it's not too bad. She won't let you get away without telling her but make it decent. I'd hate her knowing, well, imagining all this!' Billy hung his head. 'I can take it if our Ma don't know. Tell her I'll visit her when I get out. I promise. I'll do right by the old lady.'

'Sorry Bill, I didn't bring you anything, sort of last-minute visit, really.'

'No, we ain't allowed anything anyway. The warders take it all, tobacco and such and we never see it. Tell me George, how is our old Ma?' He searched George's face for an answer.

'She's alright I suppose. I haven't seen her for more than a year, though her letter said she was keeping well. She would love to see you when you do get out, Bill. Let me know, see if I can help out somehow.' They chatted for a few more minutes, then the two brothers stiffly nodded as they said goodbye, before a warder marched the shackled Billy away. George swallowed hard, wondering how he would tell his ma what he had seen.

Billy's words echoed in his mind later. Once more George doubted his rash decision to come to Canada as he rode on the train back to camp. He sat brushing dirt from his knees, thinking about his life. He wanted to understand, perhaps help Billy in some way though he slowly realised he could do nothing, but he would protect his Ma. He'd never describe the place to her, never say how her son had become so emaciated. He had promised that but what could he tell his ma about her eldest, about her Billy? George vowed he'd write more often to his brother. In the back of Chuck's cart, a lot later, he felt confused.

'Billy was always in trouble so it's not surprising he hasn't made a success of this country, though I'm not Bill!' he murmured to himself. He shook himself.

'You cold?' Chuck asked.

'No, it's just this blasted cough.' As they sat on the box watching Nellie plod along, they were both silent. His doubts crept back.

'If only I had got a decent job, something I could build on,' he whispered as he meandered back through the gates, coughing repeatedly as he showed his pass.

CHAPTER 20: Dorcas, June 1924

By Whitsun, there was little stock left in the shop to sell and that meant even the regular items were reducing and not being replenished. As Dorcas' little cash book revealed the margin was now so small, that she wouldn't be able to meet the rent by the autumn. She must tell him she was coming, make a move and he'd be forced to sort it his end. She felt she'd done her bit, managed for nearly a year on his promises. She wanted to keep their spirits up, and let them see what this new land offered.

The piano had been such a joy to them. Dorcas was glad Tilda had learnt to play but it was time for it to go, before they left the village and their money ran out. Memories of Dorcas' father must overcome as she wrote the advert for sale on the post office noticeboard.

Everyone understood it was only in their final days she could part with their furniture, but the piano was not an essential, it was a luxury. She needed the money but she could not imagine who would want it. Pianos were fashionable though many in the village could not afford one. Few people could play, and many homes would not have the space.

She was surprised when Miss Berry, Peter's teacher at the school, asked him about it after she had seen the postcard.

'Mam, Miss Berry has asked if she can see it. When can I tell her to come here?'

'Miss Berry? Really? Wherever would she put it? She's only got her little place over the chemist near the square.'

When she arrived Miss Berry looked it over, gently touching the keys and listening to the sound. Dorcas smiled at her, wondering.

'Yes, I would like to buy it and take it before the end of term if possible. I will arrange for some men to collect it when it is convenient with you, Mrs Haddon.' She nodded and delved into her bag.

'Please don't mind me enquiring but wherever will you put it?' Dorcas asked.

'Well, that's the thing you see Mrs Haddon. I haven't enough room in my little place, so the headmaster has kindly agreed to my suggestion. It will be kept in the main room at the school and I will be allowed to play it after school and at weekends and holidays. The school will benefit from my playing and so will I.' She nervously tucked her stray hair beneath her felt hat.

'It sounds ideal.' Dorcas smiled, thinking how shy this woman seemed.

'Yes, I had lessons when I was a girl though I've not played for years. It is high time I took it up again. And when I'm gone, it will be my present to the school, you see.'

Dorcas was oddly reassured and imagined her father's look of delight too. 'There's a stool with it, though you might need to recover the seat I'm afraid. I think it's a splendid idea. I wish I could afford to give it to you but …'

'Oh no, this is my gift to the school before I retire, something to remind us of the good days the children have enjoyed.' Beatrice Berry patted her bag, looked flushed and opened her purse. Dorcas felt happy and hoped Tilda would too. The money would get them to London and pay for the few weeks they might need before sailing. She would write to George to say they were on their way at last. She hoped he'd be pleased.

The following week at the end of a lesson, Adam, hat in hand, reminded her he was leaving the village in two weeks for his new job and Tilda's lessons with their time of friendly chats would soon end. He touched Dorcas's hand briefly and she smiled though her heart was in her mouth as she swallowed hard. He had made the past months interesting, though it was more a certain excitement she felt when he entered their home, a heightened tension in Dorcas. Had he felt it too? She dared not wonder. Her heart became heavy, dreading the thought of not seeing him again, never hearing his gentle laughter, never warming to his glance. Soon she too would leave the village, off across the seas to a strange land, to a new home … and George.

Dorcas felt no excitement, no anticipation of this promised life. Doubtless it would mean a lot of hard work again along with heartache at leaving her home, her mother and brother as well as others she loved. She dared not include Adam in that list, although a picture of him was foremost in her thoughts. She offered him tea, but he refused, saying he'd not stop. His eyes met hers as he hesitated, though nothing was said while something in his look made her sad. Maybe it was for the best … for them both.

With all the things Dorcas had to deal with, the last-minute worries, she was confused at how often she thought of him, remembering the feel of his hand and his quiet smile. When Adam talked of music, of art or poetry, he became animated and watching him she had relished those moments. Other times when they both had held back, with emotions shared but unsaid. Dorcas again reprimanded herself. 'You are a mam of all these children, but you are behaving like a silly schoolgirl,' she told herself standing alone in her scullery looking in the mirror over the sink, pulling out the odd grey hair.

George had been gone for a year and it was only two days before she would leave for London and start on the trip to Canada. The money she had made selling the stock from the shop had dwindled making her decide it was time to go. She had not worked all her life to end up destitute, she mentally argued with George. They must start out before every penny had gone. It was her only income and she did not want to think about the problems ahead.

On a Tuesday morning in late July when the school term was about to end, Dorcas went to the market square for the last time. The sun had gone in and clouds scuttled across the grey sky, their shadows darkening the grass of the summer hillside and casting stark shade across the canvas stalls.

Dorcas felt pleased at last she saw a conclusion to these troubled months, though sad at all the familiar people and things she would miss. After buying some food for their supper she strolled around the village stalls, remembering all that had happened here, where she had played as a girl, shopped as a bride and worried as a mother. She felt confused leaving the village, although she had often wished to escape the narrowness of the streets and of the villagers' minds. What would it be like in the new place?

She looked for a small gift to leave her mother when she went to London. Perhaps she would find something at one of the village stalls. There might be a trinket or a keepsake. On a covered table in the far corner she found a china fairing in delicately coloured porcelain, second hand but perfect for her mother's mantelpiece. It was a cameo of three shawled women wearing Welsh hats, whispering together at a neat tea-table. Just the sort of thing her mother would treasure to remind her of their gossips. A tear came which she whisked away, buying the ornament and the stall holder wrapped it in newspaper.

From behind her she heard a whisper. 'Mrs. Haddon … Dorcas.' It was him. Obviously not working today as he prepared to move back to the city, he was shopping too. He caught up with her as she hurried away from the stall and put his hand out.

'Your basket looks heavy,' he said taking it from her. 'Look, if you come to my place, I can leave my bag there and help you with this to your house. We'll have to hurry. I'm afraid it looks like rain.' he said glancing upwards. Reaching his door, he fiddled with the key. Dorcas felt breathless, a tightness in her throat, overwhelmed by sudden emotion.

'Do come in for a minute please. I have something to give you, a gift to remember our friendship.' he said. Hesitating, she stood in the doorway. The wind was strong and drops of summer rain were splattering onto the mat. 'Please come in, you'll get wet there. We could have a cup of tea if you wish?' At first, she refused. Shyly she glanced through into his single room, embarrassed yet fascinated to see his home, the place where he spent his evenings. Carefully she closed the door. As he took her hand and led her to a lumpy chair then filled the kettle, she sat. 'A cup of tea's not much after all the meals you've given me,' he said. She looked about her, noticing the books on shelves around his bed. A curtain strung across a corner hinted at his clothes. He found cups, saucers and milk from a cupboard and apologised he had no biscuits as he'd eaten the last the night before. He went to a phonograph winding it and carefully placing the needle, gentle music filled the space. She smiled and sat back in the chair.

Together they laughed over the tea, talking about things they had done as children, both dreading the parting. 'I have this little gift for you before you go into the 'wilderness!' my dear Dorcas,' he said and, reaching into his bag, he took out a small book of poems. He put it in her hands. 'I hope it will give you some moments of private pleasure. It must be difficult with so many around you every day.'

Then, as Dorcas put down her cup, Adam bent over and caught her hand. Turning it over gently, he softly kissed the palm. The silence checked her breathing. She trembled, guilty at her reaction as she looked searchingly into his eyes, very aware they were alone. Adam scanned her face, his warm brown eyes asking her questions, querying her feelings. She gazed back at him, wishing to tell him how much she felt for him. Her lungs tightened, and she began to weep. The look of love between them was something unspoken, yet as tangible as the rain which trickled down the window above them. Her feelings for him were compelling and a deep understanding mingled with primitive longing, hovered between them.

Adam moved towards her as she nervously stood. His hand went about her pressing her slowly towards him and she found herself in his arms. She felt safe and vibrant as she clung to him. He kissed her softly and her lips responded. Her hands were around his neck as she pulled him towards her. It felt so right to be close to him. He kissed her again, lifting her up. Their kisses became passionate, both overwhelmed by an urgency to fulfil their desire. Their bodies moved, responded. They were together, no-one else existed. Their love became urgent, absorbing them both and he pulled the pins from her hair letting it fall about her, burying his face in it, whispering his love, his lips on her neck. Dorcas desperately wanted him, her body warmed and melted with his touch and they sank together onto his bed. Their love fired their burning need. Fumbling, their clothes discarded, mutual passion overwhelmed them as they became fused together. Passionate but considerate, he took her. She surrendered herself willingly, becoming pliant, responsive. She wanted this. Closing her eyes in abandonment, she knew she loved him, truly loved him. She felt she always would.

In a gesture of tenderness Adam covered her with his shirt, whispering in her ear. Dorcas lay back with closed eyes, absorbing the joy of this secret love, wondering at the lingering sensations he had released. The powerful warmth of his body comforted her, his kisses felt like sensual promises. She was confused; amazed by her own vital response, at his expertise, at her total surrender. She felt as she never had before, with a new exquisite meaning to their love. Their eyes met, understanding so much. A feeling of closeness and warmth thrilled them both, as they lay locked in each other's arms.

Her mind was whirring from the sensations of his body reaching out to hers. It had moved her so much. Dorcas thrilled to the passion, a fulfilment she would never forget, that she would treasure. These few moments, this complete giving and receiving of love, would be a precious secret in her heart. She understood there was no possibility of their love in the future yet here was something powerful and overwhelming which reminded her of who she was deep inside. A passion that had not happened for a long, long time. Adam had done this. Such joy but it must remain their wicked secret, so unlike her, a complete departure from who she was. She blushed at the thought, closing her eyes at the warmth of her response. She relaxed to his murmurs.

For minutes she lay locked in his embrace, on the rumpled bed, slowly regretting that reality, but thrilled to have experienced his love. Like a sweet after-taste she cherished the sensations her memory was relishing. Her body still trembled. Her beating heart slowed and her breathing eased, as reality returned. Dorcas told herself sternly, this must end. What had she done? How could she have let this happen? She summoned the strength to rise and to leave him. She fumbled with her clothes.

Adam knew it from the look in her eyes. He whispered in her ear. 'Please, please forgive me, I adore you, Dorcas. You've made such a difference to me these past months. I didn't mean this to happen, I really didn't.' His look was sincere, earnest. 'What can I say? At least let me carry your basket up the hill, dearest.' He clasped her to him, burying her face in his chest.

'No, absolutely no!' She pulled away. 'What has happened must stay a secret, not spoken of ever. Please promise me that? I will not see you again, I cannot, you know that. Today must be the end.' His look of distress made her move closer. 'I will always remember this Adam, and I believe I will always love you, my precious man, but this is to be locked away for us both. Please promise me. Promise!' She pleaded, her hand stroking his face, as she saw his look of anguish. Tears came to her eyes and gently he wiped them away with his thumb. Dorcas carefully dressed herself, her hands shaking, pinning up her hair and covering her head with her shawl, to protect herself from the rain and possible prying eyes. She wanted to carry these moments with her, locked deep inside her heart.

'I will always love you Dorcas and remember our times together. If there is anything I can ever do? Thank you for the love you have shown me since we met,' he whispered as he placed her fingers to his cheek, 'and for today!' Turning her hand, he kissed the palm tenderly. 'You and your lovely family have made my lonely time here a joy. I really don't want to leave you, though I know you must go and so must I.' Adam tightened his jaw to contain his emotion, though his liquid eyes betrayed him. 'I will remember you until my dying day.' He handed her the book. She sobbed once, putting her head against his chest. He hugged her and gently kissed her hair. She pulled away, looked up at him and turned, her eyes closed in anguish.

Picking up her basket she hurried through his door and up the hill. She guessed he was standing watching her. Dorcas dared not look back. Her tears were lost in the summer rain, her hand over her mouth holding in the emotion. She knew she must leave this behind though her heart hammered in her ears. Her whole body felt different, alive. Today must be forgotten, erased, she told herself, realising this was impossible. A single sob escaped as she opened the scullery door and returned to reality.

Distracted throughout the evening, later at night she lay in her lonely bed, her eyes open and damp with tears. She could not think. Her heart hurt and certainly the pain inside made her feel wretched. What had she done? What magic had Adam performed, her body's reaction responding in the darkness? She told herself she must sleep, for tomorrow would be busy, but no sleep came.

Confused about her life Dorcas realised she was several different women really. Much of the time she was business-like, dealing with customers and salesmen, but also caring and thoughtful when she was with her children. Had she sometimes treated George as one of the children? She thought hard. Their love was still there she knew, although few opportunities came to show him a gentler side in the bustle of their family life.

She now felt there was another woman, one she had never met, who was folded within her and that girl had blossomed with Adam. Feeling cherished, feeling young, relaxing in the romantic music with the memory of his gentle touch, becoming warm within her body. His caresses had revealed a response she had never known before and one she would never forget. She stroked her upper arm, touching her breast and shivered as she lay on the pillow. How could this happen?

There was no future here. She must go to George and become again the sensible force in her family. She loved each of her children so much. Everyone needed her to steady the ship, to steer them through the upheavals ahead. Dorcas knew she must do this. Her children were at the beginning of their lives, and she loved each one of them. Even George needed her. Big as he was, he always looked to her for answers. Dorcas had no alternative. She must embrace this new life. Accepting the inevitability, she turned over and pulled the blanket over her shoulder closing her eyes. Her tears trickled into her pillow.

CHAPTER 21: George, June 1924

George had coughed for more than two months, feeling the pain in his lungs tighten. Although he had no alternative and recognising he must cope, each day he felt more exhausted. It sounded deeper, was uncontrollable, and he started to get the shivers at times. He sweated in his bunk, tossed in his blankets and dreamt wildly. He dragged himself out of bed each dawn, for he had watched others go down with these lung-wrenching coughs and had seen the dismissive treatment of the overseer. Each morning he coughed and hacked away in the latrine, the sound echoing around till men avoided him, not wanting whatever George had brought to their camp. He would stand, his back against the concrete wall in the early morning, and breathe as deeply as he could, trying to control his racing heart. He was losing weight. He worked on, for no one ate who did not work, and he had already made new notches in his belt to keep his trousers up. The unending work and his cough were making their mark. In the past George had taken a bowl of soup in to share with sick men at their bedsides but there was little nourishment there. It was no work, then no food. There was no-one here to do anything for him.

One morning at the mine face, George went to collect his barrow and tools from the store. He felt hungry despite having eaten breakfast. At the store he found an argumentative queue and he realised the men were again short of equipment, which happened frequently. The youngster counting tools out, was complaining they had not enough barrows, 'Tis nan my fault, I just does as I'm tol'.' The lad had loads of angry men to deal with and was cross and confused.

George piped up, 'I need one too and if I don't get it soon there will be trouble. So, shift yourself, lad. You hear me? Find some! Get the foreman.' Eventually the queue moved, as a handful of men grabbed their tools and barrows. After another long wait George got his.

As he hurried to wheel it away to the mine shaft, he heard a voice shouting. 'Haddon, Haddon. You're wanted in the office. Leave that and get along here pronto.'

'Oh no. Not more trouble.' George's face fell. How much more could he take? And if he was any later, they'd surely dock some of his day's pay. He clenched his teeth in frustration. 'Bloody hell!'

Clinging to his barrow he trundled it towards the office, praying it was nothing to do with the Spaniard back at the other camp. He constantly feared if either Bert or Jim got discovered, they would involve him and there would be an inquiry or maybe worse. When he slept, he often dreamt of that night, remembering the weight of the man as they swung him out, the glimpses of his battered head in the moonlight and the dull sound of his body crashing on the rocks below. In his nightmares, George was pleading, trying to explain to the Spaniard, how it happened and how sorry he was. He shook himself, coughing as he pushed his squeaking barrow along the rutted path.

When he arrived at the crowded office door, he squashed his way in and saw others who were already on the plumbing team and he hoped it might be just that. The foreman looked up.

'Oh Haddon, there you are. What kept you? They tell me you're some sort of trained plumber so, as there is a major crisis with our pipeline, we need all the trained hands we can get. You're to join the team for today to start with. It's got to be mended fast. Robertson here will tell you what to do and get yourself along there sharpish. All the rest of you, you know the drill. You'll be needed for a long stint I'm afraid. This job might take several days, and doubtless we'll be working throughout the night, so you won't get much sleep.' Men groaned quietly. 'Listen men, it's essential you get as much as possible of this repaired in the next couple of shifts. We'll set up some lanterns tonight to help. Right, get along all of you.' George was delighted. At last someone here was using his skills. It had taken months before this had happened at the previous camp. He followed Robertson and listened hard to his instructions. This was his opportunity. He would show them, he must..

George worked with the team on the seized pipeline for a couple of hours, when they were startled by a deafening explosion in the tunnel. Eyes widened, each man knew what it meant. There had been an enormous blow-out at the mouth of the mine where the men were blasting through rock. 'My God!'

‘Bloody Hell!’ Every man turned towards it, their eyes staring, mouths open. Dropping their tools and running to the mining area, they saw the devastation. Men thrown everywhere, blood-strewn rocks burying some, the dark hole split at a crazy angle amidst clouds of dust and rubble. The sound rang in their ears, reverberating, sucking the air away. Men shouted, and some screamed in pain. Others moaned as their lives bled away.

'Help, help me,' pathetic voices called. George worked with others, dug men out, throwing rocks aside with a frantic urgency before the voices ceased. Gently and swiftly they carried the victims to safety. The doctor and his few first aiders started to work on some of them there on the ground.

'You'll need disinfectant, hot water, cloths. Where will we find them?' George yelled. Robertson pointed, and George ran, bringing back all he could to the doctor.

'Put them in that hut. George, press down on this quickly, this one's bleeding badly.' Harry, a plumber, helped George to lift men onto the big tables in the hut and they ripped away a man's trousers. George closed his eyes at what he saw.

‘Keep your hand there and don’t let that go,’ the doctor yelled, his eyes trying to give hope to an impossibly damaged man. Battling with the warm blood which seeped between his fingers, George pushed flesh down apologising for the pain to the man who lay on the table. How could he do this? George felt sick. The man passed out, shuddered and then died.

Later they worked bringing more tables into the hut and saw men carrying the dead into another hut. Every man worked non-stop, but they were silently grateful they had not been at the mouth of the mine that day when everything exploded. George realised it was only by a fluke he had not been there. If he'd not had trouble collecting his barrow earlier, he'd already have gone there and might not have been found for the plumbing crisis. Closing his eyes at the thought, he thanked a god he was not even sure about.

It was said there were about a dozen hurt and several more men dead. The whole camp worked on for hours. When George eventually walked away, as the trees' shadows lengthened hours later, he wondered who would let Dorcas know if he'd been hurt or even killed. She might not have heard for a long time … or ever? And how would she manage, he asked himself … and what about their children? He felt terrified as he realised what might have been and what he had seen. Ordinary men: angry, surly and desperate men admittedly, but real human beings blown apart in seconds. Men he had spoken to, shared tables with and heard shouting in their sleep, so many gone, becoming flesh, identified only by their fragments of burnt clothing. And everywhere the acrid smell of smoke from dynamite mingled with a lingering tang of blood on George's clothes.

Throughout the war as a father in a protected job, George had not been called to the front, hadn't seen the ravages others hinted at. For him it was an enormous shock and his imagination relived the scenes. When today's disaster happened he had functioned automatically, done what needed to be done, helped with men in terrible pain. Afterwards, when he sat on his bunk, he could not believe what his eyes had seen, what he had held. For days he was numb, working distractedly, unable to think of the devastating scene, jumping at the sound of blasting. Others were silent too. He wasn't alone in that.

Men dug graves amongst the trees for the five men who had died. The sound of sawing and hammering went on into the night as hasty coffins were made. Simple funerals for them together took place the following day and those who could, attended. Scruffy workmen who had washed their hands and faces stood cap-less remembering some mates. George realised he did not know their names. They had been just workers, men. Thinking hard he remembered Clive, a short, stubborn miner who was only a name now. Who would remember him?

A padre read something, and the men shovelled dry earth and rocks onto the makeshift coffins. George felt a secret horror at how fast it was all over, and they were expected to return to work, for the pipeline still needed mending. No time for sentiment here. A renewed sense of caution seemed to blow through the camp for a week and there was no laughter. He noticed how the dead men's things disappeared, gone from their bunks in hours. Were they to be sent to families with a note of condolence? Or were they to be absorbed into someone else's bag of goodies? He felt he should ask but did not want trouble. He knew his questions would make little difference. They were as good as prisoners here.

George's mind hardened as the days passed, leaving him feeling old and very alone, wondering why he was here. He thought long and hard about going home, about admitting this had been a mistake, but his pride and a weary sense of no alternative possessed him. He must make a last effort to try to earn enough for them to come, for that promised future he had written in his last letter, his glimmer of hope for his family. Besides, he doubted if he had enough money for the ship back, that would not be subsidised as his passage here had been.

Over the next few weeks George was needed on the plumbing team every day and Robertson praised him several times. He hoped he could keep this new position though the pay was the same. There were no extras though at least the work was not so mind-numbing as his previous jobs. Things were looking up at last, he repeatedly told himself. He'd try to think about his future soon, once his cough got better.

CHAPTER 22: Dorcas, July 1924

The next day, with the shop closed and the children nearing their final day at school, Dorcas planned to use the morning to visit her mam but beforehand she wandered into their shop. Her footsteps echoed, as she looked about the empty shelves, remembering the good times. The excitement when they first opened the shop so long ago, and the disaster when the storm caused a flood and how she and George had spent the night sweeping water out and sandbagging the door. She smiled at memories of George's frustration at his early wobbly shelves in their first years of marriage and how he had sat and puzzled out the best way to store paraffin out in the yard, terrified it would cause a fire. She did miss him. She must tell herself, remind her drained self. Not long now. She put on her hat and closed the door.

She must see her Mam and her confused brother Ernest for the last time, despite their brief visit the previous weekend, coming down the mountain to the centre of the town on the carter's wagon. Before she left her mam had said her goodbyes to the children with gifts of her own toffee apples and a large box of home-made fudge for the journey. The old lady had hugged them all, even a very embarrassed Roger, who was not sure how to say goodbye to his grandma. Dorcas found it incredibly difficult trying not to let the children see her tears.

Her mam's comments hinted at their disagreement about George's demands and her plans to follow him, but her mam would always condemn her for accepting George's decision. The old lady hated losing her daughter and her only grandchildren, anxious they may never return from this far-flung country where George had disappeared on some mad whim of his. Dorcas understood the implications for her mother more each day … and what would become of Ernest when Mam could no longer manage? When she was no longer there to look after him, help him dress, explain things? What would he do, how would he cope? Where would he go? Who would take care of him?

Dorcas weighed it up, but felt she had no other option. She must think first of their children's future, yet she hated the whole idea. As she walked up the hill she searched for an alternative solution, telling herself it was nothing to do with yesterday's folly, trying not to think of Adam. Why had she let that happen? She shook her head. She must put it behind her for ever, though she knew she could not.

She climbed in the early sunlight, as her visit to her mam would take a couple of hours. The mountains cast shadows over the valley still, with the sun peeping through the gaps as she looked upwards. She would miss this she told herself. Sounds from the town square below were joined by children's voices calling in the school yard. The mine wheel whirred on.

Breathing deeply and hoping to make this a loving farewell, Dorcas promised herself she'd not allow its memories to be tainted by more disagreement. This might be their last time … no … she choked back her tears, she'd not think like that.

As Dorcas climbed higher, she studied the skyline. For the past year she had been too busy, too distracted, to notice the mountains. They had always been there, standing high, dominating their lives. Nearer were the tips, the slag heaps, the useless waste climbing for ever higher, higher, black and silent in front of those grey-green mountains. Today the slag was tinged with streaks of purple by the sun's rays. All this had always surrounded her, with the mine and its tentacles stretching across the village below. She was surprised to realise she'd miss it all.

As she approached her mother's cottage, one in a row of three on the mountainside, built of stone to house shepherds long ago, she saw girlhood memories again. Dorcas swallowed hard. Ernest met her at the gate. His tall figure stumbled towards her. They hugged, his mumbles excited, his joy childlike.

'He has been waiting for you since sunrise,' her mam called. 'He understands you are going away and is concerned. He can't imagine life without you. I have told him I'll read your letters to him, but he'll not settle, he's confused.'

'Sorry Mam, I couldn't leave until the children had gone to school and May was very reluctant this morning.'

'I'm not surprised at all. Poor little lamb doesn't understand what's happening, well really, none of us do!'

The old woman crossed her arms over her ample bosom and sucked at her teeth.

'Mam please let's make this visit a good memory not only for us but for Ernest too. He will think about what we say for a long time, remember!' Dorcas said. She smiled across at him wondering how much he understood. It had been so long since he had been damaged in the mine, since so much of that laughing man had disappeared in darkness.

'And you think I won't?' her mam tutted raising her eyebrows. Today she looked older than Dorcas remembered, her spirit dimmed.

'Can I put the kettle on, make us some tea?' Dorcas needed time to mend fences, to leave her mam with love, not recriminations. Tea always helped to soften Mam.

Dorcas gave her the fairing and saw her smile when she saw the gossiping figures. 'It is going on my shelf to remind me of our chats,' she said, and Dorcas hugged her hard. 'When you've gone, I'll look at it and remember.' She pointed towards the table. ''There's some shortbread in the tin I made 'specially for this morning. Put some out on a plate Dorcas, 'cause Ernest will eat it all if you put the tin out.' Her mother started to fuss, and her mood brightened. She chatted about a scandal in the village and mentioned another price rise at the grocer's shop, and as she prattled on Dorcas looked at her. She felt the sorrow of the moment. Would she ever see her ageing mam or even her brother again? This seemed wrong. She should always be there to help them both. She looked about the room, a place she'd grown up in, where she'd played and studied. Mam repeatedly smoothed her best lace cloth spread on the table to mark the occasion. It brought a lump to Dorcas's throat. She turned to the narrow window to control her feelings. The sunlight coming through the panes changed the back yard into her childhood skipping area, the place where, as a girl, she'd helped hang washing and her brothers had teased her. Carefree days before the accident which had killed her brother Delwyn and maimed Ernest, before her dearest father's funeral … before George. An hour later Dorcas looked at the kitchen clock, ten minutes fast as usual knowing she must say her goodbyes and leave. Get this over and done with. She stood up. How do you say goodbye for ever? She bit her lip though her mam was more prepared than she.

'Come and say cheerio to Dorcas, Ernest. She's got to get back for the children.' Ernest limped towards her and hugged her tight. Dorcas held herself stiff. She remembered what a joker he had been so long ago, always full of fun, so lively and now so damaged.

Then her mam patted her back. 'I hope it is a lovely place, my dear, and things go well for you. Be careful on your journey. It's so far.' Her voice choked. 'Tell George I expect him to take care of you all for me. Send me one of those picture postcards when you get there so I can see where you are. And Ernest will steam off the stamp. You know how he loves them.' Her mam fidgeted with Dorcas's collar tucking it in and patting her as she had when her daughter was just a small girl. Dorcas saw her mam's tightened lips and knew tears were near. 'Oh, and this is a little something for your new home if you have any new Canadian visitors for afternoon tea. Show them you come from a good home. I made it especially for you, my girl.' She put a wrapped packet in Dorcas hands. 'It's one of my special tablecloths, I made last winter. Now, off you go and take my love with you.' Her mam opened the door and, with a quick kiss, almost pushed her out. Somehow, she had become her mam's child again, a lump in her throat. Her mam's words were for Ernest's sake she knew, but she felt rejected. Tears started, and she swallowed hard, fumbling with the wobbly latch on the gate.

She hurried out to the path, not daring to look back, overwhelmed. 'Dear Mam, she realised I couldn't have left her otherwise,' she whispered. Dorcas was so distracted she hardly noticed the long mile down the hill before she came to the village shops.

'I must make one more visit this morning and then it's done.' She turned off by the chapel, breathed deeply and opened the lych gate.

When Dorcas entered the graveyard the yew trees cast their shadows across her path. Carrying her basket with the flowers she stepped between stone angels and lichen-covered headstones. Kneeling at her patch she watched a small bird picking at a stone. In the silence she became aware of the birds singing. Tears pricked her eyes. The tiny graves were beside each other. Two little girls who would not be going with her on this adventure. She placed a small bunch of daisies on each of them, remembering the baby and the tiny girl she mourned. Dorcas wiped away her tears and turned to the two older graves nearby. Her elder brother's funeral had been just a box of rocks, no body found, only a memory buried under the coal. Her dear dadda lost forever too. There was so much she wished to share with him. She sobbed loudly in the lonely graveyard, head in hands.

As her tears dried, she thought about what she had to do. How could George expect this of her? This was not his childhood home, not his parents. Her shoulders ached, bowed down with the enormity of what waited for them all. Anger flared her nostrils as she muttered at him, cursing the unknown.

Since that fateful morning last summer, things in their world had moved on and Dorcas realised she'd changed too. She doubted if she would hold her tongue when she eventually saw him. No, she would tell George the truth. What this had cost her and the children. Wives had little alternative having to make the best of it. It's what women did.

Her feet heavy as she plodded home and opened the back door. Sarah sat in the kitchen with tea cups before her, kettle steaming.

'I thought you might need a drop of tea somehow,' she said. Dorcas grimaced at her as she put her hand on Sarah's shoulder, sat heavily and shared the pain of what she had done.

Then Sarah with a twinkle in her eye began to crack a joke and cheer Dorcas from her melancholy as she stayed for a second cup.

'Don't worry girl, I'll try to keep an eye on them when you've gone, put some flowers for you in the graveyard too, and give their headstones a pat. I'll write once you send me an address and I'll tell you all the news. You know me.'

'Thanks, you are a dear. It will be good to get the truth. Mam's not likely to tell me if she's got problems, I'm sure, though what I can do from over there I've no idea.' Dorcas frowned.

Sarah stood slowly. 'Well, I'm off. I better get some cooking done or I'll not be able to help you this evening with those girls. I'll bring the cottage pies in soon after they come home. I know how hungry those lads are nowadays. You'll need every minute to finish packing up this place. I'll be back before their bedtime.'

'Oh, do come in and eat it with us. It will help me to be distracted from all this.' Dorcas hugged her friend. After she left, Dorcas wrapped plates in newspaper gazing out of the window, her mind arguing constantly with George. Everything left would be sold by the landlord to pay her final rent.

By supper time, after the children packed their bags for the journey, Sarah knocked and entered the kitchen carrying two giant steaming pies. She grinned at the children, raising them high. The smaller girls ran to her eagerly.

'Have you laid the table girls?' She smiled down at them, her eyes wide with fun. Soon they sat eating the pie and the small kitchen echoed with excited chatter. Sarah's humour kept them distracted as Dorcas watched her children, wondering where they would be tomorrow. Later washing dishes and clearing plates, Tilda and the boys worked to help Dorcas. 'Right, up the little wooden hill, young lasses!' Sarah followed the four girls as they climbed the stairs to bed.

'Are you telling us a story tonight, Aunty Sarah?' Ethel asked as she turned to smile at their neighbour.

'Ai, it's me tonight, Ethel. Your Mam's got a lot to do.'

'Good,' said May, 'I like your stories.' She scampered up hitching her little nightie as she went. Sarah swallowed hard; she would miss these brief moments, knowing she'd worry about these girls especially, once they had gone tomorrow. How would they adjust to the changes? Dorcas and George would provide for them, take care of their needs but there were so many different problems ahead for this beloved family. For the hundredth time she wished they weren't going, wished George would return and things could be as they were before but she knew women had no alternative. Dorcas must follow George. Even the law supported men's rights over their wives and children. It was the way the world was.

By the time Sarah reached the girls' room, all four snuggled into the double bed, two each end. She sat on the kitchen chair which stood between their bed and Tilda's narrow one. Plumping up their pillows, she told them of a present she had for them.

'It's a book I've kept for some time … and now … ' her eyes widening as she hesitated for effect.

Olive butted in. 'You are going to read it to us!'

'Yes, good guess Olive. I am going to tell you a little about the story too and can you read what it says on the first page?' Olive put her finger on the script, trying to decipher Sarah's handwriting. 'To the four little sisters, with love from Aunty Sarah. Have a lovely read!'

'We've got to go somewhere tomorrow to see our dadda, so we can't hear it all tonight,' said Marjorie frowning.

'Yes, that's why I am giving it to you as a present, so your Mam or Tilda can read it to you in your new home.'

'What every night, Aunty Sarah?' Ethel's eyes shone as she hunched up her shoulders in delight. She so loved stories.

'Well, whenever they can,' Sarah promised. 'It's a lovely story about four little sisters like you and how they have fun growing up.'

'L... little...Women,' announced Olive running her finger over the embossed letters tooled into the leather with a picture of a girl in a long skirt looking at a storage chest in an attic.

'That's the title,' Sarah explained 'Now girls, tuck under those blankets and I'll read you the first bit about Christmas morning.' Their faces were expectant as Sarah started to read. Gradually May's eyes closed lulled by the soft voice, but Ethel and Olive were bright with imagination, while Marjorie sucked her thumb in contentment.

Sarah felt the sadness of her own future without her young neighbours and her friend, and she treasured the moment. Her hand stroked the eiderdown. She gazed at their expectant faces and tried to capture the image. Tomorrow they would be gone.

CHAPTER 23: George, July 1924

At Campbell's camp they worked constantly with no regular days off and no time to walk in the forests which isolated them. The summer heat was dusty during the day and George often felt breathless, his chest cramped and aching. The tall trees on the fringes of the camp sighed in the wind but he had no energy to walk there in the evenings. He sat on the wooden steps in the fresh evening breeze and watched the shadows seeping across the camp. He wore his torn jacket daily to combat the chills he suffered. His cough was worse, but he slept whenever he could. His days rolled into each other, one after another in an endless stream.

The pressure to complete each stage of the work meant they used the threat of fines if the daily targets were not met. Overtime wasn't a paid option, but they were driven to work longer, to complete a section. Again, he thought of his home and family, cursing his brash enthusiasm which led him here. Oh why, oh why had he left them all?

George would not last long at this pace he knew. Younger men managed but he hated it all. He sat on his bunk one night and looked hard at his broken boot, rubbing his fingers over the split seam and frayed leather. He'd repair it with sacking for tomorrow though he knew as soon as it rained, it would leak. He put the boot down, breathed deeply and sighed. His muscles ached, and he had no energy. This felt like the end for him. George stared down at the ridges his feet made in the leather and the tainted water marks of the mud and muck he worked in each day. He realised there was no life here for him.

He'd saved very little when his plans had been so grand. Tears welled up and biting his lip, he swallowed hard. No one must see his distress. Almost a year since he sailed but he had very few pound notes in his body belt. He'd work things out, have some plan as soon as he could think. He knew now he must get home; this land was not for him. He longed for things to seem familiar again, for the food Dorcas always cooked, smelling comforting, for the family's hugs, for her warmth. What would he tell her? George dreaded the thought but even that was preferable to this hell. Maybe she'd understand? He hoped so. He coughed uncontrollably, pains squeezing his chest. He longed for her common-sense approach, some care and comfort, and a long, long sleep. It did not occur to him that she would be on her way to him.

The next day he worked on until the light faded. His tiredness had slowed him, but he was adamant to get the job finished although he felt dizzy. Several times he had to shake himself to concentrate. As he hurried to complete the job before he missed his supper, he accidentally smashed down on his hand with a large lump hammer. The pain shot through him and he yelled grasping his thumb. Others looked across at him and stopped. George crouched in agony bent over the workbench. Everything swirled, and he grabbed at its edge for support. Lifting his hand cautiously he cradled it in his arm against his chest. Steadying himself he looked at his hand. The smashed thumb stuck out at a peculiar angle and the hand was swelling already. He closed his eyes as the pain coursed through his whole body and sweat trickled down his forehead. It was his right hand and he'd not be able to work for several days at least. No work, no pay. He knew the rules. 'I'm alright,' he said putting his other hand up. 'Give me a few minutes.'

'Look laddie, you better be away to your bunk with that. I'll finish this and bring yea the tools.' George silently blessed the small Scot who sorted him out. He staggered back to his bunk, grabbing at hut walls for support, cradling the damaged hand as everything whirled before his eyes. He slumped on his bunk. When the world steadied, he contemplated his future. He guessed his thumb was dislocated and probably broken; his hand distorted. If he reported it he'd be off site by the weekend, yet he knew he could not work with this. The pain made him feel faint as he closed his eyes, his cough echoing in the empty bunkhouse.

Half hour later he had wrapped his hand in some strips of cloth and got himself to the canteen. He felt he must try to eat but, after the first spoonful, he felt sick and vomited in the dust outside. Trying to look up, colours whirled. He returned to his bunk climbing beneath his blanket intending to sleep. He feared for his future. The pain got worse and he spent the whole night protecting the hand which by now was burning hot with needles of pain shooting up his arm. Biting back the moans in his throat lest others complain, he rocked repeatedly back and forth. He slept a little before dawn but could hardly get himself to the canteen for breakfast next morning.

He reported sick for the next two days slipping in and out of sleep. By the third day he mumbled he must get help. The camp doctor told him to get himself to the hospital in the city as he could do nothing on camp for him because his hand was so swollen, and his cough did not help.

'It will likely get worse with th'poison spreading further up your arm if you just lay thar in your bunk,' said the little Scot, whose name he never knew. He helped George that afternoon get to Chuck the carter who'd finished his delivery and agreed to take him back to the city. George lay in the back of the jolting cart, wrapped in his blanket, praying to get to the hospital, slipping in and out of consciousness, struggling with a fever.

George must have slept fitfully for several hours and when he woke he found himself in a cool bed with sounds of others around. At first, he had no idea where he was. Chuck had delivered him to a convent hospital that evening, and George realised a young nurse in a nun's habit was examining his hand. Gently she bathed it and re-wrapped it telling him there was little could be done with the swelling.

'For now, you must rest. You have a fever, are hot. It may be your cough. Drink the water, lots of it, do you understand?' Her French accent was soft, as he clasped her hand with his left one, feeling relieved she was close as he fell asleep. Someone was caring for him at last.

Several days passed, while he sweated with fever from his deep, bronchial cough, and called deliriously in his sleep as the blue vein of poison from his hand spread up his hot, swollen arm. The pain felt like scalding needles. Days and nights passed in a blur when there were moments when he was conscious, when he feared he'd never get home. Sister Cecilia bathed it several times each day and put a tourniquet on his upper arm for a short while to restrict the flow of poison. The doctor tried to reset the thumb but it was distorted and crushed. In his delirium, George watched her, confusing her at times with Dorcas or with Tilda, often calling to them. Over the next few days the fever subsided, and, as he emerged, he thanked her. He lay listening to the echoing sounds of the ward, gradually noticing others around him. Some tossed in the narrow beds, some wandered in and out distractedly. No-one spoke to him and he was glad to be left alone.

'Tell me George, what is "back"?' she whispered in her soft accent as she fed him soup.

'Back?' he queried.

'Yes, you say in the fever every days, "I must get back." What is it you want?'

George smiled. ' Oh, it means I must get home, back to Great Britain.'

'Ah, it is what all peoples who come to foreign country truly want I think.' A tinkling sound came in the ward and she nodded and turned away. She became silent, but George did not understand the rules of her order until he saw her move across the room and bow. Why would such a beautiful young woman dedicate her life to religion and nursing? She seemed so competent and thoughtful. He thought about the women in his life, different, caring. Why, oh why had he left the safety of his home? He watched her as she later fed him more broth. She was so tranquil he noticed. George looked at the spoon. He had no appetite.

Over the next week his high temperature dropped, and he ate again. Terrified of what his stay would cost him with most of his small savings already depleted, he must leave as soon as he could. He got up from the bed and felt how weak his legs had become. Somehow, he must make his way to something cheaper because he could not pay for more nights here, more treatment. George didn't want charity. That was not his way. He would not spend any of his precious savings on transport, he needed all he had for the voyage. Slowly he dressed and said his thanks. He walked away praying for enough strength to get back to Dorcas and home. Sister Cecilia watched him go, only giving him a penetrating gaze. He guessed that was their religious constraints but George smiled back, nodding to her when he reached the corner.

He walked for an hour then rested summoning the strength to continue. He found cheap shared lodgings for one night after a day of tramping towards the docks.

'At least,' he thought, ' I'm a little nearer.' The landlady seemed pleasant; an older widow with several regulars staying in the dingy bedrooms of a tall house. Dressed in a large floral apron, she fed him vegetables with meat pie and thick gravy, giving him a large spoon. He was grateful for a hot meal and she sat talking to him, cutting his food as he ate trying to use his left hand. She looked into his eyes, raising an eyebrow.

'I see lots of men like you. Come here with high hopes. It works out for some though not many, dearie. You'd best cut your losses, git yourself home to your good woman. Make it up wiv her.' She sliced some potato. 'You ain't made for this life, I can tell, wandering about going from one job to another. It ain't easy for strangers here.' She brushed the tablecloth, gathering crumbs in her open palm. George nodded. She went on. 'The government say they want men to come but there's nothing here if you don't strike lucky. The locals ain't going to give you a chance in hell. They don't want you taking their jobs. No, I reckon you should turn tail and nip back to where you come from sharpish.' She helped him wipe his plate with bread. 'I came out here years ago with my man and we found it hard I can tell you. When I lost him I never got around to going back.'

'Why not?' George looked up at her.

'Too ashamed I suppose. I couldn't face admitting to my folks it had been a mistake somehow. It's too late now, there's none of my lot left back in London. So, I gets on wiv it here as best as I can. I daren't think too much about the future.' George looked at her lined face and tried to imagine the young girl who had come with such hope to this new land. He was doing the right thing, he was certain.

'Let me have that blanket, I'll put it out on the line in the fresh air. Might make it smell better, though really it needs a good wash,' she said. George smiled for the first time in ages, remembering his ma who would have said exactly that.

'Thanks, Mrs Patterson.'

Later she re-wrapped his hand in clean strips of rag tutting at the awkward shaped thumb. 'They should have set your hand for you at the place you worked. Fancy sending a man away like that. Got no humanity, let alone Christian charity, they ain't!'

Before he left in the morning, she tucked a pie wrapped in cloth into his bag.

'This'll help today dearie,' she said winking at him. 'Keep your hand in that sling as long as you can, my lad.' George thanked her and stepped out into the street remembering her instructions about the quickest way to the docks. She warned him it would take a day. He walked across the broad street, feeling so weak. He carried his tools in his left hand hoisting his few possessions and his blanket over his left shoulder, his right hand in a make-shift sling she had made across his chest. Leaving the little town, he strode out as best as he could along the pathway which led to another town, rough wooden buildings in between more established homes. People were coming to Canada full of hope, governments and charities even sending children here alone to work, but the tramps on the street spoke of the problems, showed their hunger. After several miles George saw a fountain in the street by a stone horse trough. He drank deeply but resisted eating the pie. He would need it later he knew. He tramped on, one foot in front of the other, willing himself not to stop till he came to the next town. By late afternoon, feeling dazed, he walked along the busy street and past several stores. Some large gates led into a tiny park. He could sit there a while, walking through looking at the cool trees budding into leaf and with several log swings for children. The quietness was a relief from the noisy streets, only punctuated by birdsong. George longed to sleep.

He found a park bench where he sat, unwrapped the pie and ate it hastily gathering every crumb from the cloth and swallowing them, as he watched the sun disappear behind the threatening evening clouds. Several people spoke to him. He saw a small child with her mother skip past and thought of little May, his darling girl. She would be a whole year older. Tears of sadness and a little self-pity clouded his eyes. What must his children think of him? What would they say if they could see him now? George vowed they would never know the truth of this nightmare. He'd never tell. Never.

He dozed for a while then waking, he wrapped the blanket around his body to try to keep warm, terrified he'd not wake in the morning. He slept a little, dreaming of Kate and woke feeling guilty. Long after the midnight chimes of a church echoed across the park, an old man hobbled up to sit on the bench. Smiling at George showing a toothless grin, he offered him a swig of his bottle and gratefully, George took a mouthful. The fire burnt his throat and made him cough again, but it warmed him. He must get home, back to Britain where he knew Dorcas would help him. Here on this bench he could easily slip into sleep, becoming like the old man beside him, smelling of alcohol and neglect. No, he would not become just another wanderer lost in a land where he knew no one, had no family, drinking himself to oblivion.

Clenching his teeth against the cold, he decided again that in the morning somehow he must try to get himself to the docks and on a ship.

The first glimmer of light came, throwing its early beams across the sky and making silhouette weird shapes of the dark landscape around the park. Noisy birds twittered and flew about. George lifted his head, shook the dew from the damp blanket, pulled it around him and started to walk again. He drank from the street fountains and tried to ignore his hunger. He had sold his other clothes and several tools at a pawn shop, parting with them realistically at last. What good would they be to him if he couldn't get home, get better and find work? He must make enough money for his passage back.

He saw the large entrance to the docks, all bustle in the early light. Ships' hooters, dockers shouting and the noise of swinging crates banging on decks with gulls screaming, told him he'd arrived. But first he must eat. He crossed the street and bought bread from a bakery, tearing at the crust with his teeth. Washing it down with more water and brushing crumbs from his beard, he went through the big gates looking at several smaller ships.

By mid-morning he had scraped his coins together and paid the captain of a tramp ship steamer to have a spare crewman's working berth, only employing him if there was an urgent need. The ship was scheduled to deliver coal to Ireland, so George knew he must then work his way home from Belfast. In the time it took to cross the ocean he prayed he would be much fitter if he could rest.

Before he left Canada, he queued in a post office once again and spent two of his last coins on a telegram to his home and Dorcas.

'*Am coming home.* STOP *Stay there.* STOP *Love George.* STOP'

George did not know she was already in London, near Tilbury Docks with the children, waiting to hear from him.

CHAPTER 24: Dorcas, Late July 1924

As the family arrived at the enormous London station called Paddington, after what seemed an endless journey, they stared about them, amazed as they had never seen anywhere so large and tall. The vast glass dome above them and the echoing sounds confused them. The sharp smell of coal and hot metal tickled their noses as steam from the idling engines screamed out in bursts. People hurried everywhere, all sure of their way. Dorcas watched each errant child, a constant frown on her face.

'Tilda, hold May's hand,' and ' Roger, Peter, have you got those cases?' and 'You girls stay together and do not lose your bags!' With her rising panic at being in London, completely lost in the crowds, she naturally gathered her brood around her. 'Let's wait till these people have gone, children. They are in such a hurry, then we can go sensibly to the barrier,' she ordered. She sat on a seat on the platform breathing deeply to regain her sense of control. She was lost in this big station so however would she find her way around this enormous city? The older children, excited by the thought of London, glanced at each other surprised at their mother's confusion. For them it was exciting and so new.

Tilda spoke softly. 'Come on girls, hold hands and pick up your bags. Mam, we can walk slowly to the barrier.

We'll stay together we promise.' She stretched out her hand understanding her mother's vulnerability as Dorcas stood looking bemused. The little children were silent, overwhelmed, their eyes darting about the huge station, taking in the steam, the shouts, whistles and sharp smells. Most of all they looked at the giant engine resting, one of several steaming noisily, which had brought them from their home to this crowded station. The boys were amazed, thrilled by the mechanics, the efficiency and the bustle, watching the men pulling levers, releasing hot water and steam.

The little girls felt intimidated, insignificant, taken from their familiar world and thrown into this gigantic place. Each clutching the others' hands, backing away from the noisy engines. Tilda noticed the bright fashions of the younger women hurrying to the barrier, feeling dowdy herself. Everyone else seemed to be sure where they were going, pushing through with determined faces.

Ethel frowned and bit her lip as she clung to Olive's hand. 'Is this Canada, Olive?' she whispered.

Her sister laughed. 'No, it's London, silly goose!'

The boys carried cases in both hands while the girls hauled bags and satchels as they banged against their legs, bumping into each other giggling nervously. The vast Victorian vaulted glass roof which allowed in the opaque light, made everything sound different from anything they had ever heard, echoing back at them. May put her hands over her ears at a sudden hiss of steam, her large eyes darting about. Dorcas walked to the end of the platform, tickets in hand, frowning. She asked at the barrier about trams, and they directed her to an exit where she found only hackney cabs and motor taxis waiting. Terrified of the imagined cost, she took the children further along the pavement and asked at a tram queue for directions, pointing to the address on the reply to Dorcas' letter requesting accommodation for a couple of weeks.

'You want to go down there, turn right and you's almost there. Not sure which side of the road but I knows 'cause my daughter lives round here, dearie. It ain't too far,' a woman said glancing from the letter to the children. They picked up their bags and started to walk. People in the queue watched speculating about their mission.

'Up from the country I reckon.' said an elderly man.

'Good luck to 'em I say.'

'Ain't no future here for the likes of them, I'd bet.' An old woman shook her head. Dorcas didn't hear her. She worried money would be tight, but she planned they'd only be here for about a week before they sailed. She hoped George had her latest letter to say they had left, and could he please wire her the money for the tickets. They couldn't wait any longer. Walking became slower as their bustling family neared the house where they would stay. May was moaning, saying her legs hurt. Roger told her to stop complaining and to hurry along. Olive took her hand and they both grinned back at him. 'Bossy thing!'

When they found the street, it seemed strange, tall houses very different from back home. As they opened the garden gate and huddled by the door, Dorcas smiled around encouraging them all, ringing the bell. With her raised eyebrow she told them to look pleasant when the door opened. A large woman in a green overall greeted them.

'You'll be the Haddon family, I guess. Come in,' she said and they trooped into the narrow hall.

'Please take off your boots children.' Both the women spoke at the same time. A row of boots and some coats on pegs showed others lived there too. Were they visitors or family, Dorcas wondered? The children bustled with boots and May sat heavily on the hall floor hoping for help. Olive knelt and undoing her sister's fiddly laces, pulling them off.

'Come through and I'll show you to your rooms.' They climbed two flights of stairs to the attic rooms, their bags hindering them as they went. There were three bedrooms and another larger room presumably for a living room. No kitchen or bathroom of their own, Dorcas had not expected that. This was hopefully a short stay although she'd not heard from George for some time. Tomorrow she must find the shipping office to look at sailings, costs and any regulations. There had been no way she could check any earlier.

The woman introduced herself as Mrs. Gage. 'Afternoon tea will be in half an hour in the dining room and dinner is at half past six prompt. The bathroom's on the floor below but you share it with my three lodgers so please respect it. There are cleaning materials there so please leave the bath as you find it. There's a gas ring on the landing if you wish to make a drink. I've left a small kettle there too.' She nodded at Dorcas without even a smile, then she left them to settle in.

Dorcas tried hard not to smile when she saw Roger's smirk and Peter hiding his grin behind his hand. Experience told her, the family would soon be imitating the landlady. They would conspire in the way families do when in strange situations, but she mustn't encourage them. She did not want them to seem rude. Once again Dorcas hoped it would not be for long. Somehow, she felt she could tackle this. A new feeling of confidence in her own ability boosted her. She could do it.

Daily, Dorcas visited the post office to discover if there was a letter waiting for her. In her last letter to George, she had said she would visit the main post office in Paddington waiting for his reply, so he should send travel details there for her to collect. The next few days dragged by with no word from him. She began to wonder if he had received her last letter, if he had any idea they were waiting in London. He'd told her to come and she'd given up the house and shop and could not stay around. It had nearly been a year. Surely, he should have sent something by now. Dorcas' impatience was starting to show. Her children saw it.

Living with Mrs Gage's rules would not have been difficult for Dorcas alone in the cramped conditions but, with her seven children, it was torture for them all. None of them were used to being confined. All of them had daily played in the street back home, and the attic rooms were unbearably hot and airless. She took them out each morning but as she was unfamiliar with London streets, they often trooped back tired, dusty and frustrated by mid-afternoon. Then they would lie on their beds and read, quarrel or draw. May dressed and undressed her doll and sometimes the girls had dolls' tea parties, but Dorcas found herself nagging their every move. The boys especially felt confined, longing to explore, to escape but even moving about on the boards was noisy.

Mrs Gage's meals were adequate, but the smaller children did not always like her cooking. Dorcas insisted they were polite and eat most of it, and the hungry boys finished off their left-overs. Daily Dorcas found the tension rising. May especially was a challenge, though her mother realised how the little girl found everything new and different. She hoped it wouldn't be much longer.

Before they could sail, they must be vaccinated so Dorcas found a clinic where she could buy their vaccinations. Some of the precious savings were eaten up by the cost. The younger girls cried at the four injections they each had punched into the top of their arms. Dorcas was surprised at the scars they left, their delicate skin red and angry. They had to visit the photographer for their passports and wait until they were issued two days later.

Dorcas made them manage on the minimum of clothing to save on the washing which she did in the small bathroom sink, getting Mrs. Gage's permission to use the washing line in the yard. Every morning they anticipated news of their exciting journey. Every evening they climbed into bed a little more deflated. Dorcas lay in bed quietly panicking. It had been a week already.

The postmaster back in their village remembered Dorcas had left for London, so he sent Joseph on his bicycle to her mother. 'There has been a telegram for Mrs Haddon received at this office. Can you please send me a forwarding address for her?' Tutting loudly Dorcas's mother slowly copied the London post office address which was the contact for her daughter before she left for Canada and gave it to the boy. She wondered what it was about. Were they still there? Swiftly Joseph pedalled away.

When Dorcas collected George's redirected telegram after several days she was shocked how damaged the envelope was. 'Can you sign for it please?' the clerk said. Putting it in her pocket, she hurried out of the post office and crossed the busy street to the tram terminus. Here she found an empty seat and tore open the telegram intending to share it later with the children, who were with Tilda in the park. She realised the telegram had been delivered to her old home and redirected via her mother by the post master. Written weeks before it meant George had no idea they were in London. The telegram was brief and final.

'*Am coming home.* STOP *Stay there.* STOP *Love George.* STOP'

Dorcas stared in disbelief. How could he do this? No, surely not. Was his dream over? Dropping it in her lap she closed her eyes against the disappointment. 'Oh no!' she whispered, 'Oh George!' Her heart fell, and a great weight sank in her stomach. What had she done? All these months, she had trusted him. Dorcas had done as he said and it was all a mistake, a terrible mistake. Everything had gone. Their whole life had been changed and all her efforts of the last year were for nothing. No Canada, no home, no work and no money. What would they do? How would they live? Where could they live? Sharp anger made her bite her lip.

Whatever had happened to George? The telegram told her nothing. The tone, the lack of his usual bounce frightened Dorcas. The future gaped at her, its open mouth about to swallow their hopes. Tears trickled through her fingers as she sat trying to contain herself. People bustled about her and trams clicked in and out of the space, but she saw nothing. The frustrations of the past year clustered about her heart and anger began to surface, again. Cursing it in silence, her jaw tightened, and she grew resentful. Her children must not see her like this.

Never again, never would she allow him to tell her what to do. Since the day they first met he had made the decisions as was the custom. The world was changing she told herself. She would decide what happened in future. She would choose for herself and the children. If he didn't consider her opinion, she'd not help him. She sat for a long time, her anger simmering, cursing her folly, her helplessness. She wished for a comforter, someone to reassure her, to help with this burden. She told herself she must not think of Adam, there was no future there either.

She alone must decide what to do. She realised she did not want to return to the village. She could not face their silent smiles and recriminations behind her back. Even her mam would say, 'I told you so!' No, she would fight it all. She had enough to deal with and she preferred to start again where no one knew her or their story. For her children's sake she decided she must make this a new beginning. Help them go forward and not show George's failure. She determined to show them a united family, because the children depended on her and maybe George would too. She could not collapse. Wiping her eyes and tucking her hair beneath her hat, she stood, her back straightening.

As she walked, she planned. First things first. She could not afford to spend any more on their lodgings. What should she do? Perhaps she could rent somewhere so she could cook for them, give the children a feeling of family with a new home and get them into schools for September. She thought about the money she had left in her purse, money she had saved to help with essentials they would need in their new home. Dorcas felt frustrated and resentful of all her things she had sold or given away. She would need them again, every cup, every blanket, every chair. A tear came at the thought of all she had lost, precious items she had parted with, for this mad scheme of his. She planned to rebuild their life together, re-establish some sort of sense in their life before George returned.

Gripping her teeth, she decided. After this she would give him little option, she would tell him how things were, she would say how they would be in the future. His message had sounded pathetic, deflated. Stopping once more in the street Dorcas read it again before stuffing it back in her pocket. What could she tell the children?

She stood at the kerbside hoping to sort this mess herself without him. Buttoning her coat and pulling on her cotton gloves she drew herself upright as she walked towards the park. She'd managed for a year without him, while he gallivanted off. She could do this.

Her children's laughter as they played, and their greeting made her try to smile though Tilda and Roger recognised the reddened eyes and glanced at each other, but said nothing. Much later they helped to get the girls to bed and then came into their living room with Peter and shut the door. 'Mam, come on, what's it about?' Tilda asked.

'Yes, what's gone wrong?' Roger demanded looking fiercely at her. 'Has he gone off for good?'

Peter went to her side and put his hand on her arm. 'Is it Dad? Is he ill or something?' he whispered. 'He's not dead, is he?' His eyes searched her face.

'Oh no, it's not that, well not exactly.' Dorcas took a deep breath and then shared the telegram and told them the truth fighting her tears. 'I don't know what's happened dears, I just don't understand.'

'So, Mam, what are we going to do?' Roger asked, lips taut, his teeth clenched as his young face flushed with anger. 'When's he coming back?'

'Well first we are going to find somewhere to rent. It must be cheap of course. Then I'm sorry but you two must get some work to help. Peter, you can still go to school like the girls and once we get sorted, I'll try to get some work in the day time too. That should help with the rent and the housekeeping.'

'Yes, but is he really coming back?'

'Of course, but it will take a couple of weeks at least, so we need to make a plan.' Dorcas tackled the landlady the next morning.

'Mrs. Gage. I've received a telegram from Mr. Haddon from Canada. He's had a slight accident it seems, so there's some delay to our departure. We won't be going for a couple of months at least. As we only booked with you till the end of the week, I will make other arrangements. I wondered if you have any suggestions of houses I could rent?'

'Oh dear, such a disappointment for you all. Well I'm sorry, I'm fully booked from next week, so I can't help you here, but I know someone who rents out terraced houses only a short way away. They are small, quite cheap. They do have gardens where the children could let off a bit of steam. It would be better if they had a bit of space. They are a lively bunch, aren't they?' she simpered. 'I have no idea what he charges but I'll find you his address.' Looking in her book she copied details for Dorcas who smiled gratefully.

Within a couple of days, Dorcas had looked at several houses that Mrs Gage had suggested, within walking distance and only an auto-bus ride from Tilbury docks. They were each very similar and finally she chose one at the end of a terrace. Roger insisted he come with her to look at it.

As Dorcas walked in the front door the smell of new paint and recent cleaning hit her. The place had been empty for several weeks she guessed. A narrow passageway opened into a main room with a window in the front. Sun flooded through onto the bare boards making the room light. A door led to a square kitchen with a gas stove and a tiny window. She went down a step to a small scullery with a sink and a stone floor and walked out to a yard and a privy. A staircase in the corner of the kitchen went to three bedrooms. Barely enough for her family, but they'd manage. She tried to visualise them crammed in together and shook her head. Roger said nothing, realising the cosy home they had left, always aware his mam would do her best.

'This'll do Mam, we'll cope,' he grinned reassuringly, and she ruffled his hair.

They walked back to the agent's office. This was when the landlord asked for a man's signature. 'Have you not got a man to sign this?' George was not here, and Dorcas knew no one in London. She argued with the landlord, but he was adamant.

'No, I have not unfortunately!' A quick vision of her dear brother flashed before Dorcas, and she felt angry. 'I am the one who wants to rent this house with my children. Do you want my money or not?' He saw her nostrils flaring.

'How do I know you won't flit without paying at the end of the week? I can hardly take a woman with children to court if you do. I'm sorry, I must have a man's signature on the agreement.' He sat back folding his arms looking her up and down.

Roger piped up. 'I'll sign Mam. I'll have a job and you can take my word we'll pay the rent.' He picked up the pen. The landlord looked hard at him, summing up the young man. Not tall though he was old enough and strong enough to do a day's work.

'Are you sure lad? If your mother defaults it could mean prison for you, not that it would pay me any rent.' Recognising the situation, he passed the contract across the desk. 'Alright, sign here son.'

Dorcas put her arm about Roger's broad shoulders. He was only a little taller than her, but she was as proud of him as if he were ten feet tall!

Now she had to explain to the younger girls. All those encouraging talks they'd had about Canada, about a new home, a new school and new friends. She'd tell them gently that some of it would be true, but here in London, not in Canada. She hoped it would be so. Dorcas sat them down with Tilda for support. 'You see girls, the good news is your Dadda is coming back to London so we're going to make a new home here. You can help me make it nice for when he comes. Would you like to do that?'

'I'll help,' said Marjorie.

'Me too,' chirped Ethel and May in unison grinning at their mother though Olive was silent.

'Will you help Tilda with things too, Olive?' Dorcas turned to her silent daughter as Olive looked at her mother discerningly then nodded slowly.

'Is Dadda alright? What really happened, Mam? Aren't we going to Canada?'

'Well Olive you see, Dadda has not been well and he wanted to come back to see us all, so we're going to wait for him here. Well, not here but in a new house we've found. I'll take you to see it tomorrow. It's empty so we will need to find some beds and chairs and things.'

'Has he had diphtheria like Peter?' Ethel asked.

'Oh no dears. No and he's a lot better now.' Dorcas sent up a silent prayer.

'Can I help you look for new things, Mam?' Olive looked tentatively. Smiling Tilda put her hand on Olive's.

Dorcas nodded. 'Yes dear, but it will be in a few days. We may sort of… camp there to begin with. It'll be fun, won't it?' Olive looked directly at her mother and the understanding they shared made Olive part of the older group, no longer one of the 'little girls.'

'I'll help you Mam,' she whispered putting her hand through her mother's arm.

Things were not as easy as Dorcas had suggested. At the end of the week, they moved into a terraced house. At first Dorcas got frustrated with the old gas stove, which was an innovation for her. Their new house echoed with the tramp of their boots as they ran about exploring, which excited the smaller children and intrigued the older three. Dorcas stood staring out of the window at the busy street cluttered with trams and a mixture of carriages. She dreaded the starting again, the scrimping and saving to get basics. She had no idea where the shops were, the grocer or the butcher. She must explore but she had several young bodies and minds alongside her who would soon help. It was so new to them. She was anxious, but the children were impatient to discover more. They encouraged her as they shared the adventure.

The rooms were empty, and they must eat their first meal, picnic style sitting on the stairs. For one night at least, they must sleep on the floor. Dorcas had managed to find some clean smelling blankets and some cups, spoons and plates. Tomorrow she must see what she could find to improve their comfort but until they had some earnings she must keep enough for next week's rent and for food. She lifted her head and decided to worry about that tomorrow. For now, she must help the children to feel positive.

Next morning as Dorcas walked into the town she looked around. A large church dominated the skyline and she watched several women walk up the gravel path with bunches of flowers. An idea came to her. 'They're too chatty for a funeral,' she murmured. 'Must be flower arranging day.' She went through the gate feeling the sharp stones of the path through her thin soles.

Dorcas wasn't sure about God. She had attended chapel in her village since she was a child, but her mind had lots of questions. 'It's not the time to have doubts. They are likely to know the answers to my questions as much as anyone.' She approached a tall neatly-dressed woman with a cautious smile.

'I wonder if you can help me, please? We are new to this area and my friend has moved into an empty house and she has no furniture and several children. Can you suggest anywhere she might go to get some second-hand items?' she fibbed, not wanting to admit her situation. Dorcas was glad she had a tidy coat and brushed shoes.

'Well,' breathed the woman with a discerning look, ''The Salvation Army has a place in the High Street, a sort of shop with clean used items and of course there's the church poor fund if you apply to the Bishop.' Dorcas blushed and thanked her, turning away, guessing she had understood the truth. Before she reached the gate, a voice called her. Another woman, cosier looking, smiled at her and directed her to a back-street pawnbroker who she said was fair and what she called “a good second-hand shop.”

'And the local Rag and Bone man, Eddie, is a decent chap who'll carry heavy stuff on his cart for a bob or two. He'll not cheat you.'

Dorcas looked gratefully at her and was about to say, 'It's not for me of course,' in her defence, before she noticed the woman's kind eyes looking at her with understanding.

'God bless you my dear,' the woman muttered, and Dorcas touched her arm in thanks, tears swelling in her eyes as she looked away.

By the afternoon Dorcas had found the various places and chosen a few tidy though well-used pieces of furniture which she could afford with the money she had kept for their journey. Beds, a large table, several odd chairs, and some cooking utensils were being carried to their new home by Eddie. The children were excited and helped in making things feel homely. 'Thank God I have you all,' Dorcas hugged them. 'Alone,' she whispered to herself, 'this surely would be disaster. I'd not have stayed with him, not after all this. But the children will make this work for me, and perhaps for him. We'll see.' She had to admit the children's enthusiasm carried a wisp of adventure into the necessity of everything that was happening. She remembered their own furniture which she had sold only weeks ago. Dorcas blinked in disbelief at all that had happened but smiled as she felt a surge of love for these children, her own family with recognisable traits and bubbling enthusiasms. Together they would make it.

A letter for Dorcas from her mam explained how George's telegram had been delayed and she hoped everything was alright. Dorcas put off writing back not knowing how to deal with her mother's reaction. She told herself she'd tackle Mam when she had the whole story and could tell her more.

The following day she registered Peter and the girls at a local elementary school, a scruffy place which smelt of plasticine and disinfectant. At the council offices Dorcas asked if there was supply work for teaching Music or English or Domestic Science, taking off her wedding ring and using her maiden name because of the rule married women were not employed in schools. Begrudgingly she was promised a few hours per week when the term started.

Tilda queued outside shops advertising for junior staff throughout the week. She was so delighted when she found a job in a haberdashery store, Dorcas did not comment on the paltry wages. The girl had done her best. Roger had quickly got work in a factory which made motor components, long hours but reasonable pay for such a young lad. At least there seemed a way forward she thought.

Dorcas scanned the lists for any ships coming in from Canada, but none seemed scheduled to arrive. She waited for word from George. No letter came, though she guessed he'd be back soon.

Now Dorcas had another secret worry, one she could share with no-one. What kind of demon was sitting on her shoulder she fretted? What more could go wrong? This was something she must keep secret for a lifetime or it would split this family she knew. George must come home in the next couple of weeks for her necessary plan to work. Now she needed him in more ways than one, she told herself.

CHAPTER 25: George, August 1924

George slept for much of the journey across the ocean, his body demanding rest for him to heal. He spoke to anyone, his beard growing bushy and hair greasy. The food was basic but filling. When he arrived at last in Ireland, he had very little to carry down the gangplank. He had sold some tools and most of his clothes. His damp blanket felt stiff and smelled foul.

'Not far now,' he thought, 'Not far.' He walked around and sat on dock walls looking for any small ship scheduled to sail for Tilbury. He prayed he could get a berth in steerage for the little money he had. Once he got to London he'd try to sell his few remaining tools and hitch a ride home. It would be alright once he was back in London when he would no longer be a foreigner.

Before George went into the ship's office he took off his sling and stuffed his damaged hand in his jacket pocket. To get a free passage he'd sign on for some work on the short voyage. He must not look as if he could not work. The clerk was confused with the paperwork and hardly glanced at him, so he found himself walking onto a small ship with dark stacks and the grating chug of an old engine below.

'How long will it take till we dock in Tilbury?' George asked.

'Well if the weather's decent it will take a couple of days, but you can never tell,' the first mate told him. 'Meeting someone then?' he asked with a raised eyebrow.

'No, no one.' George shook his head. During the night, as he'd guessed, there were endless children grizzling and adults fighting. It was so cramped down below, the air becoming thick and foul.

'Only a couple of days more,' he thought. 'Please let it be quick!' He dared not think about home, about his family, about Dorcas, for the tears choked him, and in the cramped space there was no privacy, no time for sorrow. He curled his long legs up on a narrow bunk turning his face to the wall. Above him a man, who smelt heavily of drink, snored and muttered. George closed his eyes trying to ignore his hunger. He had his remaining possessions in a kitbag with its strap wound around his good wrist, as he slept fitfully tossed by the buffeting of the sea.

Early next morning a crewman found him in the washrooms. 'Are you George Haddon? You signed up for work?'

'Yes, yes I did.' George glanced up trying to look eager.

'Well, one of our usual stokers has reported sick so if you think you can keep up, there's a day's work for you down in the engines. Here's your pass so get yourself down there and report to Bill.' The crewman eyed him warily while George followed him out. He needed to earn enough to get back home to his village and to feed himself for the next day or so. The stoker pointed the way down into the bowels of the ship where the heat and noise hit him as he clambered down the steps. George peered around in the half light. His arm throbbed although he'd never tell. He prayed he could cope with the work, the shovelling, the heavy lifting and the scorching heat.

He lifted the giant shovel. It weighed a ton before he scooped anthracite and coke on it and heaved it up to the furnace mouth. Gritting his teeth, he repeated it time after time. No wonder the man he'd replaced had fallen ill. How could they cope with this every day? George saw the others glance in his direction, sure their watching was a test. How long before they would accept him, before they would let him work, without their constant watching. The pain in his arm faded in the general screaming of his muscles. Lord, how did they do a four-hour shift of this?

When the furnace was full he slammed the door fastening it and reducing the blast of heat which already had made his skin burn and feel scorched dry. George looked at his hands with redness on his palms and fingertips as the gloves he'd been given rubbed with the sweat and pressure of the shovel handle. His damaged thumb was awkward and numb. His palms would need to toughen up if he was to continue. The blisters soon rose, painful and unforgiving. He tried not to wince.

The foreman signalled, and he opened the furnace once more. The hungry glow needed feeding again until it was white hot and roaring. George bent his aching back to the task. His head spun, but clenching his teeth, he knew he must continue, to at least finish the shift. He straddled his legs to steady himself as the ship swayed. He needed this extra money. He could not arrive back with nothing in his pockets. He'd need a bed and enough to get sorted to get home. His thumb was completely numb and he did his best to ignore the pain from his arm. The sweat poured down into his eyes and, blinking it away, he understood why the men wore a kerchief about their brow. Shovelful after shovelful, the time warped as George watched the shimmer of the white-hot oven.

The hours dragged and when the relief stoker arrived George's legs were shaking, and his chest hurt. He was frightened he would drop where he stood. His thigh muscles quivered like jelly as he climbed the companionway and clawed his way to the ship's rail. He spluttered at the sharp rush of cold air in his lungs and hung desperately on to an upright, shivering from the temperature change. This was certainly hell. In all his life he had never felt so weak. With each shovelful the time had seemed to wobble as he blinked at the mirage of the jagged glow behind the iron door of the oven.

Slowly he held to the rails as he made his way to the canteen for food and several mugs of water, before sprawling on his bunk.

Four hours later his next shift began, and George closed his eyes as he made his way back down. Only sheer determination, the life and death struggle of it and the thought of home drove him on. He thought of his sons, his daughters and finally his wife. He shovelled for them he told himself, yet the truth was he yearned for home. At the end of the shift he staggered away going to the rail before vomiting into the wind. He could not see how he would manage tomorrow. Only after his stomach settled did he make his way down to the washroom to drink several mugs of cold water and wash his face before returning to his bunk collapsing into sleep despite the noise and bustle around him.

As the next day dawned George scrabbled into his trousers, grabbing some bread from his bag and swallowing two tankards of cold water from the bucket. If he could do one more day the ship would arrive by evening and he would be back in England. He'd have a few pounds in his pocket, not arriving back penniless. He pushed aside the thought of what he would find, how the next months would be. There was a relief in the thought of home whatever it might bring. The past year had become a nightmare, a whirlwind of harsh doubt, heartbreak and pain. Anything would be better than that.

'Get yer arse in line mate. The fire don't wait for yer to arrive, yer know!' The stoker's voice echoed in the cramped space. George picked up his shovel, tightening his jaw and opened the furnace door, stepping back from the blast of heat. The time seemed even longer as only his determination lifted the giant shovel. Just the thought of home, of Dorcas and his children fired his shaking muscles to carry on. In his mind he said their names as he tossed each shovelful on to the fire. He had done this for them. He must get home. He knew he was not the same man who had so cheerfully left, twelve months before.

At the end of this shift George went to eat, finding a quiet corner in the canteen and ordering stew. He ate it quickly wishing for more but drinking water thirstily before he returned to the hell below. Could he manage one last shift? His arm throbbed constantly, and he worried this was a sign of more trouble there.

'Please,' he prayed, 'just let me get home.' He dragged himself down the steep steps and took up the shovel, telling himself they were nearly there. His blisters stung, his muscles screamed and his back was knotting with pain. Working in a vest, he glanced at the swollen arm, knowing he'd have trouble ahead. Every shovelful was a trial. His cough echoed through the space, while he grabbed water from a bucket when he could. After what seemed like a lifetime, men came to the top of the steps, replacing them all. He put down the shovel, every limb shaking, glancing across at the silent man who replaced him. They shared a grimace.

Back at his bunk he slept hoping someone would wake him when they docked later that evening.

He woke to the sound of sirens and the hullabaloo of arrivals. He guessed there were other ships arriving too. Gathering his bag and his few remaining tools, with the unopened pay packet, George followed the excited families and several single men who were making their way to the gangplank. His legs were weary. With his kitbag over his good shoulder he held the rail as he carefully went down the wet ramp. His aching arm was swollen tight inside his sleeve. Everyone else seemed elated to have arrived but his knees went weak when he finally was on the dockside. He leant his back against a wall for several minutes.

A large grand liner from Canada was also docking along the way and the dockside was crowded with arrivals. He knew he must hurry, or he'd get held up with the crowds. George felt hungry and fingered a few coins in his pocket. Perhaps he could buy a pie then, if he could find a station, he'd get a train and arrive at their town by midnight perhaps. He hoped to sleep somewhere sheltered and then walk to the village and maybe he'd be back home by the following morning. His head swum, and he stood still amongst the jostling crowds, regaining his balance.

Everyone was being greeted by families or friends it seemed. A lump came into his throat. Turning to hide his confusion he put his hand onto the wall to steady himself, his forehead against the bricks, eyes closed. Sadness and relief flooded through him. George was back. The voices were English, and he was nearly home. He breathed deeply. Almost there, he thought swallowing hard, almost safe.

George threaded his way between the bodies with their baggage, rain dripping off his hair and down inside his collar. All around there was confusion. People standing looking up, others weaving through the crowds, officials trying to make headway with porters pushing loaded barrows. He looked towards the gates wondering which way he should go. He tried to remember from the first time he'd been there with Bert and Jim. No, he'd not think of it. He was no longer that man. This was so confusing with the noise and the gusts of rain which blew along the churning water. The drops got heavier. That meant he'd be soaked before he got to the station and wet all the way home. He pulled his jacket tighter. 'Bloody hell!' he whispered, shaking his head, raindrops scattering from his hair.

As he reached the gates he shifted the kitbag to the sore shoulder showing his papers and passport to the official who stamped them quickly and gestured for him to move on. He hurried into the road, and heard his name called. Worried, he turned back to the official with a frown, but realised it wasn't him who had called.

A small figure was scurrying across the road and caught his eye. Who was it? He stared. No. It couldn't be. He was dreaming. It was. It was … Dorcas. Dorcas was here. He stood blinking, his mind tumbling, amazed as she bustled towards him, dark umbrella battling with the wind. 'George, George, I'm over here.' He couldn't believe she would be there, obviously waiting for him. His Dorcas. Why was she not back at home with the children? Had she come all that way to meet him? How did she know? As he rushed towards her she laughed then burst into tears. He hugged her desperately, his arms enclosing her in his tight grip, she, ignoring the battered umbrella, and he, his screaming muscles. Minutes passed. He felt his fear drop away. He was home. He brushed his lips across her hair in a kiss of utter relief.

' Oh George, George how could you do it?' Sobs came from her, and she put her face against his jacket, surprised by some familiar smell of him. Looking up, she recognised his need for her and sighed.

'You don't know how glad I am to see you,' George murmured, closing his eyes in relief, his chin on the top of her hair. 'I never thought you'd be here. How did you find out?' He kissed her cheek and she hugged him, as guiltily, he remembered a different scent, another's hug. 'Come on let's find somewhere out of this rain,' he said.

''There's an auto-bus which goes past here, and it'll take us to the place we're renting. I'd done what you said and moved here before I heard you were coming back. I didn't know.' They came out onto the busy pavement glistening with rain. 'Come on, it's not far and it's warm and there should be a nice cup of tea and something to eat, if the girls have done as I said,' Dorcas took his arm and guided him up the road. ''This is the stop. We'll not talk yet. We've a lot to discuss when we get home, and I can see you're exhausted.' As they sat on the bus Dorcas smoothed her hand across his wet hair looking closely at George and frowned. Her George had aged.

He closed his eyes in confusion, his mind racing. Please God, she must never guess about the gambling, or Kate or that Spaniard. All must be buried, never hinted at, never ever remembered. Would she notice? Was he different? Could she see anything in his eyes?

Glancing at his reflection in the dark windows of the auto-bus, Dorcas saw he was thinner, quite worn out. Shocked, she guessed there would be things he'd never confide to her, that she would never hear. She looked at his face, lined and sagging. George had lost weight, was almost scrawny but still her George. She guessed he had gone through a great deal as she had. He'd not be alone in that she knew, thinking of Peter and remembering Adam. It had been a long year for her, for both of them she realised. Pursing her lips, Dorcas decided she could not tell him about it, though the children would chatter a lot.

She took his hand and felt him flinch. Nothing was how she had imagined. She looked down and saw his blisters. Coal-dust hardened skin and raw patches showed her more than she could have guessed. What had he been doing? He looked as if he had to work his passage. Had he come on the big liner she'd seen?

His thumb stood bent at a funny angle. His threadbare jacket, once worn with such pride confirmed her fears, obviously no money. What had he been through? Would he ever say? Overcome with unexpected sadness Dorcas raised his hand to her cheek and his face crumpled. He scuffed away his tears.

'Don't George, don't. You're back now, that's over and we'll look after you.' Why was she so moved when she had intended to tell him of her own battles; to make him guilty and contrite; to show him all they had lost. Somehow in those few moments her anger with him had slipped away, dissolved. Only pity flooded in. Watching him she realised he was like one of her children, vulnerable, desperate, wanting her approval, her forgiveness, her comfort. Could she do this? Somehow, she saw she must. She had no alternative, for the sake of them all, for the family she had borne she must make this work. She took a deep breath and squared her shoulders.

When they stepped off the auto-bus he followed her along a narrow street to an old terrace of tiny houses and as she swung the gate inwards, the door opened, and he saw his children's faces staring out. He stopped, tears choking him. He came upright pulling back his aching shoulders. He wasn't sure how he'd face them all, whatever could he say? Three steps and he was at the door.

'Come on all of you, let us both get out of the rain,' Dorcas said and he followed her into the cramped hallway. George could say nothing. The children became quiet, with shy looks.

A smell of cooking and airing reminded him of family life. May pushed her way through and hugged his knees. His tears dripped on her as she looked up delighted to see him. He heard her distinctive giggle and smiled down. Using his left arm and swinging her up to his chest, her kiss and hug hid his tears for the moment. He moved into the room and the other girls hugged him cautiously, almost shyly. He saw how much they had grown, had changed in this year. They were almost young women. He looked in amazement at Tilda remembering a young Dorcas. George blinked in disbelief.

Surprisingly his sons hung back, Peter eventually coming to him and shaking his good hand. The lad was taller, almost eye to eye with his father but much thinner, gaunt in fact. George felt puzzled.

Roger turned away towards the kitchen. Surprised, George watched him go but felt Dorcas's hand cautioning him to say nothing. Her sharp look told him Roger was finding this difficult, something George had not realized. Did his elder son not welcome him back? Dorcas covered the moment by drawing out a chair for him. They began to talk as he smiled around at them noticing differences, recognising his beloved children had grown, all changed. A year he had missed.

Tilda brought a cup of tea, with a piece of fruit cake and George's eyes were drooping. Dorcas told him he must get to bed and they'd talk more tomorrow.

In the unfamiliar bedroom he cautiously got out of his shirt before she came in carrying a stone hot water bottle and then silently she helped him off with his boots. She hung his trousers over the bed rail and gathered up his clothes to wash.

'I'll sleep in with the girls tonight, give you room to rest,' she said. Giving him a kiss on his forehead she whispered, 'So glad to see you back, my dear,' as picking up his shabby boots, she avoided his eyes. 'These could do with a bit of polish, I'll ask Roger to give them a shine.' The awkward moment was avoided as he pulled covers over his exhausted body, closed his eyes and she gratefully crept out.

Before dawn the next morning Dorcas slipped out of her daughter Tilda's bed, into her brown coat spread across the covers and crept to the top of the stairs. The house was still. Only dim light showed her the way, but the bare boards might creak. She tiptoed. No one else was awake. Snores came from each room as different as their voices. She softly went down to the kitchen, slipping her boots on by the scullery door and going out to the lavatory in the yard. The grey promise of day gave a silver sheen to the wooden fence which surrounded the yard. The metal latch was damp with dew and she shivered as she opened the door.

Within minutes the familiar sickness came and standing, Dorcas felt dizzy remembering the sensation. She leant back against the rough brick wall and breathed heavily trying to control her stomach. The stench of the place mixed with disinfectant made her retch again. Only a glimmer of light fell through the gap at the top of the wooden door. She watched the spiders dash away across the wall. A terrible dread filled her mind. Could she keep this a secret, her secret? She knew she must. This truth would destroy their marriage and their family more surely than his telegram last year. She hadn't meant this to happen.

Just once. It had been only once and like so often before she would carry this burden. Dorcas cursed her foolishness on that July afternoon, but she knew she would never forget Adam, always remember his touch. What she felt for him was deep within her, locked away for ever but to think of him warmed her whole being. Yet she must forget him.

It had not been revenge. Only a few amazing shared moments, a realization of their love but if George ever knew he would see it as her answer to his efforts to find work during that long year. She guessed he would soon turn whatever had happened to him over there in Canada into a hero's story. as his brave struggle for them all. He would never question her difficulties, her fears or her needs, never understand the boys' disappointment over his broken promise for a new life. He would barely ask.

Dorcas could not tell him of her tears or her heartache. He wouldn't listen if she tried, but for the children's future, for her beloved family, she must keep it together. Fear of the alternative, of George's fury, must keep her sweet to him when she silently wanted to curse for all they had lost. Their home, their livelihood, and with this secret, possibly their family. For the first time in their life together she would be unable to tell him the truth. Their marriage had shifted, had changed, though he must never know. From now on she knew she alone would steer this family, whatever he said. He had surrendered the right with his glib telegram. Angry tears filled her eyes, spilling down her cheeks and dripping from her chin. This is what he had done. In this, at least, their future would be a lie. Their love would be different, changed. But she would manage somehow. She clenched her teeth.

It had been barely four weeks since that afternoon. Her family would continue. Now he was back she determined to go to his bed tonight. Her marriage would go on. It must. Of that Dorcas was certain, whatever the future held. She patted her belly. She would do whatever she had to, whatever it took, so her family would survive. She must learn to lie, to cheat the man who was her husband for nearly eighteen years. Slowly she walked back into the silent house, not noticing the sparrow shaking its feathers on the sill. Questions filled her mind. Standing at the kitchen sink, drinking a mug of cold water, looking in the speckled mirror, she saw she must be devious. George had changed her.

CHAPTER 26: Late August 1924

George slept exhausted till mid-morning, all his muscles aching as he stirred. He flinched as they tightened relentlessly. He stretched his legs touching the brass rails at the foot of the bed and shifted sideways. If he stayed still, he was warm and comfortable. Muscles, which had for so long screamed, were now slack and forgiving. He raised his arms above his head and yawned.

Frantic memories flooded his thoughts of the furnace glow and the thumping engine, troubling him. He rolled his stiffened shoulders, feeling the strain of the recent stoking, muscles cracking, his naked body damp with sweat. Reluctantly, he opened his eyes and remembered as he took a deep breath, rolling his neck from side to side, and then his lids drooped as he sank back into an abyss. Here he did not need to wake, just relax. He was back. He slept soundly again, his mouth slack with an occasional snore.

Gently opening the door, Dorcas crept in, and gave a wry smile as she looked at her husband, blankets tossed in a muddle spread across the bed. Watching him, looking at his familiar shape, his blond hair spiked from sleep and his florid cheeks, she saw he was like one of her children, vulnerable and still needing her. Seeing him yesterday, coming from the ship, he had been so dejected, nothing like her image of him. 'Dear man!' She would not add to his defeat. She could not.

She gathered clothes from the bedrail, sniffed the coal smell and wondered. Rough patches, and cobbled stitches told a tale. His year had been no better than hers. She knew anger but must supress it. So many thoughts of the past year and their future problems made Dorcas shake her head before silently closing the door and going down to her cramped scullery. Steam rose from the copper where another pile of clothes lay beside it waiting for her. With all the children out, she would get started. Dorcas fed the fire beneath with sticks and took buckets of hot water to the sink. She knew this was her future, always more work. She thought of her father's warnings about only being a man's skivvy. He had been right, but for now she must deal with today's tasks. What would her Dadda think if he could see her now, a mother of seven children living in London. She tied on her apron with a sigh.

Hours later as the rays of the early afternoon sun fell across his face, George stretched and woke. He thought back, remembering the sun on his face when he had gone to the river with Pierre. Those few days relaxing, listening to the silence, building a fire, and eating the salmon they had caught, gave him regrets. He had hoped to do it with his sons one day, picnic with the whole family in the wilderness of Canada. He sighed, it was not to be. Now the reality was here and now. He vaguely thought of Bert and Jim. What had happened to them? Had they made their fortunes or gambled it all away? Then dark memories of the Spaniard's death returned. His stomach churned. He prayed the truth never surfaced. That was a secret he could never share.

He turned as he heard quiet sounds from below. What was she doing? The smell of soap wafted up. Washing he guessed. His brain followed his body and he recognised the relief he had felt the night before, almost a warm comfort to see them all. Such joy! He was back in Britain, back home, safe. Well maybe not quite home but at least he was back with Dorcas … and his children. He was surprised at how much the eldest three had grown, Tilda at seventeen and Roger, nearly fifteen now he supposed, then Peter thirteen perhaps. He grinned as he thought of his clutch of four little girls including cheeky young May, who'd enthusiastically told him she had started school.

He stretched luxuriously across the double bed, each muscle aching, no more bunks for his large frame. Oh, how good it felt to be back with her, with them all. After some minutes he realised he had to make some effort, get up and find out what had happened, but for now he turned on his back and stared at the stained ceiling. Large cracks in the plaster and flakes of distemper threatened to fall. Hell! What sort of a house was this? He looked about him. Thin curtains and bare boards told their tale. What had Dorcas done? So many questions. How had this happened?

Below in the steamy scullery, Dorcas examined his coal-stained clothes. She would have to find him some more, these were threadbare with what looked like burn holes. She peered at them, frowning, the light from the tiny window showing stains, the reek of sweat and coal, telling its tale. Tears and holes which he had tried to sew, his large stitches cobbled together. Puzzled, she dunked them beneath the grey suds and scrubbed them on the ribbed, rubbing board. If she worked too hard, they would disintegrate in her hands. 'He must have worn them constantly for the whole year,' she mumbled as she looked at frayed collars and cuffs. Had he bought nothing new, no work clothes? She guessed he had stories, and she knew she would both laugh and shout at him in the coming days.

Yet there was just one thing she must do first and do it soon, before he got organised. It was vital. Now might be the best time, with all the family out and hours before any of the children returned from school. She must do this, take advantage of his need. She glanced in the mirror above the sink turning each way to catch the light. Maybe he wouldn't notice the lines by her eyes, her extra grey hairs. She smoothed them with her wet fingers and sighed. Their whole family's future would hinge on the next few hours. She crossed her fingers and breathed deeply, smoothing down her damp apron. It had been less than five weeks she reckoned. She determined to do this. She would make him some tea and take it up.

Dorcas' thoughts were interrupted by footsteps on the wooden stairs. Of course, he was coming down to the privy, she realised. He smiled at her, his blue eyes still fuddled with sleep, and a deep tiredness. He walked slowly, a little stooped, not the upright man he had been a year before as she watched through the window. Barefooted, he had lost weight, though his muscles were still there. A bit stringy perhaps, but hard and taut. His hands and arms showed stains of coal. Carrying the basket of wet clothes, she hurried out to the washing line in the yard.

George watched her there pushing wooden pegs onto the line of his work clothes, as he came from the outhouse privy. He stood for a long minute. As he watched her slight figure, he felt a familiar warm memory. He longed to hug her. 'Good morning my love.' He grinned, so relieved to be here and with her. She smiled back at him, the sight of his nakedness, covered only by her shawl which he had hastily thrown around his middle, reminding her of times past.

'Afternoon you mean. Oh George, what can you wear? I've washed most of your clothes and it'll be hours before they're dry,' she grinned, looking across at him with a raised eyebrow. 'I'll have to find you something,' she muttered shaking her head. He was still handsome, still the man she had married. She could do this. She saw it would not take much. She knew her George.

'Oh, don't worry about it.' he whispered. 'I can think of more urgent things. Are the children all out? They will not be back for a while, will they?' He stood behind her, raising one eyebrow and putting his arms about her middle as, pushing aside her dark plait, he bent to kiss her neck.

'Yes … for long enough.' she murmured as she turned her head. She leaned back against him, remembering a lifetime of love and argument but with a new sensation of sharp reality which the past year had given her. Dorcas would use this moment for her own ends. This was the only way she might save her marriage, her family. She put the peg-bag back in the laundry basket for now. It could wait.

Her future, the children's happiness, even George's illusions for their life together all depended on this. Lovemaking had solved many problems for them before, but none so vital as this. He must never guess. She closed her eyes in a wish. She would do this for them all. It was the only way, guilt making her blush, but he read her pink cheeks as her answer. He kissed her neck again, nuzzling her. She turned in his arms, stroked his fair hair, ignoring the silver temples and on tiptoe kissed him on the lips, opening her eyes wide. 'So can I,' she whispered, winking.

George lifted her off her feet, carried her up to the bedroom and laid her gently on the tangled bed. He gazed at her as she unbuttoned her blouse. The basket of damp washing remained in the yard, half-full for nearly another hour, as they renewed their love.

It had been a little rushed, awkward even, and at his urgent pace but as they lay together in the sagging bed, she sighed. She looked around the dingy room thinking, hardly a boudoir but he would not notice.

It was done. Dorcas relaxed. She closed her eyes pretending to doze but thinking desperately. This made all the difference. Now her secret would be protected. Only she would ever know. This would never have happened if he had not gone to Canada, she told herself. Though she knew she would always treasure her memory of a rainy July afternoon, the feel of Adam's caresses, his understanding, her unexpected responses. It had awakened a different love she would never forget.

Together now, for their family's sake, George and she would solve all the other problems which lay ahead. She'd share all those and he would try to help. She'd never know what he had experienced in Canada, but vitally he must never know her guilty secret. She was tired of dealing with it all for him, sorting the house full of all their belongings and the shop with all that stock, the children, Peter's illness, then travelling here. She had done it without him, because of his damned telegram. Then the heart-breaking shock of no life in Canada, no home, no money. All those promises but she would do her share to rebuild their future. She must. She owed him that.

This was her only secret and she prayed she would keep it locked away. Her stomach trembled. If the truth ever came out it would destroy their life. George would never forgive her, while the children lost faith in their family.

While he went down to the kitchen to shave, she breathed deeply, got up and dressed, tying her apron back around her waist. She would put the last of the washing out before the children returned. There would always be washing, even more next year. Dorcas shook her head, her lips pursed and hurried back to the yard.

Their love had altered, and she hated to guess about the coming months, maybe many years.

CHAPTER 27: Autumn 1924

Later sitting at the kitchen table, George drunk tea and ate several slices of bread with jam. He looked about the small room, shabby and so unlike the home they had left. Various wooden chairs and a dark stained sideboard of indeterminate age stood on the bare floor. The scuffed chair he sat on wobbled.

'What happened to my chair? This chair's wobbly. I'll have to fix it later,' he said, thinking of his glue pot and a mallet. He guessed there would be lots of things to do around the house, so he must get some second-hand tools. 'Did you bring any of my tools with you Dorcas?' he called. She looked at him, her head on one side, flicking her eyes to the ceiling.

'Oh, heavens George. How do you think we could have carried tools all the way here? We had to leave so much behind including your chair. I did bring your cushion cover though. The children were loaded down as it was. We came by train. Be realistic George.' Hands on hips she stared at him, shaking her head. He had no idea what their journey had been like.

'Oh, I suppose so.' He nodded. 'Well sit down, love. I want to tell you all about Canada.' She sat, her hands smoothing the wrinkled cloth as she drank tea and listened, watching his hair as it flopped across his face.

Were there more silver streaks there now? He looked older, certainly leaner. Dorcas puzzled what it had been like. The images she imagined were so different from the ones in George's memory, but he tried to enlarge about it, his hands gesturing, becoming animated. The alarm clock ticked on, as he told his tale, the sun beams moving across the floor. He talked earnestly about the work camps, the drudgery, the endless difficulties and people who treated him unfairly. He told her of the explosion and the indecently fast funerals, his few days fishing by the river and the convent hospital that had cared for him. Secretly she wondered if he had provoked any of their dislike with his self-assurance, his slightly cock-sure manner. But she sympathised with his injury, and his fever as she stroked his sore hand. The thumb seemed permanently bent now, distorted and still painful. He told her of his swollen, poisoned arm.

George was so full of stories, so he did not ask much about her, about her whole year of coping. She felt strangely glad. She dared not say much, not now. She was too tired of it all. It was behind her, something shared by her children. There were new problems here, new mountains to climb, but he did not see them. Would he ever? His optimism might help them all. He was beginning to create his past year as an adventure, himself the hero, battling the odds, doubtless hiding any uncomfortable truths Wanting to break his flow, she made him more tea and brought potatoes to be peeled onto the table. She worked as he talked.

For her the whole year had been so difficult, she wasn't ready to talk yet. What she had felt, the way she had struggled had become private, closed off, left behind in the village. Only she and the children knew the depths things had reached, the worries and intense moments they had all shared. It felt too soon to talk, to try to explain. He hadn't been there, he wouldn't understand. Having to leave so much behind, her home, the furniture she had polished, treasures she had cherished, and more than that, leaving her mam, her brother and her memories, was too painful. A deep resentment at his acceptance of her presumed role as mother and homemaker gradually grew inside her, whereas he had become the hero who had suffered in Canada.

Dorcas held her tongue and went to the scullery, hating the damp smells and the dingy walls, the draughty door next to the tiny window and fondly remembering her cosy Welsh home. She told herself it was now the past. This afternoon there was a meal to cook for her family who were always hungry when they came in, and only she could do it. She chopped vegetables hoping there would be enough as she glanced up at George propping his big frame in the doorway, watching her. He smirked obviously delighted to be back. She sliced carrots aggressively, flicking her knife. Things might have changed for him, but not for her.

The chattering girls bundled in the door, Olive neat and prim, Marjorie tall and plump with Ethel, their little mouse of a daughter and then bouncing in, yelling 'Dadda, Dadda.' six-year-old May jumping on his lap. 'I can write my name myself. I can!'

The family talked for the whole weekend, recounting different tales of their year apart, interrupting, only half listening to each other. moaning and laughing, worrying about the future, speculating what was best to do. Their different viewpoints often caused arguments, the same event being seen from entirely opposing angles.

The children listened avidly, as George exaggerated and coloured his tales. Encounters with bears and wolves peppered his stories and Dorcas wondered how much the girls believed. Becoming tired of his tales, she crocheted as they sat about the table on a bench and chairs, the lamp light reflecting on his animated face. His children loved him. George always exaggerated but she knew these stories were unlikely to be completely true. May clung to him and they each sat near except a silent Roger, who helped with chores at the slightest excuse. His sullen face told Dorcas how he felt, and she touched her son's shoulder with a glance as he passed her to get more coal from the yard. He was mature enough to doubt some of his father's tales.

It was obvious over the next weeks that the children found it hard to accept George's authority on decisions, when for so long Dorcas had listened to their requests. She glanced at her husband noticing his puzzled frown and the frustration he felt. In bed one night she tried to explain to him, to excuse their confusion, though his decisions rankled with her too. Why should he have ultimate say with the children's hopes? Soon the older children avoided issues, quietly allowing their mother to sort out their problems. George did not always know, and Dorcas did not always tell him.

One thing George did know, which took his thoughts by the end of the week, was that he must get work. They needed money. As he looked about the house, he saw how they were scraping by with the rent a priority and food taking every penny, same as a year ago, he thought. He noticed the furniture was worn, doubtless all she could buy. Living on what Dorcas had saved from their life in Wales and what Tilda and Roger had started to bring in with their work was not enough. He watched Dorcas's constant frown.

When winter comes, he thought, we will not have enough for coal or warmer clothes. She has done well but I must get work somehow. I'll do whatever it takes. It's my job to bring in a decent wage, to provide for my family. Maybe we could get an allotment again, there must be some in London. That would help to feed the family, noticing how much the children ate, especially the boys. They were certainly growing.

As George's body repaired, he needed things to occupy him, to get out of the house into the workplace, to somewhere he might feel like a man again, to do something. Things hadn't changed in the past year but after queueing and asking endless questions, he was lucky and got a hint of work. George hurried to see the foreman who was taking on men for a new project, something he had overheard as he stood shuffling his feet in a work queue. By a miracle his story of his efforts to find work in Canada struck a note with a foreman from the London County Council where plumbers were needed on updating some government buildings. Within two worrying weeks he had a job, not well paid but with a feeling of stability. He was secretly triumphant. He could do this.

The autumn leaves scattered over the road, golden at first then sodden as the months passed. George's hand still hurt, so he used the other one more, hiding it from foremen whenever they were near. Dorcas rubbed it with warmed liniment and strapped it up overnight when the pain persisted, unstrapping it before he walked to work.

With Tilda and Roger working and Dorcas now teaching part-time, the rent was paid, and they all ate. George began to feel hope. At least they would manage through the winter now with their older children paying their way.

Sometimes lying in bed, he thought back about his telegram. Had he been rash, unfair to her, to them all? A guilty feeling came over him. Things hadn't been so bad back in Wales, they might have managed if he had stayed. He pictured the shop, all those shelves he had built. Tools and drawers full of parts, overlaid with the smell of paraffin and wax candles. Who was serving there now? Was it still a shop? He would never know.

Just before sleep captured him, thoughts of Kate came to him, memories of her red silk skirt, her welcoming smile, the perfume and the husky voice. She had taught him so much, things he'd never contemplate with Dorcas. He turned away from his wife as though she might hear his thoughts as she slept. Where was Kate, was she alright? She had been quite something he admitted, awakening him to new feelings. He had barely given her a thought for so long, but he felt himself blushing as he lay in the dark. He would never know anything but at times he woke unsure of where he was, praying he hadn't said her name, hadn't whispered in his sleep, yet he knew he would always remember her. Sometimes the dreams came. He hoped she was happy, hoped she had found something more.

Dorcas wouldn't be able to work soon. Maybe they'd stay in London for the moment, probably till spring when the new baby was due. That had been a bit of a mistake he secretly admitted though he grinned to himself. At least he could still do that!

George felt good about his job, part of a new political promise by Ramsey MacDonald's new government against a background of industrial strife and health issues. It was Ministry of Works buildings needing new facilities. Schools, offices and clinics, much of which were dilapidated, rotting and Victorian, were to install new flushing lavatories and washrooms, no more buckets in privies, with proper kitchen facilities. It was familiar work, unlike Canada, and he understood the language, mostly. Gradually it became familiar again except a few cockney slang phrases by the London navvies who dug in the street, but who in their turn constantly cursed the Irish brogue of those other men whom they always scheduled to work in the foulest wet mud of the lowest paid jobs. George saw there was a hierarchy here too. He heard their malicious prejudice but kept silent. It was not meant for him this time. He was glad he was a plumber, mainly working on pipework and welding.

He came home each evening dirty and mud-splashed taking water from the copper to wash in the cramped kitchen. He determined he would soon get a second-hand geyser and install hot water somehow making it easier for them all. Dorcas tutted but washed his overalls several times a week, rubbing an iron over them though she knew they would soon be mucky. She wasn't going to let him down. She wanted to prove to him their love was still solid, though her feelings were mixed. Each morning George looked neat as he walked out of the gate, upright, with his lunchbox in hand.

As the winter bit and pipes froze, he found useful solutions to urgent problems for the foreman and was regularly consulted when a difficult issue arose. At home he managed to repair an old bike the boys found on a scrap heap near his works. Now he was mobile, able to move between sites as the foreman wanted. George enjoyed learning what was in the plans for the next week and suggesting how they best tackle any problems. Having worked for himself he was used to thinking things through. With his bright ideas and practical solutions gradually a work relationship was building with the foreman and he felt appreciated. Others saw his determination to get a job right, explaining and helping, and he found new friends amongst his workmates who knew they could rely on him too. George's enthusiasm inspired their team through difficult days, helping with the progress of the work, which gave them all enough overtime to pay their bills. The feeling of satisfaction boosted George's mood enough to spill over at home.

Dorcas knew when he had a good day by his low whistling as he came in the front door. It marked his interest in the children's stories. Every Saturday when he returned from work at dinner time May would rush to his side, reaching for his hand and delving into his pocket for some pay-day sweets piping up with 'Dadda, my Dadda.' and charming him once again. He sat on a kitchen chair as she climbed onto his knee, arms about his neck possessing him when the other girls crowded around. Dorcas watched from the kitchen door, wiping her hands on a tea towel, glad he was back, and the children were happy. 'That girl.' she mumbled, shaking her head.

Yet no similar bond grew between George and Roger. His elder son still treated him with caution for several months, eyes downcast, polite mainly but distant. George did not understand and complained to Dorcas. 'I can't seem to talk to the lad anymore. I don't know what's wrong with him. He wasn't like this before I went to Canada, we used to be good mates. I think you've spoilt him Dorcas.' Roger had worked part time with him, eagerly listening to George's explanations, but now the lad's attitude towards his father had changed, with either silent frowns or sharp answers.

'Oh George, most growing lads resent their father a bit. I expect you did too.'

'But Tilda's not like that and she's older than Roger,'

'But she is a girl, George. They're different.' Dorcas tried to get George to accept Roger's silent surliness, though secretly she knew the reason.

Also, she tried to make Roger realise his father was back and deserved respect. The lad closed his eyes as his mother spoke quietly in the kitchen. Finally, he looked at her, his expression stiff and unforgiving. 'Yes Mam, I know, but he went away on some adventure and left you to cope. Don't expect me to forget all that, 'cause I can't,

I just can't. Tilda and I were terrified when you were nursing Peter. He wasn't there. He should have been.' Dorcas saw how tears threatened and ironically, he looked so much like his father, feet spread apart, shoulders back. She guessed this was not the end of the battle. It would go on and on.

She put a hand up to his shoulder, feeling the muscle and realising how much broader he had become in the past year. She smiled but sighed. 'Just try, son. Your father thought it was for the best, he truly did. What's done is done, remember? We must all make the best of it.'

Dorcas loved them all but often felt tired of their loudness. She had worries enough without their arguments. The country was still in crisis, endless changes in government and insecurity for working people still in December 1924. Talk of strikes and dole queues in all the newspapers and yelled from news' stands. Nothing had changed. Their first Christmas in London was barely weeks away and there was nothing to spare. She must make some celebration, some effort for them all but she felt weary. This pregnancy was exhausting but she dared not complain. No one else was to blame.

Christmas 1924 was frugal for their family, but they each remembered last year and were glad to be back together. The smaller girls made cards for Gran and Sarah posting them with lots of messages. Homemade decorations, paper chains and useful gifts made the day fun and they all helped as best they could. She needn't have worried as their enthusiasm helped. Her Christmas Eve shopping gave two small chickens, which she cleaned and cooked with last minute vegetables and a homemade Christmas pudding. She had made a cake weeks before for Marjorie's birthday and Christmas combined. Yet Dorcas wondered what this new year might bring. Would she manage it all?

CHAPTER 28: Dorcas, January 1925

For some weeks Dorcas was no longer teaching. After the end of the war, once again married women did not work, with only labouring jobs for the poorest. Women who were mothers were expected to stay at home, though she hoped there would be work again at some time. She asked about for any work she could manage. In January she got some finishing work for a local seamstress, all sewing by hand at home, but it helped. They paid miserly rates but it was all she could do. George worked overtime most days, Roger was earning in the local factory and Tilda had a small pay rise. Peter ran errands for a local shop and did a paper round in the mornings before school as well as a long day's work in the market each Saturday.

The family pulled together and now they all knew after Easter there would be a new member of the family. Roger said nothing, blushing at the news, but May was very confused as to what this would mean. Would she have to share her Dadda? She pouted at the idea although she liked her new infant teacher and had made several friends, animatedly telling them exaggerated tales of the bears and wolves as if she had been in Canada too.

Olive and Marjorie found their new school different, but it was eight-year-old Ethel who seemed unhappiest. The older two got laughed at for their speech, their Welsh sounds with words picked up and joked about and it hurt, but together they coped. Dorcas insisted they ignore it. Olive defended her sisters and learnt to put the bullies in their place with a sharp word, and Marjorie for once was glad of her sister's fiery temper and clever tongue. Only Ethel cried at night and hated the journey to school, because the teasing was new to her. Her old school had seemed cosy, familiar with Tilda always there but this big, strange school with its noisy playground, loud bells and large classes, was frightening with rough boys and unkind girls.

Dorcas tried to comfort her daughter, but Marjorie was the one who looked out for her sister. Whenever her little figure was huddled against the red brick walls, head dipped towards the ground, Marjorie went to her and held her hand, often bringing her into a game with some understanding new friend. Ethel would put her hand over her ears as soon as bells echoed across the playground. Dorcas guessed it would take months before she would truly settle. How could she put courage into her daughter? She watched as Ethel started to suck her thumb again.

Dorcas made efforts to minimise her size but, as she had been pregnant so often before, no-one took much notice. Any neighbours who noticed said nothing to her face but commented amongst themselves. Large families dominated the area, so it was all familiar. She was no different.

Anxiety concerning the birth stayed at the back of her mind, but she planned how she might disguise any awkward questions. With no calendar in the house, and everyone so busy and full of the newness of their home, with extra ways of adding to the family income and the new people they were meeting each day, they took their mam for granted. Dorcas just said it would probably be 'after Easter.'

With only a weekly wage and a large family to feed, Dorcas walked to the shops several days a week, then carrying two heavy bags home on the bus. When she arrived inside, she took off her hat and coat and collapsed in a chair exhausted. She missed Sarah at these times, her friendly gossip with a ready cup of tea. In London people did not greet each other, especially newcomers, in the way they did back home. They seemed much less friendly, more rushed. No one stopped her to chat. Dorcas still felt like a foreigner.

She watched for the chapel sales, where there were second-hand clothes at times. She bought large items which she and the girls unpicked as they sat before the fire throughout the winter, sometimes with pin pricks and sucked fingers. They washed and pressed the fabric before making new garments for themselves with their mam's help. Dorcas would set the girls to unpick any good lace or ribbons, to cut off buttons to store in a colourful tin along with any press-studs or other fastenings. Scraps would go in the ragbag to become dusters or to be used to make a new rag rug. The girls knew nothing must be wasted though they looked in shop windows longingly, dreaming of fashionable outfits.

As the new year progressed Tilda tried to shop in her lunch hour for anything heavy to save her mam carrying too much and Olive started to go to the market for bulky items after school. The family did their best, but Dorcas found housework more tiring now. When she looked weary one evening George commented and then directed the children to have more chores, his voice taking on a heavy-handed tone Dorcas recognised.

'There, Dorcas, you see? Only a matter of getting them organised,' he said sitting before the fire and picking up his newspaper, his feet up on the fender. 'Don't keep dogs and bark yourself, you know.' May rushed to take off his boots, simpering at him. Dorcas closed her eyes, clenched her teeth but said nothing. Men!

CHAPTER 29: April 1925

As the last of any wintery days blew rain across the windowpane, Dorcas watched the scurrying clouds anxious about the birth. The house was clean if crowded, with bare floors and second-hand furniture, but that was so for many neighbours. The baby when it came would have to sleep in a padded drawer for a while. She must wait for the birth to be successful before such plans. She knew things might go wrong, though she prayed this hidden memory of Adam would be fine. She sometimes sat, sewing on her lap in the afternoons, eyes closed and remembering his arms around her, the sound of his whispers. Finally, she would shake herself and dismiss her thoughts. 'Be realistic girl' she muttered. The baby kicked at times and she thought of it as a real little person at last. She no longer wished for a reprieve but only she must ever know her secret.

Dorcas found a few baby clothes, second-hand but clean, at a sale at the local chapel. She had sewn and knitted so this child would not go naked. Sarah had sent two dainty matinee jackets she had crocheted within weeks of hearing the baby was on its way, but no one else knew yet back there, back in the valley. Dorcas had not written about the baby to her mam yet. It was a chore she dreaded. Mam would blame George again.

How could she manage this without questions? She lay beside George anxiously staring into the darkness wondering and remembering. Would her secret remain hidden or would all hell break loose? The child kicked within her and putting her hand on her stomach to calm the little one, she prayed the baby would wait until the last possible moment to be born. Only she knew the true date in early April.

Easter gave them all an extra day's holiday on the Monday so the four girls with Peter in charge went on a sunny outing to the countryside for a Sunday School picnic. Dorcas saw them off with their sandwiches and a large bottle of her lemonade with earnest promises they would be careful. She sighed with quiet relief, thinking it was a God send. Her back had ached for days and she guessed it would be soon. George was out working on a neighbour's blocked sink for some extra shillings, and Dorcas sat heavily taking advantage of the quiet day, her mind whirring with thoughts of the next few hours. Tilda had not gone with the children though Roger had cycled with friends in their small group to a local river to fish. Tilda sat in the kitchen hemming her dress in the late morning, concentrating on not letting her stitches show and doubtless dreaming of wearing it on some exciting day.

Dorcas knew she should do this now as the pains increased. She slowly waddled into the tiny sunlit garden taking care with the broken path. She might be able to do this. She had been having labour pains since breakfast, though she said nothing. If her plan worked today it would be ideal ... if all went well.

Putting a few clothes out to air in the sunshine, she stood breathless, grasping the wooden airer, waiting for the pain to ease. Dorcas looked at the window where Tilda sat concentrating on her seam. She knew if she called her daughter, Tilda would hear and look up, but she wasn't looking at her mother. From her past Dorcas guessed this might not take long.

She had avoided contacting any nurse or midwife, hoping it would only be necessary if things went wrong. Many poorer women managed to give birth with family or friends. Tilda would try to help her and she would not know the signs, wouldn't question the timing like a professional midwife might. All Dorcas had to do was to stage a fall. Standing on the far side of the airer, she collapsed to the garden path and lay there calling Tilda. Her daughter came rushing out, eyes staring.

'Mam, oh Mam. What have you done? Why did not you ask me? I'd have done that. Have you hurt yourself?' Tilda put her arm beneath her mam's back and lifted Dorcas to her feet then slowly helped her mam inside. Dorcas sat and took her hand.

'Tilda, I think the fall has started the baby off. Please help me upstairs. I'll be alright on the bed.'

'Oh Mam. What shall I do? Shall I get Dadda?'

'No, he'll be no use, sit with me, we can manage this I'm sure.'

'No Mam, I should get help. I don't know what to do.'

'Just do as I say and help me now, please dear.' She put a reassuring hand on her daughter. 'No, don't leave me please Tilda.' Her daughter's terror was obvious.

Slowly they managed the stairs, one at a time then she sat whilst Tilda padded the bed with draw sheets as she was instructed. Dorcas then chose to stand gripping the rail at the foot of the bed knowing this helped her. Determined she would hide the timing of this child she mentioned several times she shouldn't have fallen in the garden. Clamping her teeth, she muffled the moans which rose within her as Tilda held her hand and rubbed her back. At last Dorcas felt the familiar change and lying on her bed and gripping the bed rail behind her she began to push. Within a quarter of an hour her baby girl was born, as Tilda watched in amazement instinctively holding her as she slid out, soon crying.

Dorcas lay back exhausted, breathing deeply then after a few minutes took charge again as she always did. Tilda was tearful but helped, following her mam's orders. Carefully cleaning the little bundle of humanity, she wrapped her in a blanket and gave her into her mam's arms. Dorcas cradled her gently, looking for clues of Adam in the squashed face but saw none. The baby looked a little like Olive and Ethel. She would join the family, another daughter to share their home, but always a silent reminder. Dorcas gave a sob, remembering so much, wondering about this child's future.

Then she looked at Tilda, who was wide-eyed and concerned. She reached out her hand to grasp her eldest daughter's hands. 'Well done Tilda dear. I can't believe you were so calm. You'll never know how glad I am it was you. No-one could have helped me more. Thank you.' As her daughter leant towards her, Dorcas hugged her.

'Now I'll get some warm water from the kettle and clean you up, Mam.' Tilda settled Dorcas over the next half hour, bundling sheets and cloths with messy newspapers away in the bucket in the corner. 'What about a cup of tea?' she asked as she brought in the tray with the teapot, pride beaming all over her face. She couldn't believe she alone had helped in the birth of her tiny sister. She took the baby from Dorcas and sat cuddling her on the foot of the bed. The baby gripped her finger with her tiny fist, and opened her eyes, blearily staring up at her. The little mouth moved.

'I think she smiled Mam, she did. She smiled.' A new bond was formed, and Dorcas lay back and closed her eyes. Fortune had helped in her deceit, she had managed it. The tale about the fall would be the cause of the "early" birth, if anyone questioned, but Dorcas guessed George would never think about it, never count the weeks. Breathing deeply, she felt she could rest now. She had hidden this secret for all their sakes, not just her own. The worry of the last months was behind her. Now she would move on, rebuild their life together, without a nagging fear. Dorcas relaxed on the pillows hoping to sleep.

When George returned, he burst into the house and yelled as usual, 'Dorcas, Dorcas. Guess what?' Searching about for her, he peered into the garden. Tilda came to the top of the stairs.

'Shh. Dadda, Shh. Mam's up here.'

'Well tell her to come down. I've some good news,' he shouted.

'She can't come down.' Tilda looked excited and George's eyes widened.

'What's the matter? What's she done?' He rushed up the stairs and into their room where he saw Dorcas in bed. 'Oh, heavens. Are you … Oh?' At that point he saw the tiny bundle in her arms. His eyebrows rose and his mouth opened, but no sound came out. George did not believe he had missed all the drama. 'I was only along the street, why didn't you call me, Tilda?'

'She was marvellous George, but there wasn't time. It was rather quick. I had a fall in the garden. But come and look at your new daughter.' George looked into Dorcas' eyes, sending a memory of his return and their first spontaneous, brief reunion. He grinned, crinkling the lines about his eyes.

Dorcas held the baby out to him. Cautiously he took the bundle sitting down on the bed and peering at the little face. 'She looks like Olive,' he whispered. The baby gazed at him, eyes blurred. George stared back and smiled. This one was special. He had always been kept away at birthtimes in the past by useful women who had helped Dorcas, his largeness and loud voice being their excuse. But this time … this time he was right there holding this wriggling, tiny person, protecting her from the world. His size hadn't frightened her, she seemed very content in his arms, closing her eyes.

Dorcas hid her guilt with a yawn and smiled shaking her head, a slight blush colouring her cheeks. At least she ought to let him have some ownership, some part of this baby. 'What do you want us to call her, George?'

He felt so proud silently determining he would take special care of this little daughter. As her tiny hand grasped his rough finger, he remembered the afternoon after he returned, his hopes to renew their love and grinned at Dorcas. 'Who'd have thought it, such a tiny scrap. Thank God you're safe.'

He carried the baby to the window, his back to the women, before touching her soft cheek with his callused finger, as he reflected on his desperate need to repair his marriage when she was conceived. A tear dripped on to her blanket. 'Another beautiful daughter.' Unbidden a guilty memory brought a lump to his throat. His memories of the brief love of last year, when he was the other side of the ocean, of a rustle of scarlet silk, haunting perfume but a generous smile and most of all her kindness. Without thinking he whispered, 'Katherine.'

'Katherine?' said Dorcas unsure.

Blustering he hid his mistake. 'Yes. I fancy Katherine, perhaps call her … call her Katie. What do you think, love?' He blushed.

Tilda piped up. 'Katie, yes, I think it's lovely. She looks like a 'Katie' don't you think Mam?'

Dorcas smiled. She was happy it had all worked out, so Katie she became. No-one ever questioned his choice. The whole family would adore their tiny sister and probably spoil her too, although Dorcas wondered about May who most of all wouldn't find this easy. She lay back taking a deep breath.

'Tell me George, what was your news then?'

'Oh, just the promise of some more work from along the road. Several people have had trouble with their drains. Nothing like as exciting as yours though.' He bent and kissed her.

Dorcas slept for an hour then woke as the four younger girls burst into the house discarding boots, with Peter. George sat on the stairs his fingers to his lips. 'Wash your hands girls and then I've something to show you.'

Peter looked puzzled then as the light dawned, he mouthed, 'Is our Mam alright? Tell me.'

'Yes son, she's fine,' George nodded. 'Come on girls, up here.'

Olive grinned. 'I bet I know what it is.'

Full of excitement they hurried after George to the bedroom. Suddenly shy, they all stood at the end of the bed and looked at Dorcas, who was holding the baby. 'Come on then girls. May, Ethel, come and meet Katie.' They crept up beside their mam, sitting on the rumpled bed, eyes wide. Olive and Marjorie stood beside them looking at the baby. Gentle touches happened as Katie slept. Peter stood silent at the foot of the bed. The whole business of babies was an embarrassment to him still, knowledge of his parents' involvement causing him to blush. Tilda stood in the corner smiling broadly. After several minutes she called the girls to come downstairs and help with the meal deliberately allowing Peter to be alone with his mam. Cautiously he approached the bed. 'You positive you're alright Mam?'

'Yes, I'm fine. Here hold her for me for a minute.' Cautiously Peter held Katie, gazing down at her tiny face, touching the minute fingers which grasped his slender ones and grinned. He peered at her pink fingernails. He had never seen anything so perfect, he thought. Dorcas thought Katie had another protector now. Her steady, thoughtful Peter would care for her whatever happened in the future. She sighed.

Roger returned that evening, red faced from the wind and carrying a fish which he took through to kitchen and dumped on the draining board, talking of his day oblivious to the rest of the family's chuckles. Peter was grinning widely and said, 'Wash your hands well Roger. For goodness sake, get the stinky smell off them. Then you can go up and meet our new sister.'

'What, she's had it? Is Mam alright?'

'Yes, go up and see.' George jerked his head in direction of the stairs. 'She's great, they're both great.'

Roger went into the bedroom slightly embarrassed but as soon as he saw his mam with the baby, he felt overwhelmed. Such a tiny thing, how did women do this? He knew what he had heard but it was only words, sometimes crude ones too, but the reality of new life was amazing. He had been merely a boy when May was born, but now he knew much more. Dorcas made him hold the baby and he felt protective.

Over the next few days they all treated Dorcas and the baby with great caution, each one wanting to hold and care for this new family member and their beloved mam, before the normal pattern of family chatter and opinion burst back into their lives and Dorcas found herself back in charge.

Although George did not know and Dorcas prayed he never would, their whole family was now in a different place, truly in a new land.

THE END

About the Author
Leonora Wilson

Leonora learnt sewing at her mother's knee and the joy of stories from a tinny radio. After years of teaching both primary and adults, she found time to scribble. Sitting in her sunny study, looking through French windows into her beloved garden, her stories grew, many based on tales of past family and dotted with treasured heirlooms.

Printed in Great Britain
by Amazon

47930934R00188